Only One Summer

by

K.M. Daughters

Sisters of the Legend, Book 2

Only One Summer

Cover Art by *Kim Mendoza*

The Wild Rose Press, Inc.
PO Box 708
Adams Basin, NY 14410-0708
Visit us at www.thewildrosepress.com

Publishing History
First Fantasy Rose Edition, 2019
Print ISBN 978-1-5092-2919-2
Digital ISBN 978-1-5092-2920-8

Sisters of the Legend, Book 2
Published in the United States of America

When she charged through the door like a bolt of lightning, Vinnie's agitation increased with a pulse-revving blast of pure lust. Despite how ladylike and buttoned-down Summer appeared in business attire, she moved that curvy body with unabashed sensuality. Every male in the room eyed her with open enthusiasm. She had but to say the word and she'd never pay for a drink…or a meal…or hell, anything else her heart desired.

Summer reached his perch at the bar in four strides in *very* leg enhancing sky-scraper heels. He popped off the stool and stood to greet her, grinning into sparkling jade eyes. "Hi," he said. "You look beautiful, Summer. Almost makes me forget my problems."

She tossed back her head, hooting a laugh, and threaded her fingers through her spiky, gleaming, fiery auburn hair. "You are ever the flirt, Vin. Come on, let's get a table." She clasped his hand.

He sauntered over to the hostess's lectern linked with Summer, the heat of envious men's stares on his back.

"Table for two." He surveyed the mostly empty dining room in the greenhouse-like setting. "How about over in the far corner?"

Settled at the table of choice across from Summer, Vinnie accepted a menu from the hostess setting it down unchecked on the snow-white table linen. "What do you need from me to get my shield back? I want to return to duty as soon as possible."

Dedication

For Daddy.
You taught us to find the magic.

~*~

Acknowledgments

Our heartfelt thanks to Ally Robertson for her sweet, tender touch and wise editing. We love working with you, Ally.

Thank you, Brian, for helping us with all things legal.

Thank you, Rhonda, R.J., Lisa, and everyone at TWRP for tending the garden so well.

Thank you to our world traveler friends who had some fun lending their names to secondary characters.

To our families: you are our everything; thank you for your love and support.

And thank you, Lilly, for believing that we're famous authors—you make us feel that way.

Praise for K.M. Daughters

BEWITCHING BREEZE
The Carolyn Readers Choice Award
"*BEWITCHING BREEZE* cast a spell on me, and I couldn't put it down."

~*N.N. Light's Book Heaven (5 Stars)*
"Full of both heart and adventure!"

~*Author Joshua Grant (5 Stars)*

~*~

FILL THE STADIUM
Winner Booksellers Best Award
"A vivid fictional creation. The book's well-orchestrated ending sections shouldn't leave a dry eye in the house."

~*Kirkus Reviews*

~*~

REUNION FOR THE FIRST TIME
Winner International Digital Award

Prologue
The Legend of the Three Butterflies

1740, Outer Banks, North Carolina

Mary Bender Avery sang softly to her babies, peering into her mirror and jabbing the pearl encrusted comb into her auburn hair to secure her chignon in place. *"Rock-a-bye baby in the treetop…"*

Turning toward the cradle she grinned back at her daughters who appeared enraptured by their mother's singing. Such lively intelligence sparked in three pairs of wide, identical, grass-green eyes that Mary half expected the six-month-old girls to join her in the chorus. She had no doubt that the Sacred Source welled strong in each triplet. Together? Mary bit back a smile. She was certain that parenting them to adulthood would test her and Daniel to the core. A smidgen of guilt tightened inside her remembering the supernormal challenges that she and her sisters, had provided their second mother.

May the Sacred Source hold you in her arms forever, dearest Hazel.

Among her many gifts, Mary literally remembered the day twenty-three years ago when she and her two four months old sisters first met Hazel Avery.

Still as a statue and struck dumb, the childless widow had gaped at the electrifying metamorphosis of three red butterflies into three identical foundlings on the sun-bleached sand. Offshore, smoke billowed, and canon fire thundered as marauding pirates plied their trade.

Heedless of personal safety, Hazel left the cover of a copse of palm trees and hustled toward the babies. Extending her index finger, she hazarded a touch of a chubby leg. Satisfied that her yearning heart hadn't deceived her brain into conjuring children out of thin air, Hazel gathered the wiggling creatures into the folds of her cape and then lumbered away from the shoreline with her sweet-scented burden.

None of the other settlers questioned her tale of fictional kin's demise that brought her "great nieces" to her home to be raised as her own children. The triplets' deceased mother, Sarah, would surely have approved of Hazel's simple ways and loving heart—especially with respect to the girls' gifts. Mortal though she was, Hazel accepted the impossible and treated their burgeoning powers as if nothing more than everyday talents.

As babies, the girls favored creatures that flitted and flew, like butterflies or hummingbirds. As preteens they were all about dolphins, surfing, leaping and skimming the waves as Hazel shaded her eyes with a hand on her brow and demanded that they come forthwith to complete chores or sit at table. As they entered adulthood, they appreciated Hazel's earthy wisdom and respected her dictates that they use their powers with discretion and only for good.

Hazel dedicated the rest of her life to providing a legacy for her girls, opening an inn bordering the beachhead where she had encountered her instant family. She named the establishment, The Inn of the

Three Butterflies. Mary and her husband, Daniel, lived in and kept the bed and breakfast after Hazel's gentle, Sacred Source be praised, death. The first of her sisters to become a mother, Mary had fulfilled the prophesy of *The Legend*... And shared with her adoptive mother the challenges of raising gifted identical triplet daughters.

Mary finished dressing just when Daniel poked his head through door. "The preacher is here, love. Ready?"

At his wife's nod, Daniel strode over to the cradle and halted, gazing down at the triplets with the customary love-saturated expression in his eyes. Opening his arms bent at the elbows, he waited, grinning at his daughters. Mary gently lifted Sarah and transferred the small, bundle into the crook of her father's right arm, smoothing the drape of her lacy christening gown before turning back to the cradle. Hazel was next transported to Daniel. Mary lifted Elizabeth into her arms and then followed Daniel out of the room.

The large crystal bowl that Mary intended to use as a Baptismal font had been one of Hazel's most prized possessions. Daniel had carried a beautifully hewn wooden table that he had built and carved himself for the occasion out to the beach and set the Christening bowl on top. As Mary emerged into the bright sunlight onto the porch at the back of the inn, she spied the preacher standing behind Daniel's table, the sun-dappled, turquoise Atlantic a stunning backdrop. Anne and Rachel, Godmothers for their nieces, with the respective Godfathers/their husbands, Seth and Michael in tow, scurried to meet Mary and Daniel. While each couple relieved Daniel of two of the babies, Mary strolled over to Jess and Raleigh, neighbors and dearest of Hazel's friends, and presented them with Elizabeth. The three sets of Godparents and Goddaughters assembled in front of the Christening font.

Mary beamed throughout the lovely ceremony, her mother's heart bursting with pride at her babies' comportment, believing that they not only looked angelic, they also, acted like angels.

Preacher Ames took his leave, and Mary and her sisters settled the babies in a pram on the shaded veranda and then bustled into the inn to serve refreshments and sweet cakes to the small gathering of guests. Gazing out the window frequently to watch over her daughters, Mary's soul filled with contentment at the sweetness of her life.

As she handed a cup of tea to the widow Holmes, rapid movement in the corner of her eye had Mary turning toward the window. Three red butterflies circled above the pram's blanket and then flitted and glided, riding the ocean breeze.

Chapter 1

Present Day, Northern New Jersey

Senior Special Agent Vincent Carlucci slept comatose-like, sprawled atop his king-sized bed, limbs extended to the max, like a boxers-clad starfish. After the previous eighteen-hour surveillance and ten-hour workday before that, Vinnie had collapsed on the bed intending to luxuriate in REM's sleep as long as his body desired.

The operation's demands had paid off, though. Breaking up the Port of Newark based drug ring had topped the Field Office's duty list for nearly a decade. Vinnie and his team might even receive commendations for the successful Op that he relived now deep in a dream state.

So, when the pounding started, his groggy, semi-awakened brain interpreted the booms as echoes of last night's firestorm. With effort he swam up to the surface of open-eyed consciousness; but he still took a few seconds to process the loud banging and accompanying din.

"OPR, Carlucci! Open the door!"

OPR? What the....?

He shoved off the bed. Rubber-legged he wrestled on sweatpants while the banging and hollering continued. "Hold on," he bellowed.

Irritation propelled him out of his bedroom and down the hallway. He flung open the door, scowling into McMillan's freckled face. "What the *hell,* Mack?"

Mack held up a document at eye-level and then extended it toward Vinnie approximately an inch from his nose. "I'm executing a warrant. Move aside."

Vinnie swiped the document out of McMillan's huge paw as the OPR officer elbowed past him into his condo. Spinning on his heel, Vinnie tailed him leaving his front door gaping open.

"What's this all about, McMillan?"

"Where's your laptop?"

Vin's scowl deepened. "My laptop?" he said, utterly clueless at this unbelievable invasion.

McMillan bulled a path down the hallway through the kitchen and into the small living room. On his heels, Vinnie pointed to the card table cum desk to the left of sliding doors leading to a balcony just large enough to accommodate the two folding chairs outside that faced the railing.

"Over there," Vinnie said.

Rooted to the spot, Vinnie observed Mack's every movement, filing it away for possible future reference. He didn't know what drove this intrusion, but he *did* know he had nothing to hide from the Office of Professional Responsibility of the FBI. Somebody would pay for disrupting his hard-earned sleep.

Opening the MacBook on the tabletop, McMillan touched the on/off switch. "Password?" he barked.

"One-nine, lower case t, capital R, lower case icia, eight-oh," Vin recited. Peering over his shoulder, he watched Mack bat buttons rapidly.

First the OPR officer clicked on System

Preferences, and then chose Sharing Preferences in the drop-down menu; finally, he clicked an arrow into Remote Service.

Mack pulled out a folded slip of paper from his breast pocket. His eyes dipped down to reference the paper, raised to study the computer screen and then down again before he gave a nearly imperceptible nod of his head. He closed the Preferences windows, pulled down Vinnie's surfing history in Safari and had the audacity to open his email application and scan the page contents.

"I *repeat*, Mack, what the hell is this about?"

The man pointedly ignored the question. Instead he fired back, "When was the last time you logged on? What do you use the computer for? Do you conduct official FBI business on this device?"

"Um…" Vin threaded the fingers of his right hand through his bed-rumpled hair. "I haven't been home in a couple days. I mostly use it personally. Emails, online purchases, etc. Very occasionally I might search background stuff associated with a case. Why?"

"You use it for banking."

A shudder ran through him at the statement versus a question. "Sure. Bills payment, that sort of thing."

Mack jerked down his chin, a clipped military-like acknowledgment in the affirmative. He powered down the laptop, closed the lid and disconnected the power cable. Slipping Vinnie's computer under his arm he turned and began marching toward the door.

"Whoa." Vin sprinted after him. "Where do you think you're going with that?"

"Paper in your hand authorizes me to seize this device," he said over his shoulder. Breezing through the door, he said, "Direct any future questions to your Special Agent in Charge."

With that, McMillan swept the door closed behind him, a click of the latch.

Vinnie stood suspended in disbelief. A few seconds passed before he launched into action heading toward his bedroom. "You bet your ass I have questions for the SAC," he grumbled.

He took a five-minute shower; shaved off two days of beard scruff, the electric razor's vibrations buzzing in his head; and then dressed in a crisp, starched, blue pinstriped, white shirt; pressed gray slacks and a navy-blue blazer. In motion toward the door, he swiped car keys up from a dish on a small oak table in the condo's foyer and exited into the hallway of the seventh floor of the multi-family condo building. Aside from his tiny balcony, Vinnie prized the shared roof feature of his unit here that had set him back four hundred and fifty thousand when he transferred from a rent-controlled apartment near the NYC Field Office and bought in Hoboken with the new assignment to the New Jersey District office in Newark.

Scraping up the down payment had hurt considering he had spent a fair portion of his savings financially helping his sister, Tricia when her husband left her for another woman. But the promotion after he had spear-headed the investigation of a charter boat fleet smuggling drugs on Outer Banks, North Carolina, put his salary right where he needed to qualify for the mortgage and still set aside some money each month to replenish his savings account. Although a bachelor with little thought to putting down roots, Vinnie derived unexpected satisfaction from owning a home—

especially one with a fifteen-minute drive on a good day to the Field Office.

He slid into the seat of his 2015 Ford Fiesta, the used car of choice with his new suburban dweller status for both affordability and the almost extinct cigarette lighter and ashtray at his fingertips. He shoved the lighter home and then inserted the relic car key into the ignition switch and started the engine. After firing up a Marlboro, he sucked in a gratifying lungful of nicotine laden stimulant, wrenched the wheel counterclockwise and hit the accelerator.

His headlights beamed pale lemon light onto the asphalt as he rocketed out of the parking space. He glanced at the digital readout on the dashboard. Six AM. Random deductions swarmed in his brain. The pre-sunrise rousting was well calculated. His recent duty had him sound asleep and vulnerable. The kudos the SAC had lavished on him for the Op's success just hours ago, in retrospect, were designed to foster phony security. So, he wouldn't hide—presumably, evidence.

What? My computer?

Nothing made sense. He genuinely hoped his Special Agent in Charge had decided on a very early start to work. Because today was a really good commute day. Fourteen minutes after leaving home, Vinnie pulled into a space, slammed the car into Park, pocketed the car key and shoved open his door. In one swift motion he shoved out of the car and swung closed the door, a resounding and satisfying boom. No need to lock the car. If safety weren't a given on FBI property…well then, where? Besides, Vin owned very few material things of value to him, car included.

Reeling from sleep deprivation and the surreal

circumstances that propelled him toward imminent confrontation, Vinnie made his way through the parking garage into the red brick building. Through the doors, he trudged past retail shops to the elevator banks. Inside the car, he scanned his security credentials allowing him to press the seventh-floor button. The doors swished closed and the rapid ascent to the top floor heightened Vinnie's shaky condition.

Now delivered to his destination, Vinnie paused outside glass doors leading to the top brass inner sanctum where the SAC and his band of six Assistant Special Agents in Charge had offices. He had seldom visited his new SAC's office. Vinnie's work since his promotion to Senior Special Agent had mostly entailed autonomous Ops in the field. His reputation in the Bureau had never brought reprimand from any superior officer allowing him to steer clear of office politics or call-on-the-carpet meetings on the other side of an SAC's desk.

During the rare occasions that Vinnie was at a desk himself, he veered to the left off these elevators to a partitioned, door-less area along the perimeter, affording a nice Passaic River view through a bullet-proof window.

Confident that he would correct what had to be a mistake, he scanned his security credentials, opened the door and headed toward the boss's office. His confidence was shaken as he spied McMillan and another OPR goon, whose name escaped Vin, down the hall, emerging through the SAC's door. Vinnie had never tangled with OPR before in his career. McMillan was the only semi-colleague he knew in the new assignment apart from his team. Their workout schedule frequently overlapped, and they had grabbed an occasional beer together after work. Had the budding friendship with Mack somehow exposed him to this injustice? Had Mack set this up?

Vinnie sped up to catch him, but Mack and his underling marched rapidly out of sight down the far corridor. Mounting fury had Vin barreling forward. He pulled up short in front of the SAC's closed office door and rapped twice rattling the glass pane.

Senior Agent in Charge Brian Ashley's gaze redirected from papers on his desk boring directly into Vinnie's eyes. He gave a minute nod of his head and continued to stare at Vinnie. Interpreting the gesture as permission to enter, Vinnie advanced toward him, shot through with adrenaline fueled righteous anger. From his superior officer's tight-lipped expression and dull-eyed glare, Vin guessed that whatever this collusion with OPR involved, his bulldog SAC would not apologize to him.

"Sit."

Ignoring the command Vin said, "Sir. I want an explanation of OPR's actions in my home this morning."

Flattening his palms on his desk, the SAC rose canting his torso toward Vinnie in rooster-like aggression. Although Vin had five inches and fifty pounds on his boss, he knew better than to underestimate Ashley. Even looking down on the man, Vinnie felt instantly cut down to size.

"I'm glad you said 'want', Carlucci," he said through clenched teeth. "For a minute there, seemed like you came storming in here like I owed you an explanation."

Vinnie narrowed his eyes trying to take his new boss's measure having yet to create much of a working relationship with him. He knew Ashley hadn't opposed his assignment here—had supposedly welcomed Vin's addition to the New Jersey district. And the SAC's reputation was stellar: brave, fearless, honest and above all, fair.

"I apologize if I seem combative," Vin said carefully. "But McMillan rousted me out of bed and confiscated personal property without explanation except for waving around authorization—presumably stemming from you."

"Right."

Vin knit his brow at the clipped response. His pulse accelerated at the affront. "All due respect, sir, but what the hell is going on here?"

"I'll overlook your tone, Carlucci. For now." Ashley sat down in his chair, propped his forearms on the edge of his desk and folded his hands. "A large sum has been misappropriated from the Informant's Fund. Tech analysts have traced the EFT to an IP address. This morning Officer McMillan verified a match to the computer seized at your home."

Vinnie brought a hand to his brow and squeezed his temples. "You've got to be shitting me."

No mistaking the storm clouds gathering in Ashley's eyes. Suppressing the impulse to rail at the man, Vin bit out a deferential, "Sir."

Reconfiguring his face to project composed superiority, Ashley continued, "I prefer that this…investigation remains within this building. As of now, you are the sole subject of this investigation."

"What do you mean 'subject'? You honestly think

I took money? I have never…would never take a dime from the Bureau."

"Don't force me to bring charges, Carlucci. If you return the money all you'll lose is your badge."

Swamped by teeter-totter waves of dismay and outrage, Vin glared at Ashley, his chest heaving. His heartbeat pounded out seconds of silence as he struggled to formulate a response to this unthinkable pronouncement. The truth, hopefully, would win out. "I didn't take money from the Informants Fund. I have no explanation about the IP address mix-up. But it *has* to be a mix-up. What can I do to clear this up?"

Ashley sighed and gazed past him—at the door, at the floor and then, bam…laser-focused on Vinnie. "You accessed the Fund for the Port of Newark sting."

"I did. All the paperwork is in order, I assure you."

The SAC's taciturn expression didn't change with receipt of the assurance. "The paperwork does *not* support withdrawal after you paid the Informant—a withdrawal that landed in *your* bank account—and vanished from your account the same day of deposit. We're dealing with a significant sum here. Four hundred thousand dollars in total."

Reeling, Vin repeated, "I have no explanation because I didn't—"

Ashley rose from his chair, ramrod straight and official. "You're suspended from duty pending the outcome of the investigation. For now, it's internal and in the purview of OPR. You will be charged in a court of law if the investigation leads there."

He held out his arm with his hand palm up. "Your badge, Carlucci."

Vinnie complied robotically, staggered by

impotence. He obviously had no voice in this. *How could this be possible?*

"Need anything personal from your desk?"

Vin wagged his head.

"Wait here," Ashley commanded, skirting his meant-to-impress cherry wood desk. "I'll ask an Aide to escort you out of the building."

"That isn't..." Vin protested to Ashley's back.

The sun just breached the horizon as Vinnie drove away from the red brick and glass building. Untethered and dazed, the nearest he came to an action plan was to divert to a Coffee-To-Go drive-through and order a large triple-shot.

Chapter 2

Summer Layton stretched out on a striped beach blanket next to Breeze and Skye, soaking up Indian summer sunshine. The rhythmic pounding of waves against the shore had a pleasant, hypnotic effect on her generally overstressed psyche. That warm lazy day with nothing to do was the perfect way to spend sister time.

Summer deeply needed the mini-vacation before she took on new challenges. Accepting her new job, leaving the District Attorney's office, packing, and moving into a new home had left her drained. She found her footing here, grounded with her two sisters on the beaches of Outer Banks where they had grown up. They had talked late into last night about her decisions. Summer was grateful for Bree's and Skye's unconditional support. Identical triplets shared a connection far beyond siblings' bonds. Her sisters' approval meant everything to her.

"What is he doing here?" Skye's curt voice had Summer sitting up and squinting toward the water.

"Who?" Bree said. She bumped against Summer's leg as she propped up on her elbows. "Oh. That's just Vinnie." Disinterested, Bree settled back down on the towel.

Vinnie more than captured Summer's interest, however. Clad in red swim trunks contrasting his olive skin; his toned body; those long powerful legs covered with sable hair; and his athletic movement across the sand riveted her attention.

"Looking good, Vin," Summer called out. But Vinnie didn't glance in her direction.

"Damn, that is a fine hunk of man," she muttered. "Hey Vin! Over here," she yelled louder. Again, no answer.

"Quit that," Skye said. "I don't want to talk to him."

"Fine," Summer huffed, aware of Skye's low opinion of Bree's one-time, college boyfriend.

No law against looking. Summer trained her eyes on Vinnie's muscular back as he dove under a wave. "What did he ever do to you, Skye?"

"You're kidding right? He almost got Bree killed and what about the danger he put Ella in?"

"Well, to be fair, Ella put herself in danger."

"Believe what you want Summer, but I want no part of him."

Shading her eyes with her hand, Summer continued gazing at Vinnie's increasingly distant form in the sundrenched seascape. Oddly, no other sunbathers shared the beach. About to lie back down on her towel, Summer noticed a disturbance in the ocean. Screeching seagulls winged above the area where the water churned frothy white.

The dorsal fins cutting the surface near Vinnie sent a chill through Summer making the hair stand up on her arms. "Oh my God. Sharks!" she shouted.

Summer jumped up and waved her arms wildly over her head. "Vinnie! Get out of the water!"

He kept swimming toward the horizon.

"Skye do something!" Summer screamed.

"No."

"You have to do something," Summer implored, her voice trembling, nearing hysteria.

"No. I don't," Skye insisted as she casually thumbed the pages of an art magazine.

Disbelieving, Summer turned toward Bree. "Talk to her. She has to help him!"

"No, she doesn't," Bree said calmly.

"What is wrong with the two of you? Bree you love him."

"Nope. I'm married now."

"No, you're not. Not yet," Summer spat out as she ripped the T-shirt over her head, tossed it onto her towel and took off toward the water's edge. She pumped her legs with all her strength, but the soft sand reduced her to slow motion.

Determined to help him despite her sisters' unwillingness, she sloshed into the ocean. The waves swelled larger, gigantic, batting her backward with each small gain forward that she made. Battling the undertow, she yelled his name and briny saltwater filled her mouth. Tears streamed down her face. She couldn't reach him in time.

"Please, Sacred Source, help me," she whispered. But no help came.

A wave dashed her against the shoreline. Dripping, her chest heaving, she stood up, ankle deep in the sand. The sharks surrounded Vinnie. She called his name again. And then he disappeared in the foaming water.

Summer opened her eyes and bolted upright in her bed, her heart pounding erratically. The clock on the bedside table glowed 3:00. With shaking hands, she gathered the soft silky sheets around her shoulders. The nightmare left her disoriented and she had no idea where she was for a moment. She relaxed some when she identified the freshly painted butter colored walls of her new condo's master bedroom. But the dream, a combination of recent reality and nightmarish tragedy, left her deeply shaken.

Vinnie Carlucci might not have been eaten by sharks in the real world, but she knew he was in trouble. No member of Summer's family *ever* ignored a dream. She had to call Bree. Swinging her legs over the side of the bed, she arose and strode toward her kitchen. Without turning on the lights, she snatched her iPhone off the charger, thumbed the home button, and selected Bree's number in favorites.

Leaning against the granite counter she gazed straight ahead oblivious to the breathtaking lights of New York City glittering across the Hudson River beyond her windowpanes. She had no reservations about calling her sister in the wee hours of the morning. Bree answered the call before the first full ring.

"Hi, Summer. I woke up a few minutes ago, grabbed my phone and have been waiting for your call."

"Did you see the dream?" Summer asked.

"No. But I knew you needed me."

After Summer described the nightmare in detail she said, "What do you think?"

"Obviously, Vinnie needs your help." Bree cleared her throat. "I haven't actually spoken to him in a while. We've been playing phone tag. Returning his most recent call, I'm embarrassed to say, has not been a priority. Things have been crazy with the wedding plans."

"So exciting. How's that going? Can I help with anything?"

"Thanks, but no. Mom is organized - as usual. Oh, there is something else, though. We were thinking of coming to the Christmas show at Radio City. Can we stay with you?"

"Of course, you can. Tell me the dates as soon as you decide. Jacob knows everyone in the city. I'll ask him to get us tickets."

"How are things going at the new office?"

"I love it. I have to keep pinching myself to convince me that I'm not dreaming. I should have left the DA's office years ago."

"You weren't ready. The time was right now."

"I think that's true. Speaking of dreaming…" Summer yawned and covered her mouth with her hand. "Sorry. Is it okay with you if I reach out to Vinnie?"

"Of course. The vision you had demands it, I think. I'll give you his new number. But I would wait until later." Bree chuckled. "If I remember correctly, Vinnie likes to sleep in."

"That is certainly too much information." Summer's bawdy laugh echoed through the dark condo.

"Don't be crazy. You know Vinnie was like a brother to me."

"I'm sure he would argue that point."

"Well, that would be his problem." Bree sighed.

A beep sounded. Summer took the phone away from her ear, glanced at the screen and smiled at the familiar number displayed. "Skye is calling," she told Bree.

"Of course, she is. Go ahead and talk with her. I'll text you Vinnie's number. Give me a call after you touch base with him. Love you."

"Love you too."

After talking with Skye, who was less sympathetic about Vinnie's probable trouble than Bree, Summer exercised in the gym that she had installed in the fourth bedroom in her condo. A deliciously hot shower capped off her workout. She dressed in a dove gray suit and black silk blouse, poured her second cup of coffee, and then sat with her legs tucked under her on the white leather couch in the spacious, sunken living room watching the sun rise silhouetting the Manhattan skyline. Pink and gold bands of color cast shimmering rainbows on the cream-colored walls of her living room.

Satisfied that seven AM on a workday was an acceptable hour to call him, Summer referenced Bree's text message and connected to Vinnie's phone number.

"What?" The gruff voice rang in her ears.

"Well, good morning to you, too."

"What's good about it? And who the hell is this?"

"Sorry. Thought you'd recognize my voice. It's Summer Layton."

"I apologize, Summer. I've just had a bitch of a morning. Is Bree okay?" She noted the genuine concern for his old flame.

"Bree's fine. Hope you don't mind, but she gave me your number."

"Of course not. What can I do for you?"

"Are you in some kind of trouble?"

"Wow. I thought the SAC was more straight up than he is. And I sure as hell didn't expect the DA's office to call me and gloat. Especially not you, Summer."

Summer knit her brow. "I have no idea what you're talking about. I called because I had a dream about you and…"

"Was it as good for me as it was for you?" He hooted a laugh.

Unamused, Summer met the innuendo with dead silence.

"Uh…"

She let him dangle.

"Sorry. I'm pretty turned around today."

"That's why I'm calling. I woke up at three AM and knew you were in trouble because I dreamed that sharks attacked you. How can I help?"

"Are you for real? Why would the Assistant DA offer to help me? More like you're trying to help yourself… I didn't do anything wrong. I don't need your help," he bellowed in her ear.

"Screw you, Carlucci." Summer pounded the disconnect button and slipped the phone into her jacket pocket. "Stupid ass.

"So much for being a do-gooder." She nabbed files off the round, marble-topped coffee table in front of the sofa and stuffed them into her briefcase.

Shrugging the strap of the briefcase over her shoulder, she stomped into the kitchen, filled her travel mug with coffee and then strode down the hallway leading to her front door. Her phone rang just as she placed her hand on the door handle. Halting, Summer pulled out her phone, glanced at the screen and plopped her briefcase on the floor.

"What?" she barked, giving back his earlier greeting in kind.

"I'm sorry."

"I don't have time for this, Vin. Whatever's wrong, my offer to help you is genuine."

"I…"

Cutting him off to continue her rant, she held up a hand as if he could see the I'm-not-finished gesture. "For your information, I don't work in the DA's office anymore. And even if I did, do you really think I would call and try to hurt you?

"Despite your rudeness, my offer to help if you need me is still on the table. Give me a call when you figure that out."

"Don't hang up again," he managed to interject before she disconnected again. "Are you still there?"

She sighed. "Yes. Tell me what's going on with you. Why do I have this feeling that you're in big trouble?"

"Because I am. I lost my badge this morning and I don't know why."

"Oh no, Vin. Hold on…" Scooping up her briefcase she hurried back into the living room dumped the satchel on the coffee table and fished out a legal pad and pen.

"Okay, I'm ready to take notes. Don't leave out even the smallest detail."

He related the facts from the moment McMillan took his laptop until his boss, Ashley asked for his badge.

Pleased with his succinct reporting, Summer took notes verbatim.

"Who exactly is Ashley?"

"My boss and the Senior Agent in Charge of the Newark Field Office."

"I don't recognize the name. Probably Jacob knows

him?"

"Jacob?"

"My new boss. How much did they say you stole?"

"Four-hundred grand."

"Damn, that's a sizable number."

"Look, I'll shoot straight. I'm a good Agent, maybe even great, but when it comes to computers, I only know the basics. When I have a problem, I get my nephew Barry to help me. He's only fifteen and runs circles around me. I don't know a thing about manipulating IP addresses and the only funds transfers I have ever done was from my checking account to Tricia's at the same bank. I don't need to be a tech expert. We have IT guys in the Bureau to handle all of that for us."

Summer absorbed his unnecessary explanation. Even if Vin were a tech wizard, she absolutely believed he wouldn't use the knowledge to steal money. She glanced at her watch.

"Vin, I really think I can help you, but I have to get to work. Is there any way you can drop by my office today, so we can develop a strategy?"

"Well sure. I don't have anything else to do."

"Give me a minute to check my calendar." She opened the App and scanned the entries. "Does four o'clock work for you?"

"Like I said, I have nothing else to do today."

"Great. Four it is." She added the appointment and then thumbed the home button.

"Summer do you think I should hire a lawyer?"

She laughed. "Sweetheart, you just did. I told you I don't work for the DA's office anymore. What I didn't tell you is that I work with Jacob Levant."

"Holy shit, Summer. Even *I* know that name. Levant is linked to the biggest trials on the Eastern seaboard. There's no way I can afford him."

"No worries. He might consult, but he won't charge you. I'll be your lawyer."

"I don't think I can afford you either, lady."

"You won't have to pay my fee. But trust me; I won't let you off cheap." She chuckled and was gratified that he laughed along with her.

"Thanks," he said. "I needed that."

"I will help you Vin, I promise."

She gave him directions to her office and disconnected the call. Now all she had to do was figure out who had framed him.

Chapter 3

Summer smiled as Johnny Kelly, looking snappy as usual in his charcoal gray uniform, swung open the door ahead of her precisely in time with her stride. She didn't need to hesitate for a millisecond exiting the building. The doorman ushered her to the yellow cab idling at the curb, opened the door for her and beamed her a smile after she tucked into her seat. The man was a magician who intuited her every need.

An urban dweller before taking the new job in New Jersey who had mastered the fine art of hailing cabs whenever and wherever, Summer had yet to buy a car. In the months since her career move brought her to suburban living, she had taxied from her condo building or booked Shared ride cars in the burbs where cabs weren't as plentiful as in New York City. Having twenty minutes commute time each way during the work week available to read briefs or use her tablet had proved well worth the fares. Summer might not buy that car at all.

Rather than preparing for the full calendar awaiting her at the office during that morning's commute, Summer's mind drifted to the "vision" that had prompted her connection with Vinnie Carlucci. The first half of the dream had actually occurred in July. After Jacob recruited her to his law practice, Summer had spent time with Bree and Skye lazing at the beach where their family's Inn of the Three Butterflies perched like a grand dame, her white columns beneath the wraparound porch's overhang gleaming in the sun. Her sisters' much-needed support of her life changing decisions had encouraged her to move forward with confidence.

The sharks' menace, however, provided the nightmarish fantasy element that portended Vin's real-world predicament. Despite the circumstances, Summer looked forward to meeting with him later that day. She didn't know him well having first met him about a year ago after rushing to Chicago to Bree's bedside. Skye had yet to forgive Vinnie for what she viewed as overstepping the bounds of friendship involving Bree in his FBI investigation that resulted in a gunshot wound to her sister's shoulder. Didn't matter to her doting sister that Bree had volunteered for that fateful encounter.

Maybe Skye disliked Vin for more than his debatable responsibility for Bree's injury. Monogamous Breeze had ended the fledgling dating relationship with Vinnie her sophomore year in college claiming, with proof Summer guessed, that he was anything but monogamous. Although Bree squelched romantic attachment to Vin, his undeniable charm and wit proved irresistible, and she remained Vinnie's faithful friend. Summer marveled at that since the last thing she'd seek with the physically magnificent man was friendship. Or monogamy.

"Here you are, miss," said the cabbie.

Summer thrust her arm forward and deposited the twenty-dollar bill in Felipe's outstretched hand. He had functioned like her personal driver these days orchestrating her movements around town through her doorman's and her text's dispatches.

"Pick you up at what…six o'clock?"

"Sounds good for now, Felipe. But I'll text later on to let you know for sure."

He moved to open his door.

"No need to get out," she said. "I've got it."

She collected her briefcase and zipped out of the cab. Crisp autumnal air filled her lungs, an invigorating charge to her step in four-inch Louboutin pumps. Swinging through the door fronting Jacob Levant and Associates, Summer felt steady, capable…confident.

Jacob waylaid her entering her office suite. "Morning, Summer. Have a minute?"

She beamed him a smile. The man, deservedly known as a "super lawyer", exuded rock-solid integrity. Milk chocolate eyes gazed at her with his unique directness that conveyed both acute intelligence and genuine kindness. His daily attire was impeccable: starched white shirts, power ties and custom-tailored suits. Summer more than liked her once formidable adversary, now her mentor. She admired Jacob and loved working with him.

"Sure. I'll grab a coffee and come to your office," she said.

"I'll get your coffee and meet you in your office. Be right there."

She drifted into her office and skirted the vintage, elaborately carved, wooden desk. Setting the briefcase down on the built-in leather blotter, she tapped the return button on her computer keyboard, entered her password and brought up her calendar.

Summer glanced up as Jacob breezed through the

door toting a mug in each hand. He set the drinks down on the coffee table, a circular, mini-version of her executive desk and sat in one of the four armchairs grouped in the suite's sitting area. She strode over to the table, linked a thumb through a mug handle, sat down across from Jacob and blew on the surface of the steaming liquid before taking a sip of coffee.

"Mm, thank you," she said.

"Welcome. Listen..." He picked up a mug and took a swig of coffee. "I have a meeting at State at three with Liam Donahue. I want you to go instead."

Summer arched her eyebrows. "Really? I thought I was working second chair on that case. Do you have a schedule conflict?"

"Nope. I want you first chair. Lonergan is the prosecutor."

"Ah," she said nodding her head. "I guess I know a thing or two about how to beat Lonergan. He was an ADA with me before he got the DA appointment in New Jersey."

Jacob gave her a wicked grin. "Exactly. Are you up to speed with the charges?"

"I will be by three."

"Good." He stood up cueing her to rise from her seat and turn toward her desk.

He stopped in the threshold. "Oh...take my car. I drove the Mercedes in today so you could use it. I'll have Bruce pick me up in the Rolls tonight. Bring the car back tomorrow or whenever...You know you can go lease a car on the firm any time you want."

After the man had quadrupled her salary, not to mention the yearly profit sharing in the offing, Summer was awed by Jacob's generosity. "Thanks, Jake. I'll get around to it."

Absorbed for the next hour in reviewing Donahue's file preparing for the afternoon meeting with the inmate in Trenton, Summer blinked as a calendar alert tone sounded.

Vin. 4:00 PM.

Need to reschedule that, she thought as she opened her internet browser and googled restaurants equidistant between State Prison and Newark, where Vinnie…used to work. She made a note to ask him where he lived.

New Brunswick situated halfway between Trenton and Newark—and boasted the location of the "Best Restaurant in New Jersey". She clicked on the Open Table reservations button and then composed a text on her cellphone: "Need to interview a client at State Prison at 3. Can we meet at The Frog and The Peach restaurant in New Brunswick at 5:30? Happy hour and great bar menu…my treat."

Phone in hand, she minimized the reservation window and continued perusing the client file. She paused to glance at her phone's screen when the text notifier chimed. "Sure," came Vin's reply.

After completing the online reservation, she returned to her work.

****

Vin had never experienced nervousness waiting for anything or anyone—in this case a woman—until today. As a veteran in surveilling individuals in the course of duty, he had long conquered pre-Op nerves and impatience no matter how long the wait. Even though he was only fifteen minutes early, had met Summer before *and* the meeting with her today should help him toward reinstatement at the Bureau—all good, unintimidating things - he fidgeted on the bar stool, ill at ease, gazing fixedly at the restaurant's entrance.

When she charged through the door like a bolt of lightning, Vinnie's agitation increased with a pulse-revving blast of pure lust. Despite how ladylike and buttoned-down Summer appeared in business attire, she moved that curvy body with unabashed sensuality. Every male in the room eyed her with open enthusiasm. She had but to say the word and she'd never pay for a drink…or a meal…or hell, anything else her heart desired.

Summer reached his perch at the bar in four strides in *very* leg enhancing sky-scraper heels. He popped off the stool and stood to greet her, grinning into sparkling jade eyes. "Hi," he said. "You look beautiful, Summer. Almost makes me forget my problems."

She tossed back her head, hooting a laugh, and threaded her fingers through her spiky, gleaming, fiery auburn hair. "You are ever the flirt, Vin. Come on, let's get a table." She clasped his hand.

He sauntered over to the hostess's lectern linked with Summer, the heat of envious men's stares on his back.

"Table for two." He surveyed the mostly empty dining room in the greenhouse-like setting. "How about over in the far corner?"

Settled at the table of choice across from Summer, Vinnie accepted a menu from the hostess setting it down unchecked on the snow-white table linen. "What do you need from me to get my shield back? I want to return to duty as soon as possible."

"First—" she angled the menu in her lap. "—You need to stay away from the Agency and let me handle any communications as your Advocate."

"Sure. I can do that."

"Good. Give me contact information for your boss."

"Yeah. The SAC." Vinnie scrolled contacts on his phone. "That's Special Agent in Charge. As I told you on the phone his name is Brian Ashley."

Locating the contact, he selected Ashley and then shared the contact with Summer as a text. "He's a bit of a prick, although in fairness I haven't worked with him long enough to judge."

Vinnie bent his head over his phone's contact list again. "You really want to talk with McMillan in OPR. That's the Office of Professional Responsibility. Sean McMillan. He's the guy who seized my computer. OPR is running the internal investigation. Apparently the $400,000 *is* missing."

He twisted his lips and shook his head. "I have no idea how that's linked to me. Do you think this will go beyond internal?"

"I honestly don't know. If they think they have enough solid evidence against you, they'll have to file formal charges since you can't return the money to hush the whole thing up. You can't give back what you didn't take in the first place. Please try not to worry. I'll arrange meetings at the District Field Office tomorrow if I can synchronize my calendar with theirs. Don't think about it, Vin, until we have all the facts at our disposal."

Her luminous, moss green eyes softened as he frowned. "I know it's easier said than done. How about some food? I'm starving. And this place is supposedly #1 in the state."

He had no appetite, but the prospect of lingering over a meal across from sexy Summer Layton helped to lighten his mood.

"By the way," she said. "I hope this place was convenient for you. I know where the Field Office is, but I forgot to ask where you live."

"Hoboken. Off Elm."

"No kidding. I live in Hoboken, too. On the Hudson."

Vinnie puckered his lips and whistled a long note. "Way beyond my pay grade."

****

His whistle drew her attention to his full lips and a shimmer of attraction sent a delicious shiver through her. Summer had expected to relate to Vincente Carlucci in a sisterly way. He was her sister's long-time friend, like a brother to Bree. By extension... But sitting this close to him, inhaling the subtle, musky scent he emanated, if Vinnie was her brother, then surely, she contemplated incest.

She was powerfully drawn to him and her breath caught in her throat at the slightest touch of his huge hands. Just the brush of his fingertips against hers when he passed her the basket of bread sent shock waves through her system.

Unnerved, but intrigued, Summer inwardly sent up a prayer of thanksgiving to the Sacred Source for sending the dream that brought her and Vinnie together.

After providing the server with drinks and appetizers orders, Summer relaxed, deciding to do some personal exploring. "Even though you've known my sister forever, I know very little about you, Vinnie. Do you have family in the northeast?"

"I do. My kid sister Tricia, her two children and Mom and Dad. Their houses are in Dickinson, New Jersey. My parents also have a time share in Palm Springs. Trish is separated from a true asshole, Wallstreet type named Barry. You think with all the money the guy moves around in his job; he would have provided better for his family."

"That's a shame. What does she do for a living?"

"She's a high school science teacher. Totally brilliant. And her students love her." The smile that bloomed on his face dimpled his cheeks, softening his chiseled profile…boyish and appealing as hell.

She returned the smile. "You're proud of her."

"Very. My nephew, Joey? Smart as his mother. And funny, too. Trish's eldest, Barry, Junior, however, is currently working hard to hide his light under a bushel of resentment over the pending divorce. I spend time with him as often as I can. I think the "guy time" is helping him. At least he's nicer to my sister these days."

"Hmm," she said.

"What?"

"I guess I wouldn't have taken you for a family type."

"No?" He narrowed his eyes and gazed at her with penetrating directness. "What type do you take me for?"

She met his gaze, unblinking. "I think you're more the thank you ma'am—next…type."

Vinnie's aqua blue eyes danced as he leaned over the table, close enough that her temperature rose a couple degrees from his brawny nearness. Transfixed, she leaned toward him, a foot away. "Are you going to contradict my opinion?" she teased.

The corner of his mouth twitched. "No, counselor. I'm going to take the fifth. What about you, Summer? Serious about some lucky man?"

The appearance of their server had them simultaneously drawing away from each other. Drinks were set atop cocktail napkins in front of each of them. Summer clinked her wine glass against his pilsner. "Cheers."

She took a sip of ruby red Cabernet Sauvignon eyeing Vinnie over the rim of her glass. Amusement gleamed in his expressive Mediterranean Sea eyes. A hint of beard stubble darkened his cheeks adding ruggedness to his features. A close-cropped cap of shiny, coal black hair begged her touch. Those full lips framed even, white teeth. The body that she fantasized he possessed beneath the starched shirt and conservative blazer captured her imagination. What would his reaction be if she invited him to her home? She had certainly never been tempted to do that after the first business meeting with anyone.

"You haven't answered my question," he said, breaking her reverie.

"Oh, right." She set her glass down on the table. "Nope. I'm not dating anyone. You?"

"Nah. I haven't been involved with a woman in a long time. Work, you know?"

"Yes, I do. It's a little calmer working for the Defense than the DA's office. But not much."

Vinnie leaned closer to her again, a cocky smile playing on his lips - apparently on more solid ground with Summer the woman than Summer Layton, Esquire. "I have a lot of free time on my hands. Maybe you could spend some of your down-time with me?"

I'd like nothing better. Shifting toward him she touched the back of his hand softly. "We'll see."

The arrival of their appetizer selections separated them again.

Nibbling on a pita triangle coated with artichoke cheese dip, Summer continued to enjoy Vinnie's company. How lucky that she might help him *and* possibly enjoy a no strings fling. Unless her instincts were off the mark, he was as attracted to her as she was to him.

Living in that moment, she delighted in his thrall, feeling fortunate that she had finally found a kindred soul.

Chapter 4

Summer raked her fingers through her hair and stretched her aching back. Glancing at the time on her computer screen she widened her eyes at the 4:00 p.m. displayed. Buried in the Donahue file since nine that morning, she had lost all sense of time, working straight through lunch.

Her stomach hollow, she stood stiffly, bent at the waist and clasped her ankles in a quick Downward Dog. Rounding her back, she inhaled and then tucked in her abs to straighten her spine into an upright position. She grabbed her mug off the corner of her desk and stalked out of her office to refuel at the coffee machine.

As Summer zipped past her assistant's cubicle, Barbara popped up from her seat and raced to intercept her. "Ms. Layton, I'll get that for you."

"No need, Barbara, I want to stretch my legs. And please call me Summer."

Her assistant stuttered, "I, I...couldn't possibly call you by your first name. Mr. Levant would have my head."

Summer smiled as she gently touched Barbara's hand. "You let me worry about Jacob. I insist."

Summer strode straight to the barista caliber machine in the kitchen. She focused on the caramel colored stream of fluid into her mug, poised to snatch the cup out from under the spout the second the machine stopped with a hiss. Sipping on the coffee she returned to her office, savoring the blast of caffeine.

Barbara tailed her. "Do you want me to continue to hold all your calls?"

"No thanks. I've finished plodding through the file."

"Okay. Here are your messages."

Summer accepted the stack of pink message slips and drifted to her desk where she stacked the slips based on priority. *Finally,* she had a return call from Sean McMillan about the seizure of Vin's computer, but still no word from Vinnie's SAC after her multiple calls.

Well, Mr. Ashley you might dodge my calls, but you will not ignore me. She pressed the intercom button on her phone console.

"Yes, Ms. Layton?"

"Summer." She chuckled. "Don't make me come out there. Barbara can you please get me the street address for the FBI Field Office in Newark? And please note on my calendar that I'll be out of the office until late morning tomorrow. I plan to meet with the Special Agent in Charge…

"Whether he likes it or not," she said under her breath.

Three slips of paper had Vinnie's name on them—calls timed about two hours apart. Picking up the phone she dialed his number.

"Hi, Summer," came his resonant, utterly masculine voice sending a now familiar zing of pleasure through her.

"Hey, Vin. Sorry I didn't get back to you sooner. I was buried in a case file all day."

"No problem. I've been at loose ends and was hoping you had some news for me."

"Nothing yet. McMillan left a message and I'll call him back as soon as I get off the phone with you, but Ashley is apparently dodging me."

"Man, so frustrating."

"Exactly. But I intend to wait at his office door tomorrow morning. Do you know what time he generally comes in?"

"Yeah, seven or so."

She nodded. "Good. I will not be ignored."

His throaty laugh rumbled in her ear. "You are one tough broad. I'm glad you're on my side."

"Squarely." She stifled a yawn. "I'm going to call it a day. I missed lunch and I'm starving. Want to grab something to eat?"

"I would love to, but I have plans. Some other time?"

"Of course. No problem," she retorted rapidly.

Her invitation had slipped out unchecked and she strongly regretted opening herself up to rejection - not her style.

"If you're interested, would you like to come with me to my nephew's birthday party?

It's a family party at my sister's house. My parents flew in last night. I think they cut their vacation in Palm Springs short because of the mess I'm in. Even though they said they're home because of Joey's birthday."

"I don't want to horn in on your family party."

"Horn in? You haven't met my parents. Having my lawyer with me might prove very helpful." He huffed a laugh. "Besides, there'll be tons of food."

"How can I turn down a client? Do I have time to

run home and change?"

"Sure. How about I pick you up in a half hour?"

After giving him directions, Summer logged off her computer and left her office.

****

Clad in soft jeans and a gray turtleneck sweater, Summer shrugged on her supple charcoal-gray leather jacket and left her condo bound for the lobby to wait for Vinnie. Chatting with the doorman, Summer didn't realize that the beat-up Ford idling at the curb in front of the building was Vinnie's car until the driver door opened, and he appeared, grinning at her.

"Hi," she greeted him.

Picking up on her cue, Johnny beat her to the passenger door and swung it open for her. She slid inside inhaling the pleasant scents of tobacco and woodsy aftershave. Very manly. Very appealing.

"Nice ride, Vin. They can't accuse you of spending stolen money on a car, that's for sure," she teased.

"Sorry, if it's not up to your standards, princess."

No missing the sarcastic tone in his voice. "Don't be so touchy. I was only kidding. I don't own a car. And even if I did, my standards are minimal. If the engine turns on every time I want it to, and the car takes me to my destination without breaking down, I'm happy. If you saw the car we shared during high school you'd know I'm telling the truth. It was a lime green Pinto. Your car looks like a Ferrari compared to that ugly heap. But Dad kept it in tip-top shape. Sometimes I wish I still had that car. So many memories."

"You three must have been something in high school. I wish I had known you then."

Summer hooted. "We were something, all right.

39

So, tell me about the birthday boy."

"Joey is amazing. He turns ten tomorrow. The kid is all smiles and wonder."

Even in profile, Summer couldn't miss Vinnie's eyes light up talking about his nephew.

"My mother calls him her little prince. Good thing he's a great kid or I might be jealous. I was always Ma's little prince."

"My guess is you still are."

"Well, maybe I am." He gifted her with an irresistible grin. "I treat her like a queen. She deserves it."

For her, a man who loved his mother and wasn't ashamed to show it was extremely sexy. Devoted to her family, Summer's heart melted at this side of Vinnie's personality.

They drove in silence for a while. The jazz station on the radio supplied pleasant background music. He turned into a driveway with a For Sale sign posted in the middle of a manicured lawn.

"Is this your sister's house?"

"Yes. She has to sell it because she's divorcing Barry the bastard. Don't get me started." He turned off the engine. "I'll get your door," he said as he exited the car.

Impressed with his chivalry, she waited patiently while he rounded the front bumper and opened her door. She accepted the handhold he extended, his huge, warm hand enveloping hers, and allowed him to tow her out of her seat.

The front door of the brick house swung open and a mini-Vinnie bolted outside and barreled down the walkway toward them.

"Uncle Vinnie you're finally here!" The little boy sang out.

Amused, Summer stood slightly apart from the pair watching Vinnie bear hug his nephew and ruffle his mop of shiny black hair.

"Joey, I want you to meet someone." He turned toward her, the sweetest smile on his face. "This is Summer."

"Hi Summer. Cool name."

"Hi Joey. Nice to meet you. Happy birthday."

"Thanks. Come on in. Nana is here, and she made our favorite stuffed shells. She made a Nana cake too. She hid it in the fridge downstairs, Uncle Vin. But I saw it." Joey zipped away and disappeared through the open door.

"I assume a Nana cake refers to your mom's baking?"

"Right. She's famous in the family for her homemade birthday cakes. No one makes them like her."

Vinnie popped open the trunk, lifted out a jumbo birthday gift bag and slammed the trunk closed one-handed. Bending his arm, he angled his elbow toward Summer. Tucking her hand around his firm bicep, she strolled up the paver brick path with him and entered his sister's house.

The family swarmed the hallway and Summer was caught up in introductions. Summer especially loved witnessing Vinnie's loving interaction with his sister considering her own all-important relationships with Bree and Skye. He enveloped the petite blonde in a hug and then hung a possessive arm over her shoulder while Joey and his grandparents milled around in the foyer.

"My goodness I thought Bree had come with you, Vin." Tricia walked toward Summer and gave her a warm hug. "I'm sure you hear it all the time but, wow. Other than your hairstyle, I can't tell you guys apart."

"Really?" Vinnie gazed at Summer. "I don't think I would ever confuse Summer with Bree. Summer's eyes shoot sparks of green fire when she gets mad and her laugh starts at her toes and bubbles up to her chest."

Surprised by his...sort of poetic description of her, Summer narrowed her eyes and searched Vinnie's face for telltale signs of sarcasm. His sweet smile radiated fondness.

"Hmm..." Tricia gazed fixedly at her brother a couple moments and then chuckled. "I'll try to avoid making Summer mad, but I do look forward to sharing a couple of good laughs. Maybe after a few glasses of wine—like now. Come on in."

Vin steered Summer into Tricia's spacious kitchen and introduced her to his mother, Rose, who sat on a barstool chair, her short legs dangling. She was a cherubic, smiling, dumpling shaped lady with pale blonde, Julie Andrews pixie-cut hair like her daughter, porcelain skin and the same sparkling crystal blue eyes as both her children. Instantly, Summer felt warmly accepted and melded into the vibrant family circle.

"So nice to meet you, Mrs. Carlucci." Summer accepted the glass of Cabernet that Tricia handed her.

"Oh, please call me Rose. Everyone does."

"Okay if I sit next to you, Rose?" Summer tilted her head toward an empty seat.

"Sure." She patted a freckled hand on the seat cushion.

Summer wiggled onto the high-legged chair and set

her wine glass down on the counter. "Joey mentioned that you made your special Nana cake for his birthday."

Rose knit her brow. "That scamp."

Summer smiled. "Guess I shouldn't have ratted on him. He snuck a peek. And he can't wait to eat it. I'm looking forward to having a piece, too."

Rose snorted. "It's a protected secret recipe," she said her eyes gleaming. "I don't share it with just anyone. Would you like to know how to make it?"

Summer returned Rose's wide smile. "I'd be honored."

"Pillsbury."

"Excuse me."

"I use the Pillsbury yellow cake mix and the plastic container of Pillsbury milk chocolate icing. That's it. That's the big secret. Vinnie and my grandsons believe it's a special family recipe." She faced Tricia. "Who knows? Maybe your father, too. Men…"

Rose burst out laughing, a deep rich belly laugh that brought tears to her eyes. Her laughter was contagious catching up Tricia and Summer in the joke.

"Your secret is safe with me." Summer, usually not a hugger, spontaneously hugged Rose.

"I know this sounds crazy," Tricia whispered. "But I've made the very same cake and followed the same instructions as Ma. It never tastes the same. I even use the same brand of oil. Still it tastes different. My boys rated it as good, but not as good as Nana's."

"You must have a special touch." Summer grinned back at Rose.

Dinner was loud and boisterous. Everyone talked over each other. It reminded Summer of her family dinners; filled with noise, love and laughter. Even the older nephew Barry, who looked like he would like to be anywhere other than at dinner with the family, joined in the conversation.

Afterward, Joey opened presents. Much to Vinnie's and Summer's delight, Joey seemed most impressed with their gifts—the latest football and baseball video games from his uncle and tickets to an upcoming Giants/Panthers game that Summer included in a card. Jacob had told her that she could use the Giants season tickets anytime she wanted. Her impromptu attendance at the party had provided her first opportunity.

Joey bustled around the table hugging and thanking each adult. The boys asked to be excused and hurried downstairs to put their gaming skills to the test the instant that permission was granted.

"So, tell me exactly what is going on," Vinnie's father demanded; the first words he had uttered since the quick, "nice to meet you" to Summer at the door.

"Not much new since I talked to you last night." Vinnie gulped a mouthful of wine.

"Have you gotten a lawyer?" The patriarch continued.

"Of course, Pops. I told you that last night."

"Is he good? Can you afford him? Do you need money?"

Vin responded to his father's machine gun questioning with two nods and one shake of his head.

Vincente Senior scowled at his son, clearly expecting more discussion…or explanation. Summer observed the man, sizing him up as if he were her courtroom opponent. Vin's dad projected an aura of dominance, a take no prisoners directness. Like his son, he cut an imposing physical presence. Not as muscular as Vincente, Junior, his dad still had a slim, athletic body and a full head of black hair threaded with snow white strands. His eye color was a smokier blue, cobalt, storm clouds.

Vinnie picked up the cue and reiterated verbally, "Yes she is *very* good. I doubt I can afford her. But, no, I don't need money." He smiled at Summer.

She didn't return his smile, poised to deal with the opposition.

"She? You hired a girl? What the hell? Listen. I called Louis. His son is a lawyer. He's a really big deal in Garfield. He knows the mayor personally. He's really busy, but Louis said he'll take your call."

"Thanks, Pops, but I'm good. I am *very* happy with my lawyer."

"What's the girl's name?" the man sneered.

And Summer jumped in. "Vinnie's lawyer's name is Summer Layton. Me."

She faced Vin's father unblinking. "I don't like being called a girl and a former U.S. President uses my law firm, which I think tops the Mayor of…Garfield, did you say?"

Tricia and Rose stiffened in their seats and gaped open-mouthed at Summer. No one said a word.

Summer knew the advantage of waiting. As she sat serenely gazing at Vincente Senior, she could almost hear the thoughts whirling in his brain.

"I meant no disrespect, Summer," he said, his voice soft, a new tack.

"I hear a big, "but" coming, Mr. Carlucci," she retorted evenly.

"But…" he agreed, "I still believe that a male lawyer would be better suited for Vinnie."

"Everyone is entitled to their opinion. I respect Vinnie and I'm fine if he agrees with you. But this is a very serious charge against your son with more than just his job at stake." She paused to take a long sip of wine. "It would be a mistake to underestimate me. Many male opponents entered the courtroom and thought that I would be an easy foe just because I didn't have a dick in my jeans. They *all* left red faced with their pants down."

His storm-cloud eyes bored into her. Boldly she held his gaze, unfazed by his scrutiny.

A clock ticked somewhere in the silence.

"You've made the right choice, son," came the verdict.

Vinnie's father half stood and leaned over the table extending his arm in her direction.

Summer rose and firmly accepted the *paterfamilias's* handshake.

Chapter 5

Vinnie steered onto her street and braked at a stoplight. He turned toward Summer who angled her head away from him—her same posture during the thirty-minute ride. She hadn't spoken since they left Tricia's house remaining seemingly absorbed in the view out the passenger window. He eyed the swan-like curve of her long neck, the gleaming diamond stud in her earlobe and considered acting on the temptation to kiss a path along her porcelain skin—maybe nibble on her ear to capture her attention.

After the tense moments between Summer and Pops at dinner, Vinnie wouldn't chance making her angry enough to shoot green fire out of her eyes in his direction. He chose a safer path to break the silence between them. "What's going on in that pretty head of yours?"

Summer's sparkling, pine green eyes met his in response, inciting an unprecedented jolt of attraction deep in his core. She gave him a tender smile and said, "Absolutely nothing. Just enjoying some peace for a change."

He returned his attention to driving as the light changed. "Sparring with my father get to you?"

She laughed softly. "Are you kidding? Not even a blip. You have no idea how much combat I engage in every darned day. I liked your family a lot, your dad

47

included. I understand his motives for wanting the best for his son. Seems I recall that my dad went all Navy Seal on you at first meeting when Bree was shot."

Steering to the curb fronting her building, Vinnie braked and shifted the gears to Park.

He draped an arm over the steering wheel and regarded Summer. "Hard to forget meeting your whole family that day," he said. "But I *think* he's gotten past that. He was very cordial when I saw him in May."

"Yep. I think he likes you." She reached for the door handle and an urgency to keep her with him shot through Vinnie.

Did the impulse stem from loneliness and unemployment? Was her command of his legal mess prompting gratitude? Or did he just plain want her?

Vinnie liked control. Largely because he needed to protect people. He had dominated dealings with criminals, law enforcers, his loved ones and most of the women he had dated to fulfill that deep-seeded need. Not long ago, he hadn't protected his old flame, Bree, Summer's identical sister. The nightmare gunshot that had felled Bree rang out frequently in dreams even now. His only saving grace, besides her surviving the shoulder wound, was that *she* had insisted on coming with him despite his protests and then wound up in the line of fire. He shouldn't have allowed her to take control.

Now he remained powerless to take control and protect himself from the threat the Bureau had set in motion. Vin had to leave that to the scintillating woman seated next to him. She was fearless facing off with Pops. Summer offered him so much more than topnotch legal advocacy. For the first time in his life, Vinnie inwardly acknowledged the novel reversal: a woman wanted to protect him.

She was halfway out the door when Vin piped up, "My place is only about fifteen minutes from here. Want to come by for some coffee or a drink? I have some Italian cookies and a couple bottles of Montepulciano…"

Summer placed her hands over her midriff. "Thanks, but I couldn't fit another bite or drop in me. And I want to beat your boss to work early tomorrow morning."

She slipped through the door and hung her head back inside the car. "Loved meeting your family, Vin. Talk with you soon."

And then she whisked away, a blur of rosy sunset-colored hair and long blue jean clad legs in rapid motion. He sat a couple beats after she disappeared inside her building, lacking purpose; a man whose former operating mode was fast forward. With a shake of his head he put the car in gear. Vinnie traveled the short distance home keeping well to the speed limit in exaggerated law abidance in his vulnerable state.

He tossed his keys into the dish on his hall table; emptied his pockets setting his phone and wallet on the tabletop and slipped off his shoes before meandering out onto his balcony. Vin's condo floor didn't afford a birds-eye view of the city skyline, but he deemed the vista pretty damned spectacular from where he stood. He wondered at how much more spectacular the view Summer had from her place on the Hudson.

Strange that the mammoth luminescence, visible from space, of Manhattan island before him brought a sense of serenity when calamity better described the city's reality. It didn't take long for the calamity in his spirit to overshadow his enjoyment of the vista. Restless, he stepped back inside heading for the kitchen cabinet to have that glass of wine that he had offered to share with Summer.

He fished the restaurant-style opener out of a drawer and used the point of the corkscrew to rim around the cork seal, removed it and tossed the crackly paper on the countertop. Vinnie twisted in the corkscrew, levered the cork up one level and then forced the cork out with an upward pull. He tilted the bottle and the ruby-plum colored wine burbled into the large bowl of the wine glass. With the goblet in one hand and the bottle in the other, Vin returned to his perch on the balcony where he took a seat on a folding chair.

Alternating between staring blankly off into the distance and gazing downward at the local traffic and tree-lined park across the street, he sipped wine—delicious wine, actually, that he should have relished a lot more than he did. Vinnie couldn't remember the last time he had the freedom to drink all that he wanted in the safe harbor of his home without worrying about duty readiness. Tonight, he had no worries of the kind. No call to duty would come for Senior Special Agent Vincente Carlucci no matter how surreal that fact increasingly became for him.

As if the fates mocked him, his phone rang. He surged to his feet and jogged down the hall toward the chirping iPhone vibrating on his hall table.

Half-believing the caller was an annoying solicitor, he was more than surprised when he identified the incoming caller as originating from the District Field

Office.

It's a mistake. I knew it.

He seized the phone as if reaching for a lifeline and connected the call. "Carlucci."

"Yo, Vin-man. How are you holding up, Buddy?"

Vinnie's stomach sank. The last thing he needed was hero-worshipping, pesky Tyler Wellington dogging him. Tyler Cornelius Wellington. His parents' name choice had almost certainly forged their son's geeky persona from the cradle.

Even though Wellington was twenty-something, and Vin guessed a rising star in his own estimation, Vinnie thought of him as a kid. Maybe because he had exhibited such fan-boy deference to Vinnie when introduced to him upon transfer to the new post in New Jersey. The kid had wheedled his fawning way into a couple off-duty gatherings at a bar with the men under Vinnie's command. He even slept on the couch here one night because Vinnie considered him too overserved to drive and Vinnie couldn't spare the time to drive him home himself that night.

Wellington was an HRIS analyst. Translation, as far as Vinnie was concerned, a nerd who kept personnel records. But what Wellington wanted most was to work in the field and convince someone like Vinnie to mentor him to that end. He had never come right out and said so, but Vin figured it was just a matter of time.

Vinnie wondered how Wellington had gotten wind of his situation and decided a formal suspension in his employee records supplied the answer. *But wouldn't OPR keep this quiet?*

"I'm all right," Vinnie responded. "Why do you ask?"

"I put two and two together and figured out that you're in deep shit, my friend," he said. "Intel *is* my specialty, after all."

Vinnie bristled at the designation, friend. He envisioned Wellington's skinny chest puff up with his bragging and was sorely tempted to guffaw in his ear. Intel? More like Comp and Benefits, my friend. But he considered it needlessly unkind to swat away the pest, so he said, "Sure. What can I do for you, Wellington?"

"Please, sir, call me Tyler. And it's what I can do for you."

Vin stifled a sigh. In the same instant a tiny flicker of hope ignited. He believed in opening doors when opportunity presented and this offer of assistance out of the blue might represent golden opportunity. *What have I got to lose?*

"I'm listening."

"I know OPR has tagged you for missing money from the Informants Fund. Idiots."

"Uh huh."

"A vacation request form, approved by the SAC, put up a red flag. Your partner, Paul Muñoz is taking time off."

Vinnie frowned. The oddly-timed approval left a big hole in his unit with him and Paul on leave at the same time. Even so, no particular red flags waved before his eyes. "We just came off a big Op. I'd probably have vacation leave now, too."

He scrubbed a hand through his hair, frustrated yet again at his predicament. "If the SAC hadn't provided involuntary leave, that is…"

"Yeah, well. Any red flags about Muñoz's vacation plans? He's taking his whole brood to Disney World, amigo. For a full week. At the Grand Floridian to boot. Yep, mister, missus and count 'em, *five* muchachos."

The information sucker punched Vinnie enough for him to overlook the snide ethnic slur and Wellington's overall irritating personality. His mind raced to construct an explanation that banished suspicion. Paul Muñoz wouldn't steal—and worse, frame Vinnie for the theft. He had a lot of thinking to do. His deep loyalty to Paul precluded his believing what Wellington insinuated.

"Thanks, anyway, but I think Paul is entitled to a break. And, obviously the SAC agrees. I'll get everything cleared up."

"I don't know…that's a lot of money. Just sayin'…"

The kid was right. Paul didn't have enough money to take his whole family to Coney Island as far as Vinnie knew. But he wouldn't accept the information at face value.

His first inclination was to end the conversation with Wellington as graciously as possible—which he did in a couple seconds. Second, he itched to confront Paul about this incredible affront. Could the man he trusted with his life be so duplicitous? He couldn't accept that. At least for now, he wouldn't.

The best course of action? Call his lawyer. Which Vinnie gladly proceeded to do since he hadn't stopped thinking about her for a moment since she volunteered to defend him. "Hey," came her breathless response to her phone's ringing.

"Am I interrupting something?"

"Just some treadmill jogging. While I watch *Big Bang* reruns. I'm addicted. What's up?"

He grinned intending to tune in to the same show as soon as he ended the call. "A kid who works at the Newark Field Office just called me with information he thought I'd consider vital to exonerating me."

"Don't keep me waiting," she said. "Is tomorrow morning going to be a reinstatement meeting, Vin?"

"I wish. No. I learned that my partner, who is strapped for money *all* the time, is taking an expensive vacation with his large family at Disney World."

"And...whoever this 'kid' is has proof that the embezzled funds are being used?"

"No. And he isn't a kid, I just think of him that way because he's so...eager. He works in HR in the Field Office and he researched Paul's approved vacation request."

"Wait. Researched? How did he come by this information anyway?"

"I don't know fully. I didn't ask him. He has access to vacation entitlement information, etc., performing his job. I assume he flat out asked Paul about his plans. Does it matter?"

"Yes, if we're going to act on it."

"I sure want to...Paul is a good guy. At least I think he is. I've only worked with him during the few months in the new job. But his reputation is spotless, and he's *never* given me a reason to think otherwise. Until this... I want to go see him and ask him to explain."

"Nope," she responded firmly. "I don't want you to have contact with anyone in the FBI unless I'm present and either initiated the contact or we're legally obligated to meet with them. Got it?"

Vinnie heaved a sigh. He didn't doubt the wisdom

of her advice, but it galled him that he couldn't act...like himself. "Okay," he agreed. "Whatever you say, Summer."

He hung up the phone, drifted over to his sofa, and flicked on the television.

Chapter 6

Summer tossed her briefcase onto her desktop, cascading a teetering stack of folders over the edge. Papers flew to a scattered landing on the rug.

"Dammit!" She sank to her knees on the oriental carpet, retrieving the paperwork.

Barbara hurried through the door and stooped down gathering files in her arms.

"Please, Barbara. I'll take care of this. I didn't mean to make more work for you." Summer ducked her head under the desk to nab a couple sheets of paper.

"No let me, Ms. Layton. Don't get dirty."

Summer ignored her assistant's request, determined to do the lion's share of clean up since her frustration had set off the avalanche. She slapped several folders up onto the corner of her desk.

Barbara knit her brow. "I take it your meeting with Mr. Ashley didn't go well."

Summer shook her head sitting back on her heels. "It didn't go at all. The SOB didn't show up for work today. I'm positive someone tipped him off that I intended an ambush this morning."

"Well, I suggest you make a surprise visit this afternoon. Especially since they've scheduled a hearing." Barbara cast her a wicked grin. "Two can play that game."

Summer chuckled. "You know me so well. I

planned on asking you to clear a couple of hours this afternoon." She consulted her watch and groaned. "It's almost noon. I can't believe I wasted my whole morning."

Summer looked askance at her paper strewn desk as Barbara added even more stray sheets to the pile. Her stomach grumbled audibly.

"I'm so hungry that I'm hallucinating. I swear I smell pizza," Summer said.

"Yep. Pizza's here."

Summer gave a start and turned toward the direction of the deep baritone voice.

Vinnie leaned against the doorjamb, filling her office doorway on a six-foot five slant. A bulging plastic shopping bag dangled off the fingers of his right hand. "I brought lunch." He hoisted the bag up drawing Summer's eyes to the flex of his impressive bicep rimmed by the short sleeve of his POLO shirt.

A zing of anticipation coursed through Summer. From the tantalizing smell coming from the bag? Or from the man holding it, dressed in snug, pressed blue jeans and the fitted black shirt? The ebony hair curling above the V-neck of his shirt captured her attention. Summer had a wanton urge to kiss the exact spot.

"Hello, Vin." Summer rose to her feet and outstretched her arm offering Barbara a handhold. "Barbara, this is our client, Vincente Carlucci."

Summer towed Barbara upright. Her assistant smoothed her skirt and stammered, "Uh, Mi-mister Carlucci. Nice to meet you."

"Please, Barbara, call me Vinnie." He unleashed a charming, ear-to-ear smile on her unwitting assistant.

Barbara fussed with her hair and blushed crimson,

obviously dazzled by the man.

Summer bit back a smile. "Well are you just going to stand there, or what, Vinnie? I'm starving."

"Ms. Layton, you'll be more comfortable in the conference room while I straighten your desk," Barbara said, efficient despite Vin's hunky distraction. "I can bring Vinnie's file to you if you like, also."

"I'll grab the file, Barbara. Would you please direct Mr. Carlucci to conference room three? I'll join you in a few minutes, Vin."

"Certainly." Barbara advanced toward the door, and Vin stood to let her pass out into the reception area of Summer's office suite.

"Vinnie, if you would please follow me," Barbara said.

Vinnie shot Summer a grin and left.

Vinnie? Really? How many times have I asked her to call me Summer? He blasts her with one of his lady killer smiles and she's putty in his hands?

Summer banished the line of thought about Vinnie's universal effect on the opposite sex with a headshake as she slipped his file out of her briefcase - glad that she didn't have to sort through the mess on her desk. She checked her lipstick in her purse mirror, fluffed her hair and then dabbed a little perfume on her wrists before she left her office. Summer understood Barbara's flirty reaction to Vinnie. The man often made Summer feel like she was sixteen again and the most popular boy in class had noticed her.

"Okay. Let's get down to business." Summer breezed into the conference room.

Barbara finished setting out a feast—so much more than pizza—on one end of the long mahogany table.

"Oh, Vin," Summer said. "This looks delicious."

"If you need anything, I'll be at my desk." Barbara stepped toward the door.

"Whoa, hold on, Barbara. Stay and have something to eat." Vinnie cast his gaze at Summer. "Right, Summer?"

"Absolutely. Have a seat."

"I couldn't possibly." Barbara's cheeks flamed scarlet.

"Of course, you can. You don't want to hurt my feelings, do you?" Vin heaped food on a plate and held it out to Barbara.

Barbara accepted the meal. "Thank you. I'll enjoy this at my desk." She turned tail and streaked out of the conference room.

"I think you flustered my prim little assistant." Summer chuckled ambling toward him, placing his file down on an empty space on the table. "You had her eating out of your hand."

Vinnie picked up a garlic knot and met Summer in the middle of the room. He held the roll up to her lips. "How about you eat out of my hand?"

She circled her fingers around his thick wrist and took a bite of the buttery soft bread.

"Mm…" She chewed slowly, equally savoring the flavors bursting in her mouth and the burst of pleasure his nearness brought. "Where did you get these rolls?"

"I made them."

"As if." She grinned at him. "I usually don't like garlic bread, but this is amazing."

Summer plucked the roll out of his hand and took another ample bite. "Have you discovered an Italian bakery around here?"

Vinnie wiped buttery residue off his fingers with a napkin and regarded her evenly. "No. I baked a batch of garlic knots this morning."

"You're a man of many talents," she said, still not believing that he could bake bread.

"You have no idea lady." Vinnie winked.

He filled a plate with food and handed it to Summer. The touch of his hand set off a blast of desire. His gaze locked on her eyes.

"Did you order lunch?" Jacob Levant entered the room.

Possibly reading the situation accurately Jake said, "Oh. Sorry to barge in. I didn't realize you were... working in here." He backtracked a couple paces.

"No problem, Jake. Please stay. Meet my client, Vinnie Carlucci. Vinnie, this is Jacob Levant."

Vinnie extended his hand to Jake. "Nice to meet you."

"Same here." Jake returned the handshake and then cast his gaze around the buffet on the table.

Vinnie narrowed his eyes and observed Jake's actions.

"Help yourself," Summer said. "You don't mind do you, Vin?"

"Of course not. There's plenty."

Vinnie inspected Jacob from head to toe while Summer stood quietly watching him. It seemed that Vin viewed Jake as a competitor. Completely off the mark. But interesting.

At six-foot five, Jacob stood nose to nose with Vinnie. Both men obviously spent ample time in the gym, but Vin had the edge on musculature. Vinnie's short cut ebony hair contrasted with Jake's silver blonde cropped haircut. Dark versus light. Summer was always far more attracted to "bad boys".

"This meatball is delicious." Jake forked up another bite. "The last time I had a meatball this good was at a little restaurant in South Jersey. If I remember correctly it was called Via Lucci." He popped a piece of sausage into his mouth and groaned with delight.

"You remember correctly. I brought the food from there. It's my family's place."

"What a coincidence. I'm going to have to go back there for dinner soon." Jake tossed two garlic knots on top of the food on his plate. "I'll enjoy this in my office. Thanks for the lunch."

"You're welcome."

"You weren't kidding. You really made the garlic bread."

"I did. I've helped my parents out at the restaurant waiting for this whole mess to clear up. I have to get back on the job, Summer. Much as I love spending time with my folks, I'm going crazy with all this down time."

"I understand." Summer sat down at the head of the table and opened Vin's case folder. He tossed his paper plate into the trash can and took the seat to Summer's right.

"I'm afraid you're not going to like this. Your preliminary hearing is scheduled on January 15th. We'll have to appear in District Court before then to respond to the charges. I'm pushing to get that technicality out of the way as soon as possible. Then I can formally request a witness list and evidentiary specifics."

"*January?* This is unbelievable. Wait...hearing? As in the court?"

"Yes. Even though your superior hasn't given me the common courtesy of asking him salient questions, the FBI has filed charges. I had a brief phone conversation with Sean McMillan who added nothing helpful other than to confirm the basics of the charge against you."

Summer couldn't mask her annoyance. "I'm sorry, Vin, you have no choice but to wait. We have a lot of work to do before the hearing. First an arraignment takes place where formal charges are brought. As I said I'm working on the timing. Of course, you'll plead not guilty. In the meantime I'll work with the DA's office to secure that witness list and evidence against you. We'll fight back. You'll see. Time will pass faster than you think."

"That's easy for you to say. You have your job."

"You have a job, too. Your job is to help me win your job back. I can't let you feel sorry for yourself." Her voice rang with authority. Stone-faced, Summer gazed at him.

He tensed his jaw. "All right. I get it."

"Our firm has a good relationship with the prosecutor's office. I've asked for a witness list as soon as possible. I also want access to your laptop for our own tech analysis. And I need more info about your partner."

"All right. I've only worked with Paul since my transfer to New Jersey. But we connected right away on the job. You learn a lot about the measure of a man in the Field. Not only how he works in unison with you, but also what he confides during long hours of stakeouts, and such. He's a good guy and a great family man. I have a hard time believing that he would steal money and an even harder time believing that he would jeopardize me."

"Any suspicious behavior lately—aside from the Disney World vacation?"

"No. Nothing. He doesn't socialize after a shift. He goes home. He has five kids and a homemaker wife."

"Have you ever gone to his house? Met his family?"

"No."

"Is that unusual?"

"Maybe a little." He twisted his lips. "Come to think of it, he didn't come to the big summer barbecue. Everybody did with all their kids except Paul. I never thought much of it until now. I guess that is a little odd."

Vin huffed a laugh. "Damn you're good. You have me convinced that my partner did it. You must be something in the courtroom."

"I just ask the right questions." She smiled. "I'll need Paul's contact information."

Vinnie pulled his phone out of his back pocket. He thumbed the home button, scrolled contacts and texted Paul's information to Summer.

"Now tell me about the IT guy who called you and implicated Paul." She consulted a paper in the file. "His name is Tyler per my notes."

"Right. Tyler Wellington. His picture should be next to the word geek in the dictionary." He huffed a laugh.

"What do you think he was trying to accomplish telling you about Paul?"

"Tyler is an odd duck. From what I hear he is brilliant at what he does, but he wants to be in the Field.

Basically, he wants my job…or maybe Paul's."

He stared off into the distance. "Nah," he said with a shake of his head. "I don't think he had any ulterior motive. Besides, eliminating a Special Agent would do squat for him career-wise. He's a good kid. The guys rib him a lot. I don't. I feel sorry for him. I honestly think hc was just trying to help me."

"Good. Sounds like we can put him on our list as a character witness." She jotted notes in the file.

Anticipating her request, Vinnie texted her Wellington's contact information.

"I need you to think of some more people who will be willing to stand up for you."

"I'll go through my contacts tonight and send you a list."

"Perfect." She put the pen down. "Do you know anyone who would want to frame you? Are there any enemies at work that I should know about?"

"I can't think of anyone who hates me that much. Sure, I've had disagreements with guys at work. Tempers can flare when we're on the line. But we're like a family. The guys I work with and who work for me are like brothers. When we have a problem, we go to a bar, order a pitcher of beer and hash it out."

"All right. When you go through your contacts see if anyone stands out. And don't restrict your thinking to your job now. Review *all* your Bureau relationships."

Summer stretched her arms overhead noting Vin's fixation on the rise and fall of her breasts. "We're done for now. I *will* meet with Ashley," she vowed.

She glanced at her watch. "Too late today, but I'll make it my early morning mission tomorrow and, dammit every day until I get him to hold still for me."

Vinnie followed Summer's lead and pushed away from the table. He sidled to the far end and began packing up the leftover food. "Would you like to take this home?"

"Yes. Yes. Yes." She beamed him a smile. "Food for the weekend."

"Speaking of the weekend, I spoke to Joey last night. The four tickets you gave him for his birthday are for the game this Sunday. He invited me to go and wanted me to ask you along, too."

"That's so sweet of him. But wouldn't he prefer Tricia or his dad to go instead?"

"Tricia has already booked a spa day with my mother, and don't get me started on that piece of... I think I may have mentioned that Barry is a piece of work. He doesn't have any interest in going to the game with the boys."

"That's a shame. But his loss is my gain. I would love to go to the game with you guys."

"Great. Joey will be happy." He closed the gap between them. "I'm happy too."

He brushed her cheek with a soft feather-like kiss. His musky cologne filled her senses. For a brief second, Summer surrendered to the dizzy sensation Vin brought with the slightest contact. A phone rang somewhere in the outer office jarring her back to reality.

"I'll pick you up," he suggested.

"You have to pick up the boys. Why don't I meet you at the game? Let me get you a parking pass from Barbara."

Vinnie stood between her and the doorway. "Thank you for helping me, Summer." He leaned down and kissed her.

Her knees turned to water and she hungrily returned the kiss not caring that she risked broadcasting PDA should a co-worker appear.

He ended the kiss gently and stood gazing down at her.

"My pleasure." She edged past him and out the door bound for her assistant's desk.

Definitely my pleasure.

Chapter 7

"Barry, we're leaving in five minutes," Vinnie yelled up the stairs.

"Uncle Vinnie." Joey bounced up and down next to him, waving his birthday gift tickets from Summer overhead. "I looked the seats up online and they're in a suite! Can you believe it? Have you ever been in a suite at the football stadium?"

"Nah, buddy. A little too expensive for me."

"I have to get my camera. No one will believe me at school. This is so cool," he rattled off before he whizzed up the stairs, presumably to search for the camera.

"He's beyond excited." Tricia emerged from her kitchen gifting Vinnie with a sunny smile. She wiped her hands on a dish towel. "Pretty swanky tickets."

"Summer works for a pretty swanky law firm."

Checking his watch, he hollered up the stairs again, "Barry get a move on."

"Be nice to him," Tricia whispered. "He's still in knots over his father's leaving. It doesn't help that the SOB makes plans with him and then doesn't show up."

"If he had big boobs and a tight ass his father would show up," Vinnie sneered.

"Not funny." She punched him in the arm. Put some steam behind it, too. Vinnie gave her a crooked grin, appreciating his sister's fighting spirit.

"Just be nice."

"I'm always nice," he said. "To nice people."

Joey hopped down the stairs. Barry descended a couple steps behind him—thumping down each footfall like he stamped on hard-shelled bugs. The last thing the sullen expression on his face conveyed was excitement at going to a football game.

Another noticeable difference between the brothers: Joey sported bold blue and white Giants team gear while Barry wore a non-descript black T-shirt and jeans. Vinnie didn't comment on Barry's most likely calculated symbolic disinterest. He had an extra Giants cap in the car if Barry wanted to get into the spirit of the thing later. For now, he was happy the kid had come out of his bedroom.

Vinnie pecked Tricia on the cheek. "Have fun with Ma at the day spa."

"Oh, I intend to…"

He herded the boys out to the car.

Joey called, "Shotgun!" Grinning widely, he slipped into the passenger seat as Vinnie triggered the ignition.

Vin listened to Joey's running monolog with half an ear while observing Barry's reflection through glimpses in the rearview mirror. The kid bent his head over his phone, his eyes apparently glued to the screen.

"When's your next game, Barry?"

"Friday night," he muttered.

"Who are you playing?"

"Harrison."

"They're tough."

"We're tougher."

Barry's eyes hadn't budged from staring at his

phone during the minimal dialog, but Vin knew he could keep him talking on the subject of football—the one activity that kept him engaged despite depression over his parents' seemingly permanent split. As a high school freshman Barry sat the bench on the varsity team so far, but he was the starting quarterback for the Junior Varsity team. Already, his performance had college scouts' interest.

"What do you think of the matchup between Manning and Newton?" Vinnie probed.

"No comparison. Newton all the way."

"Uh-uh. The Giants are going to beat the Panthers," Joey asserted.

"Wrong, squirt," Barry snapped. "Newton is the only player to win the Heisman, the national championship and number one draft pick in the same year. He's amazing. I think he's even better than Brady."

The boys continued bickering as Vinnie steered into a parking lot following the directions Summer had texted him earlier. He handed the pass to an attendant, pulled into an available space and then shifted the car into Park.

He sent a "We're here" text to Summer's phone.

Look for the huge Giants flag closer to the entrance, came her text response.

He showed Joey his phone sharing the message and then switched off the engine. "Come on, Barry. We're going to a tailgate party."

Joey raced ahead swiveling his head from side to side scrutinizing the alleys between rows of parked cars as he passed.

Nearing the walls of MetLife Stadium, Joey halted.

"I found it!" He pointed to the left. "And there's Summer."

Vinnie's eyes locked on her. She was seated at a table across from a man about three times her size. Vinnie stared in amazement at the improbable spectacle of willowy Summer arm wrestling a bear.

Their intertwined arms shimmied, biceps bulging: Summer's a dainty curve on her slender, porcelain-skinned arm and her opponent's a thick coconut sized knot. The guy would surely fracture her delicate bones.

"Hey Vin. Grab a beer. I'll be right with you," she tossed out nonchalantly while maintaining an eye lock with the giant.

Summer smiled as she fixated intensely on her opponent, tilting his arm closer to the table. He grimaced, clenched his jaw and groaned applying counteractive force with obvious exertion.

Vinnie blinked at the lightning flash of her swift leverage. He could swear that for an instant Summer's arm seemed to swell to he-man proportions.

Bam! The loser's arm slammed down on the table evoking awestricken cheers from Vin, his nephews and a group of spectators clustered around the table. Summer gracefully disengaged her hand, rose to her feet and plucked a one-hundred-dollar bill off the tabletop. She tucked the money into the front pocket of skintight black jeans—an extremely seductive maneuver to Vinnie. He absolutely wanted to tuck his hand into the exact same spot. The couple of open buttons on her form fitting short sleeve, gauzy blouse had Vinnie fantasizing about tucking his hand elsewhere.

"Next?" She raised her eyebrows at Vinnie.

"No, thank you. I'm not stepping into that trap."
He chuckled. "How the hell did you do that?"

She gave him a wicked grin, her jade eyes dancing.
"It's all in the leverage."

He snorted. "I'll bet."

She skirted the table and bussed his cheek; a soft
kiss that had him smiling. A waft of her perfume teased
his senses: citrus laced vanilla with a musky
undertone—the heady fragrance of Summer.

"Hey Joey, Barry," she greeted the boys.

"Hi," Joey sang out.

"Hi," Barry grunted.

"Come on over here," she directed. "We have tons
of food."

The boys dove into the tail gate buffet shepherded
by the pretty lady aka arm wrestling champ.

Jacob Levant stepped forward extending a hand to
Vinnie. The man dressed like a Ralph Lauren model,
Waspy and upper-class casual. Even his jeans had
deeply ironed creases. "Good to see you again." He
shook Vinnie's hand. "She always puts on a show."

Vinnie nodded agreement, knitting his brow at the
word 'always'.

Jacob picked up on the cue. "She rented a house
one spring break in college with the money she won
arm wrestling."

"No shit. You mean that—" Vinnie wagged his
finger at the now empty seats at the table. "—Wasn't a
fluke?"

Jacob hooted. "She'd take on all comers."

"You went to school together?"

"We did," Jacob said. "Coincidentally, here comes
one of her past victims from that era."

"Ready for a rematch Hugh?" Summer boomed as the tall muscular man neared their area of the parking lot.

He wagged his head. "No way. I learned my lesson years ago."

Summer sauntered over to Vinnie toting a plastic plate heaped with food. "Hugh was the captain of the Princeton football team."

"Safety school," Jacob quipped, triggering roars of laughter from his group of friends and a scowl from Hugh.

"We were hanging out in the bar after the game senior year when Princeton played us in Cambridge. Hugh and his o-line came in to drown their sorrows. And I suggested a friendly arm-wrestling contest." Summer grinned.

"Big mistake," Hugh said good-naturedly.

"How much did you lose that night?" Jacob asked, slapping Hugh on the back.

"Two hundred dollars and my self-esteem. But I made a friendship that I treasure, so in the long run it was worth it." He hugged Summer.

"Are those burgers ready yet?" he called to the guys surrounding a grill.

"Come and get it."

"Can we have burgers, too, Uncle Vin?" Joey stuffed the remnants of a hot dog in his mouth.

"Of course, you can," Summer interjected.

Vinnie circled his arm around Summer's shoulders. "So, what's your trick with the arm-wrestling leverage?"

"Um…"

Her hesitation had Vin scrutinizing her hands—an

interrogation tactic he employed. She shrugged her shoulders palms up and then clasped her hands in front of her. Whatever she'd say next could not be trusted.

"There's no trick involved." She smiled up at him sweetly.

Vin guffawed. "Bullshit."

"You think I'm lying?" She faced him, jade eyes twinkling. "Have a seat, Vincente. I'll take you down in less than twenty seconds. If I don't, I'll confess my supposed secret trick."

He narrowed his eyes as he slipped into the chair opposite Summer. Her cheeks flushed rosy pink, and her eyes sparked gleeful at the challenge. Regret pinched as his nephews gathered around the table. This was a lose-lose situation. Either their uncle beat a wisp of a female, or...

Well, despite recent evidence to the contrary, she couldn't possibly match his strength.

Ten seconds later, Summer proved him absolutely wrong. Her handhold an iron vise, she pressed his arm flat on the tabletop with seemingly no effort at. He hadn't thrown the contest—on the contrary. And he'd be damned if he could figure out some trick involved. Shaking his head, he beamed at her, wonderstruck.

"You let a *girl* whoop your ass, Unc?"

"Barry. Language…"

"Wait 'til I tell Ma." Barry gave him a shit-eating grin.

For that alone the ass-whooping was worth it.

Vinnie gazed at Summer's beautiful face alit with victory. He had no idea how she bested him in a contest where he almost always was the victor faced with male opponents minimally twice her size. The sexy female power she exuded magnetized him—an attraction so powerful that his knees went weak.

Despite the fact that she was his lawyer *and* Bree's sister, he intended to seek a rematch the next time they were alone—hopefully with a bed nearby. "You *have* to tell me how you did that."

****

The expression on Vinnie's face caught Summer off guard. The wild appreciation and tenderness in his sky-blue eyes triggered an ache of yearning deep in her core. Would she divulge her secret to him? Only if she were head over heels in love with him like Bree was with Jack. Even then…maybe not. Her mom would likely kill her if she knew she had drawn on the power of the Sacred Source all these years to win bets in arm wrestling contests.

His penetrating warm gaze sent shivers through Summer. No denying the volcanic attraction sizzling between them…and something more. This powerful, muscular giant had a soft side that appealed enormously to her. Fall head over heels in love with Vinnie? The notion filled her with unexpected hope.

"Someday maybe I will tell you, Vin." She grinned at him, and then hugged Barry and Joey in turn. "I'm so glad you guys are here. Joey, there's no question that you'll root for the Giants with all that fan gear you're wearing."

She hooked a finger in the neckline of a bomber jacket and hoisted it off the back of a chair, shrugged it on, and presented her back to the boys displaying Panthers insignia. "Sorry, Joe, but the Giants are going down today. I'm a North Carolina girl at heart. Barry, are you a Giants fan too?"

"Nah, my dad and I are Bears fans. My dad went to school in Chicago."

"Your uncle, too, kid," Vin said.

"Right. Your Uncle Vinnie went to school with my sister, Bree. She still lives in Chicago," Summer said. "It's a great city. Have you ever been there?"

"No, but my dad said he'll take me one day."

She interpreted Vinnie's eye roll as "when hell freezes over". Summer decided to change the sensitive subject when Jake announced that it was time to go to the game, and she herded her guys toward the VIP entrance.

Summer fell in step with Vinnie and linked her arm through his. In profile, his clenched jaw and downcast gaze had her probing, "Everything all right?"

"Yeah. But I'm pissed at Tricia's soon-to-be ex. The jerk makes promises to the boys, has them all excited about big plans and doesn't even bother to show up."

"But you keep your promises?"

He halted and faced her. "Every single time."

She stood on tiptoes and planted a soft kiss on his cheek. Summer brushed her thumb across his cheek gently scrubbing away the faint red lipstick smear.

A smile bloomed on his full lips riveting her eyes on his mouth. "What was that for?" he said.

"You're a good man, and I'm very happy that you're here today."

In the next instant those full lips covered hers. Summer hung suspended in the sensual connection, lost in his clean manly scent and the taste of beer on his tongue. She closed her eyes against the onslaught of molten desire, her surroundings and reality blotted out by the most passionate kiss she'd ever received.

"Ew…what the heck Uncle Vin?" Barry's sarcasm pierced through and Summer pulled away—reluctantly.

"Wise guy," Vin said, giving his nephew a crooked grin.

Trooping through the VIP entrance, Summer struggled to regain her equilibrium. Vinnie was her client, which automatically should prohibit kisses, passionate or otherwise. But…she had had more than a few carnal fantasies about the man since she had met him at the hospital when Bree was injured. Friendly, no strings kind of fantasies. Should that kind of opportunity present now, why not? It wouldn't affect her whole-hearted defense on his behalf one bit.

The suite impressed Joey who exclaimed delight at the "amazing" buffet and the spacious, apartment-like accommodations. Seating options included leather captain chairs on the interior or three rows of leather chairs, stadium seating that fronted the suite on the exterior. Joey bounced back and forth between the two areas and repeatedly asked Vinnie to take his photo for bragging purposes at school.

When he wasn't posing for the camera, Joey seemed intent on eating non-stop.

"Slow down on the food, okay, buddy?" Vin asked, apparently to no avail as Joey made multiple selections from the Cracker Jacks and candy table.

"Tricia will kill me if he eats himself sick," Vinnie confided to Summer.

She chose a seat in the front row outside. Vinnie and the boys followed her lead occupying the other three seats in the row.

By the fourth quarter, the score was tied. Summer

loved football and enjoyed breaking down the offensive plays for Barry, gratified that his earlier sullenness had evaporated. Instead, the mopey teenager transformed into a pleasant young man who seemed genuinely delighted to talk football with her.

Vinnie leaned toward her and whispered in her ear, "I wish Tricia could see Barry's behavior with you now. She'd be hugging the shit out of you."

Warmed, Summer beamed him a smile.

In the final minutes of the game the Panthers intercepted Manning's pass and ran the ball in for a touchdown. Groans erupted from Vin and Joey as Summer jumped to her feet and shimmied a victory dance. She linked hands with Barry when he hopped up to join her.

"Told you Newton would win out over Manning," Barry informed his brother.

Despite the home team loss, their antics solicited grins from the "losers". Joey hopefully considered the overall experience compensation for the Panthers' win.

"Can I give you a ride home?" Vinnie asked.

"No thanks. Jacob sent a car."

He abruptly turned away and nudged his nephews toward the stairs leading back into the suite.

Joey ducked under Vinnie's arm, headed toward Summer, and wrapped his arms around her waist. "Thank you so much for the tickets. I had so much fun. I don't even care that the Giants lost."

"You are *so* welcome. I hope we can do it again."

Barry stood behind his brother his arms at his sides. Summer enveloped him in a loose hug, and then cupped his shoulders with her hands. Smiling, she promised, "I'll check the schedule to see when the

Bears play here this season."

His face lit with his grin. "Wow, thanks Summer." He threw his arms around her doling out a hug.

"I had fun today. I hope I see you guys soon." She trailed the boys into the suite.

"Uncle Vinnie said we might go apple picking next weekend," Joey said. "Want to come?"

Summer glanced at Vinnie. His expression was impassive.

Does he not want me to come?

"Um, thanks Joey. We'll see…"

"Sure." Joey followed his brother to the suite's exit.

She tapped Vinnie on the shoulder before he left the room. "Did I say or do something wrong?"

"No."

The straight-lipped expression on his face persisted.

"It seems like you were rushing the boys out of here after I said I didn't need a ride."

Narrowing her eyes, she regarded him. "Did my mentioning Jacob have something to do with your—shut down?"

"No."

"Wait. Are you jealous of him?" The thought tickled her.

"Nope."

She arched her eyebrows at the obviously false answer.

"Jake and I have been friends since Harvard Law School. I was his wife's maid of honor. He's the brother I always wanted." She placed her hand on his chest thrilled at the hard plane of him and the drumbeat of his heart beneath her palm. "Are you sure you weren't just a little bit jealous?"

His lips curled up at the corners and his eyes danced.

"Uncle Vinnie, are we going or not?" Barry demanded.

"Definitely going." He leaned toward her, kissed her cheek and then whispered, "Maybe a little bit."

Summer hooted a laugh. "I'm available to go apple picking with Joey in case you were wondering."

"Then it's a date," he said.

"Good. Call me Monday to go over a few legal matters?"

"Sure."

Vinnie and the boys left the suite. She watched her client retreat thoroughly appreciating his powerful, long-legged strides and the excellent fit of the seat of his jeans.

Chapter 8

The words in the document that she reviewed on her computer monitor blurred. Her eyes glazed over, her thoughts turning inward. She held Vinnie one hundred percent responsible for her lack of focus on work that morning—pretty much daily occurrences that week. He had dominated her thoughts on every level; professional, as she battled frustration and damning information involved in his case, and *deeply* personal.

Summer relived every moment in his company since the surrounded-by-sharks nightmare had triggered her representing him. At the outset, she certainly hadn't planned anything other than to assist a family friend with his legal troubles. A sensuous, compelling, ultra-virile family friend who had spurred more than a few hot fantasies in the past. In his company recently, her fantasies roared from hot to inferno. She absolutely had to investigate if lovemaking with Vinnie lived up to her imaginings.

Her preoccupation deepened considering the embezzlement charge that hung over their heads like a piano dangling on a wire. She shuddered remembering his quivering with barely controlled rage and frustration facing the bench next to her at the arraignment and declaring, "Not guilty," with unwavering clarity.

She sighed, propped her elbow on the desk and cupped her chin in her hand. Sweet memories of the

Giants-Panthers game swamped her; especially the awestricken appreciation Vinnie radiated at her arm-wrestling feat. Would he still regard her the same way if he knew? Summer had never had a problem concealing the bit of rapid-fire shape-shifting an "ape arm" that she needed to win in arm wrestling, positive that she'd escape detection. She had never failed in keeping her truth secret. Although Vinnie's investigative skills might exceed those of any other male she'd known, her secret was safe—unless she *chose* to reveal it. Why did she contemplate baring *all* to Vinnie Carlucci?

"Buried in your work, or your work has buried you?" Jake leaned against her office door jamb evoking a mental flashback of Vinnie grinning at her from the same vantage point as he declared himself the pizza delivery guy.

Summer straightened in her seat beaming at him. "A little of both."

He sauntered to her desk and presented her with a shopping bag.

"What's this?" She buried her nose in the bag fingering the polyester material of one of the items inside.

"I paid attention to your young guests at the game. Thought you might like to add to their hero worship for you."

"Oh wow." Summer lifted out one of the jerseys. "Eli Manning's autograph! Joey will flip."

A smile bloomed on Jake's face. "Good. But I think you'll make a bigger hit with the other one."

Summer foraged inside the shopping bag and brought the orange and blue Chicago Bears Jersey into view. "Mitch Trubinski? This'll bring a smile to Barry's face. How the hell did you pull this off?"

"Friends in high places."

The man boggled her mind. "I imagine I owe you a fortune." She fished inside her lower desk drawer for her purse. "Worth every cent."

"Nah." He shook his head. "Got these gratis. Glad you think the kids will like them. I enjoyed their company."

"Yeah, me, too." She leaned back in her chair.

His brown eyes held hers pinioning Summer with Jacob's famous laser beam stare. "Everything good with Carlucci?"

"Glad you asked. I need a computer expert. Can you recommend one?" She averted his dissecting gaze intuiting that his question had nothing to do with Vinnie's defense.

"I can and will." He narrowed his eyes. "But I think we both know I was referring to your personal relationship."

"Hmm. Are you concerned that my…friendship with him impedes my ability to defend him? Because I don't see a conflict there at all."

"Friendship." He gave her a half smile. His eyes sparked, amused. "Lady, Vinnie Carlucci has plenty in mind where you're concerned. I wouldn't put friendship on the top of that list."

"Oh. Don't worry." She flicked her wrist in dismissal. "He's a hot-blooded type. I can handle him."

Jake chuckled. He flattened his palms on her desk and leaned closer to her. "I have *no* doubt of that. Just remember, I'm ready to step in on his defense *if* a conflict arises and you need me."

"Thanks. But I'm good." She furrowed her brow. "Besides. You know I'm essentially doing this pro bono, right? He can't afford your retainer, that's for sure."

"I do know that. And my offer still stands." He stood upright, and half turned toward the door.

"One sec? I need that expert referral. Actually, I'm looking for a magician."

He faced her. "Right. Happen to have one up my sleeve. His name is Mike Haws. The best expert tech witness that I've ever known. The guy has worked for NASA, Boeing, you name it. Even has a patent with Boeing. He's a good guy, too. This case will appeal to him. I'll call him and head him in your direction."

"Thanks. And if you can put some heat on the DA and FBI to grant forensic access to Vin's laptop? We'll meet whatever supervision requirements they set forth. I want Mike to find out who hacked that computer."

"Nope." Jacob shook his head. "You want Mike to find the money. *Then* you've got your case."

Jacob turned and paced out of her office leaving Summer to her reverie. She checked the digital clock readout in the upper right corner of her computer gauging her next steps in her remaining workday. She decided to work late that Friday evening as necessary to enjoy the weekend guilt free. She had never picked apples in the fall before. A tomboy at heart, anything outdoors held great appeal to her. Not to mention the prospect of Vinnie's company during the outing.

****

Tricia swung open the passenger door of the black Toyota Sienna that drew up in front of Summer's building and hopped out of the car.

83

"Hi, Summer," she said. "I'll ride in back with the boys."

Summer ducked her head inside the car and said hello to Barry and Joey. They grinned at her while fixating on the small screen suspended from the ceiling in front of them.

"Spider Man." Tricia squatted in between the boys' seats offering Summer her cell phone. "Just hit Go to start directions to Chester. It's about an hour away off 78."

"Thanks." Summer settled in her seat fastening her seat belt. She faced Vinnie in the driver seat warming at his sunny expression. "Good morning."

"Morning. You look beautiful."

Happiness streamed through her at the sight of him. His hands rested on the steering wheel; his arms bent at the elbows. Even in the long-sleeved pullover that he wore, his defined biceps through the material presented an enticing picture.

"Thank you. You look pretty great yourself. Ready?" She poised her index finger over the smartphone screen.

"Yep."

She pushed Go. Tricia cleared her throat.

Summer swiveled in her seat, angled her head and smiled back at her.

Vin's sister twisted her lips. "You two done complimenting each other?"

Summer huffed a laugh. "You look great, too, Trish."

"Already told her," Vinnie added.

"Where are we headed?" Summer asked.

"In two miles turn right," squawked the virtual

assistant.

"There are several farms to choose from in New Jersey apple picking country. We love Alstede Farms. We haven't missed a year since Barry learned to walk. I love the baby photos of each of them in the pumpkin patch. Too cute," Tricia said.

"I have the photos framed. They're great. And in those twelve years or so, this is the first time I've been available for annual apple picking," Vinnie said.

"Yeah," Tricia said. "Were your ears ringing last night, Summer?"

"Why?"

"My brother couldn't stop praising your lawyering."

Summer regarded him in profile.

Vin shrugged his shoulders in response.

"That's nice," Summer said. "But I haven't done much that's praise-worthy yet."

"That's not the way I heard it."

"Vinnie?" Summer tapped his thigh playfully.

"You're good, Summer. You gave me confidence in that meeting with OPR and the SAC. I like what you told me about that computer expert. I know you'll make this all go away."

Summer's stomach sank as the nightmare dreamscape flashed in her mind. She was the only one who had wanted to help Vinnie during the shark attack in the dream. And she hadn't saved him.

But her conviction of his innocence grounded her firmly in reality. "We will make this go away. Together."

The north Jersey urban-suburban sprawl near New York City gave way to a rural landscape, the grounds undulating vine green dotted with crimson, orange and yellow topped trees. Soon the land flattened, and railroad tie fences lined the road on either side of the minivan. Vinnie steered off road onto a dirt path at the entrance to Alstede Farms. Brittle corn stalks nodded in the breeze on one side of the drive. Near the parking area a painted wood cutout of the farm's pickup truck loaded with pumpkins drew kids posing for photos. The little models pressed their faces into oval shaped holes in pumpkins in the cargo area, a square in the passenger window and a rectangle in the windshield, grinning at adults' smartphones.

"Want your pictures taken, fellas?" Trish quipped.

"Yeah right…" Barry sneered.

Outside the crisp clean air and bracing breeze filled Summer with carefree freedom reminding her of the anticipation and liberation she experienced every time she stepped onto the beach fronting her family's Inn of the Three Butterflies. She luxuriated in the "ah" moment gazing at the rare spotless blue sky as the other passengers scrambled out of the car.

Vinnie draped an arm over her shoulders deepening her sense of peaceful anticipation. The boys barreled toward a red barn-like building, whipped open the door and jostling each other for first place through the threshold, disappeared inside.

Tricia came up next to Summer. "Footlong hotdogs and fries."

Summer nodded. She looked up at Vinnie. "Are you hungry?"

"Not yet. Want to head to the orchard and pick some fruit? I'm bringing a couple bushels of apples to Ma for the restaurant."

"You two go ahead and I'll herd the boys. You know they're going to want to run around in the corn maze and pick Halloween pumpkins and gourds. Come find us when you're done."

"Will do." Vinnie offered Summer a handhold. "Your hand's so cold." He sandwiched her hand between his hands, rubbing gently back and forth to stimulate circulation. Radiating warmth enveloped her and she basked in the pure pleasure of simply being with him.

Apparently satisfied that he had shielded her from the cold, he led her toward a tent, handed her an empty bushel basket and grabbed one for himself. "One of these filled weighs about forty pounds. You okay with carrying one back here a fair distance to checkout?"

"Sure." She bent her arm and flexed her bicep. "Arm wrestling champ."

He smiled. "How could I forget?"

Meandering down the grass carpeted lane between rows of varietals in the apple garden, Summer drank in the clean air and loveliness of sharing the day with Vinnie. On a mission to stock his mother's restaurant larder, Vinnie loaded his basket with *Rome Beauties.*

"If you're looking for great eating apples, I like the *Crimson Crisps* or *Lady* varieties," he advised—a man of apparent diverse life experience.

Discovering the many facets of his personality intrigued Summer. And excited her. She couldn't remember the last time she felt this free and happy— half of a couple. Had she ever experienced that unity? Probably not. Definitely not.

She refused to analyze her feelings further, preferring to relax and revel in the day's uncomplicated enjoyment. She heeded Vinnie's expert opinion about the best baking apples and picked a combination of *Rome Beauties* and *Ida Reds* to ship to her mother Kay in Nags Head, North Carolina. She knew Mom would preserve, jelly, freeze dry—whatever - to bake up a storm with the perfectly ripe fruit to grace their Thanksgiving table and to delight patrons of the inn next season.

By the end of that afternoon her jeans and boots sported a layer of dust, her spiky cut hair had tousled every which way in the stiff breeze, her cheeks had pinkened wind-blown, her arms ached from lugging forty plus pounds of apples at a time, her cheeks ached from laughing at Vinnie's and the kids' antics and she felt refreshed and exhilarated.

She never tired of receiving Vinnie's tender attention. Summer was wildly drawn to him even though he hadn't said or done anything vaguely seductive. Without trying he exuded sensuality, perhaps owing to his Mediterranean roots, compelling *la dolce vita* mentality and innate chivalry. Despite her family's Celtic ethnic heritage, Vinnie reminded her of her dad, Mike—a prerequisite to a serious relationship according to her engaged sister, Bree. Summer and her sisters Breeze and Skye would always be Daddy's girls.

Before they left the farm's grounds, Summer helped the boys load the trunk with assorted pumpkins, gourds, bakery boxes, and gallons of apple cider. Vinnie hoisted his bushels of apples into free space in the trunk and pushed the overhead button triggering the cargo door to close. Seated in the van, Summer finger combed her wayward hair and checked email messages on her phone. Happy that nothing pressing demanded her attention, she slipped the phone in her purse.

"I hope you guys have an appetite. We're going to the restaurant now," Tricia said.

"Good, I'm starving." Barry grabbed headphones out of the seat pocket in front of him. "Can you push play on the console, Uncle Vin?"

"*Please*," Tricia said.

"Yeah. Please." He covered his ears with the headset.

"I'm starving, too," Joey piped in mimicking his brother's movements.

Tricia rolled her eyes at Summer. "I don't know where they put it. Will you join us for dinner, Summer?"

"I'd love to." She faced Vinnie. "Is that okay with you?"

"Are you kidding? My mother would kill me if I didn't bring you to supper." He winked at her.

Summer narrowed her eyes and held his gaze. "In *that* case, yes. I wouldn't dream of disappointing Rose."

Chapter 9

The noisy group clambered into the restaurant in front of Vinnie. Propping the door open with one of the baskets, he strode back to Trish's car, hefted the other basket out of the trunk and toted it into Via Lucci Ristorante.

Approaching him from the waiters' station nook to the left of the bar, his mother clapped her hands together. "Oh boy. Perfect. Thank you so much."

"Where do you want them, Ma?"

She pivoted and faced her tall, lanky head waiter. "Benjamin can you and Walter please bring these apples down to the wine cellar for me?"

"I'll take one down," Vinnie said.

"No, no. You need to be with your lady. We'll take care of this, won't we Benjamin?"

"Sure thing, Missus C."

"Vincente, you're at the round table." She shooed him up one step to the main dining room. "Want a couple bottles of wine for the table to start?"

Remembering that Summer preferred Cabernet he requested, "How about Schooner number 5? It's such a rich Merlot I think Summer will like it."

Rose nodded and approached Walter who stood behind the empty bar.

Vinnie observed "his lady", warming to his mother's reference to Summer, as he neared the table where she sat next to Tricia. Her lawn green eyes widened at every turn of her head checking out her surroundings. He read the sparkle in her eyes and her earlier spontaneous acceptance of his parents' open-armed welcome hugs as just the right level of delight.

He flat out loved this place—his parents' pride and joy as far back as he could remember. The blonde wood paneling from the floor to two thirds up the Italianate stucco walls projected an old-world warmth. Non-functioning doorbell-like buttons were positioned a few feet apart below carriage rails around the perimeter of the dining room, a nod to the gangster era when waiters in an Italian restaurant *only* came when summoned. The buzzers were a source of endless fascination to him as a kid and to all the kids who came here. Barry, and soon after, Joey, had eventually outgrown pushing the buttons at every opportunity.

The doorbells seemed to catch Summer's eye. She pointed to one, muttered to Tricia and the pair burst into laughter after Trish responded. Summer effortlessly fit in with the people, and now one of the places, that meant the most to him. He was raised to believe that faith, family and gratitude were the bedrocks of a well-lived life.

Vinnie was immensely grateful that the Lord had sent Summer into his life, despite the circumstances. Increasingly enchanted with everything about the woman, he suspected that her importance in his life would figure far beyond extricating him from a legal mess. Or his acting on the powerful sexual magnetism she exuded. She already felt like family. Was it because he had a deep brotherly love for her sister? No way. Nothing brotherly in his attraction to Summer.

He knew beyond doubt that sex with Summer would be mind-shattering. The past few weeks if she had but crooked her little finger at him, he would have *run* to do her bidding.

Now maybe not so fast. Vinnie wanted to make love to Summer. He knew beyond doubt that were the lady to agree, she might not only shatter his mind…Summer might shatter his heart.

Ole blue eyes crooned on the audio system, the prominent background music of his childhood. Taking the vacant seat at the table next to her, Vinnie smiled at Summer's humming the melody of *My Funny Valentine.* She passed him the breadbasket and then bit off a third of a sesame bread stick with a resounding crack. He could fall in love with this singular lady.

His dad poked his head through the doorway that fronted the galley leading to the restaurant's kitchen. Clad in a snow-white chef's smock he clued Vinnie in to the specialties available that day since Pops commandeered the stove. Nobody cooked authentic southern Italian dishes like his dad.

"Hey sonny," Pops said. "The usual for appetizers?"

"Heck yeah," Tricia said.

"Okay with you if Pops feeds us? You won't regret it," Vinnie asked Summer.

"Bring it on." She handed Vinnie her menu.

Ben removed menus from the table after he served Cokes to the boys. Ma brought over two bottles of wine which the waiter expertly uncorked. He poured a tasting sample into a goblet presenting the glass to Summer at the nod of Vinnie's head.

"Mm. Perfect," she declared.

The boys slathered butter on hunks of crusty bread and devoured slice after slice. Vinnie sat back in his seat, wine glass in hand, relishing the pleasant company and the animated banter between Summer and Trish.

"So, Tricia, you're a high school teacher. Are you enjoying your students this year?"

"Oh yes. This year and every year. I'm certified to teach Biology, Chemistry and Physics, so I have a variety of subjects and learning levels."

"She teaches all the AP classes, too. She has her Master's in Education," Vinnie said. "Super smart lady."

"Oh well." Tricia waved off the compliment. "Nothing compares to you Summer - going to law school and passing the bar."

"Don't sell yourself short. I couldn't teach a science course AP or otherwise. I'm just glad I got through the high school and college core curriculum requirements for science and math. In the case of Bio in college?" Summer said. "I got a D. And the only reason I didn't fail is because the final was a take home exam and the prof elevated my F to a D because she was so impressed that I obviously didn't cheat! Good thing I had no intention of going to med school like my sister."

Vin and Tricia burst out laughing along with Summer. Barry hooted a laugh, apparently not as absorbed with his bread and butter as he appeared. Ben and Walter brought platters of appetizers to the table to start the family style feast. Tricia and Summer collaborated on splitting some items: a half of a red bell pepper topped with melted Provoleta cheese sprinkled with sprigs of rosemary, and a grilled Portobello mushroom capped with melted Fontina cheese. Summer selected her own twice baked clam from the passed plate and a square of grilled polenta topped with a dollop of chicken liver pâté.

Summer took a bite of the crostini. "Good grief. What *is* this?" She smacked her lips.

"Pâté on grilled polenta. You like it?" Vinnie said.

"Mm absolutely." She swallowed, holding a half uneaten square in her hand. "How is marketing your home going, Tricia?" Summer popped the other half of the crostini into her mouth.

"We've had a few showings. I'm actually afraid someone will be serious and make an offer. Because I honestly don't know where to move. Everything is so expensive in my area. I have to stay in the district to teach at the same school. Not to mention not wanting to uproot the kids." She lowered her voice, "Especially Barry."

Summer leaned toward Tricia conspiratorially. "You *have* to sell? Isn't there any way you can stay there?"

"Joey, Barry, help me clear these plates? Maybe Grandpa can use a couple of sous chefs for the pasta course," Vinnie said creating an opportunity to give the women some privacy.

****

Summer waited for Vinnie to shepherd his nephews away from the table. "I don't want to be too personal, but Vinnie has alluded to your estranged husband's infidelity. Is that right?"

"Oh yeah. Stereotypical blonde bombshell, too." Tricia's bitter tone dripped with sarcasm.

"Well then, why aren't you suing the pants off him? Surely you can at least keep the house."

"He wants half the equity and I can't afford to buy him out."

"Bullshit. Who cares what he wants? Who's your attorney? If you don't mind my asking."

"I haven't really hired one yet. I had a conversation with a man named Brian McKillip. He came highly recommended."

"From New Jersey?"

"Uh huh. Ramsey."

"I've never heard of him, but that doesn't necessarily mean he isn't good. My network is more New York City based. Did he tell you that you had to provide Barry with equity?"

"No. Not really. I told him that's what Barry wants. I didn't really think to oppose him."

"Do you want to if it's possible?"

Tricia's eyes glowed as she clenched her jaw. "Oh yeah."

"One of my classmates in Harvard Law specializes in divorce now. And he happens to live in North Jersey. He's a dynamo. I would not want to be on the other side of this guy. Would you like me to refer you?"

"Thanks all the same, Summer. But I don't think I can afford a high-power divorce lawyer."

"Sure you can." Summer referred to her phone. "What's your mobile number. I'll text the contact."

Tricia recited the number and Summer sent the message. "His name is Chuck Roberts and I think his retainer *is* way up there. But don't worry. He'll make sure Barry pays for every penny of it."

Summer smiled as Tricia wrapped her arms around her shoulders. "Thank you so much, Summer. It would be a miracle if I could stay in my house."

"Chuck's a dream to work with. I'll call him first thing Monday and explain that you're…" Summer regrouped at the verge of referring to Tricia as her boyfriend's sister. "A close friend and very dear to me."

"Should I wait to hear that you connected before I contact him?"

"Yes. I'll call you as soon as I hang up with him."

Vinnie and the boys returned toting oval bowls of pasta at the precise moment that Summer and Tricia ended the private conversation.

"What have we here?" Summer said.

The aromas tantalized her: pungent garlic, oregano, tangy tomato and buttery laden. Tricia spooned some from all four bowls onto dinner plates for each of the boys before helping herself. She passed consecutive entrées to Summer identifying each in turn: Pasta Paul, olive oil and garlic Rigatoni tossed with a variety of roasted vegetables and pine nuts; Pasta Bruno, angel hair pasta with marinara sauce and a hint of red pepper; Bugatini Caprese, tube pasta with olive oil, tomatoes, fresh mozzarella and basil; and finally, Pasta Roger, penne with Alfredo sauce and peas topped with a golden crust of Parmesan cheese.

Summer had to sample every dish even though she was filled to bursting. Truly she had never tasted anything so delicious. When Chef Carlucci poked his head in to check on their satisfaction, Summer spontaneously popped up from the table, doled out a hug to the man and declared his specialties the finest dinner of her life.

He gave her a half smile. "Your dinner isn't over, Summer. That was just *Primo*. *Secondo* is almost ready."

Open-mouthed, Summer drifted back to her place at the table. "Dear God, I'm about to explode."

Her eyes saucers, she sat stiffly in her seat with her hands in her lap as Ben and Walter replaced the pasta bowls with platters of meat, seafood, vegetables and roasted potatoes. She selected a bite of a variety of food and nibbled the delicious fare, although she wasn't remotely hungry. When an array of desserts—Tiramisu, Cannoli, Panna Cotta and chocolate-coated Tartufo were served, Summer held up a hand, palm outward, and groaned.

"I couldn't. Not another bite."

Happy that no one pressed her to further gorge, she relaxed fingering the stem of her wine glass. The events of that day spooled in her mind—the fun, the enjoyment and the rightness of being included in Vinnie's family. In his life.

Her parents would absolutely adore Rose and Vin senior. Kay would go crazy sharing recipes and Mike would *love* the multi-courses stretching the meal's companionship to hours at a time. The unique hospitality of her family's inn was very like that of Via Lucci. Warmth, genuine friendliness and every morsel cooked and presented with love.

She gave a start at a sudden realization. The Laytons and the Carluccis would meet. Good grief. What does *that* mean?

The kids, unbelievably, vacuumed up the sweets. Vinnie munched on a Cannoli.

"I'll hit the gym tomorrow, that's for sure," he quipped.

"I think I'll hit the gym tonight." She gave him a wry smile.

Summer thanked the hosts profusely and planted a kiss on Rose's and Vinnie Senior's cheeks before leaving the restaurant. Laden with take-home delicacies that Rose pressed on Summer, Vinnie held open the door for her and his family.

Vinnie took the wheel of the minivan. "I left my car at Tricia's house. Can I head there first and then drive you home?"

His aqua blue eyes bored into hers, penetrating, smoldering, revealing so much more of his true intentions for that evening than dropping her off at her door.

"I'd like that," she said.

Chapter 10

By the time Vinnie switched cars at Tricia's house, the temperature had plummeted from autumn brisk to winter-like chill. Summer shivered in the passenger seat of his "vintage" car. He fiddled with the heat control dials to no effect, and then he stretched his right arm over the console dipping his hand behind his seat with impressive reach.

He plucked a well-worn, hooded sweatshirt out of the gym bag on the floor and handed the shirt to Summer. "See if this helps until I can get the damn heat working."

Vinnie scowled as he refocused on the dashboard dials. Before he pulled out of his sister's driveway, he helped Summer shrug into the butter soft pull over.

"Much better, thank you." She snuggled into the soft folds and inhaled his heady familiar scent. "My God the amount of food your dad brought out was incredible. I really wish my dad was there tonight. He would have loved every dish."

"Next time he's in town we'll have to take him there." Vinnie maneuvered the car into a stream of traffic on the main street. "Does he travel north often to visit you?"

"Hardly ever. But once I tell him about Via Lucci, I'm sure he'll want to come. Plus, he hasn't seen my new condo yet, either."

"Just let me know when he's in town. My parents will treat him like royalty."

"Sounds great." Summer smiled, happy that Vinnie included her in his future.

The heater vents continued to discharge cold air. Summer huffed a laugh. "Maybe we'll be warmer *without* the heat."

"Good point." Vin twisted the dial counterclockwise.

"Tricia seemed to have fun tonight. She's had a tough time. It was really great to see the two of you laughing together." He smiled.

"I like her a lot. I don't have many girlfriends, never did. But I could easily become your sister's friend."

"I'm pretty sure she thinks of you that way already. Why don't you have girlfriends? You're warm and friendly and great company." The headlights from approaching cars illuminated his handsome face. His serious expression delighted her. He meant every word of flattery.

"Thank you for saying that. But my sisters were all the friends I needed or wanted. Bree invited girlfriends to our house all the time for sleepovers. I hung around with them, but I didn't have a lot in common with girly girls. I was never into shopping or gossip. I'd much rather watch sports with my dad, especially football. He loved to watch games with me. I guess I was the son he always wanted."

"A woman who doesn't like shopping?" He placed his right hand over his heart. "I think I found a unicorn."

"Very funny." She playfully punched his arm, her

knuckles meeting the brick wall of muscle. "Don't get the wrong idea. I can do major damage on my American Express card, but I can also pass a shoe store without even glancing at the display window."

"I don't think I have ever met another woman who could say that." He chuckled.

"Anyway…" She grinned at him. "I hope Tricia accepts my help."

"Help?" He snapped his head in her direction, his gaze penetrating. "She didn't tell me she needed help. Is she okay? I thought she knew she could ask me for anything."

"Whoa. Slow down, big brother. She didn't ask me for help, either." She placed her hand on his leg—another solid wall of taut muscle beneath her palm. "Tricia told me that her husband expects fifty percent of the equity in their home. And that forces her to sell the house. I think that's wrong on so many levels. He cheated on her. New Jersey is a no-fault divorce state after eighteen months of separation, and presumably Barry is pursuing a no-fault divorce. Adultery occurs in almost half of divorces and most courts don't take it into consideration. But adultery is grounds for divorce in New Jersey."

"That sounds open and shut to me," he said.

"Not so fast. I'm not sure how far this has gone down the no-fault road. That's why I suggested at dinner that she should consult Chuck Roberts. I've never met a better divorce lawyer. If there's a way for Tricia keep her home, he'll find it. Truthfully, I think he'll negotiate a lot more than that on her behalf—including requiring Barry to pay his fees."

"Thank you for going out of your way." He

covered her hand with his and squeezed gently.

"It's no bother at all." Her hand tingled in his warm strong grip. "Hopefully, Chuck will help her."

Vinnie pulled up in front of her building and withdrew his hand to work the gear shift, leaving her missing his touch. The doorman stood ready to open the door before the car came to a complete stop.

"Thanks, Johnny." She accepted his handhold and climbed out of the low car onto the curb, shivering as a gust of wind blasted her.

She ducked her head back into the car, only marginally warmer than outside, probably because of Vin's radiant body heat. "Do you want to come up for a drink or something?" she asked impulsively.

He beamed her a smile. "Sure. Go inside before you freeze. I'll find a parking space."

"No need sir," the doorman interjected. "Just pull your car over to the side." Johnny pointed to an area on the driveway apron. "I'll keep an eye on it."

Summer waited in the toasty lobby peering through the window. Her heart raced with a hormonal rush from simply watching Vinnie emerge from the driver's seat. *Damn that man is sexy without even trying.*

Maybe too sexy for my own good. Second guessing herself, she debated whether or not inviting him upstairs was wise.

Vinnie yanked open the back door, ducked inside the car and emerged with the handles of the bags of leftovers hung over his arms. He strode through the door that Johnny held open for him.

A new rush of lust swept through her at Vinnie's smiling countenance and imposing presence.

He thanked Johnny for his courtesy and slipped

one of the bags of leftovers off his arm. Handing the bag to the doorman, he said, "Hope you like dessert."

Johnny peeked into the bag. "I surely do, almost as much as my wife, Erna. What's inside the containers, sir?"

"Vinnie, please. Cannoli and Italian cookies."

"She will love this treat. Thank you, Vinnie."

"Enjoy." Vinnie encircled Summer's waist with his arm and swept her along with him toward the elevator.

The upward momentum of the lift heightened the swoony sensations Summer experienced contemplating alone time with Vinnie. Her stomach churned as she opened the door and led him into her home. Uncharacteristically at a loss for what to do next, she zipped down the hallway and flitted around the living room switching on lights; totally unnecessary considering the daytime-like glow of the city lights through the wall of windows facing the Hudson River.

"Where's the kitchen?" Vinnie hoisted up the plastic bags when she turned to face him.

"Oh. Right over here."

He followed her into the room. She opened the door of the stainless-steel refrigerator and moved aside. Vinnie stowed the bags and then swung closed the refrigerator door, his hand grazing hers stoking an unreasonably electrifying jolt through Summer.

She moved clear of the swinging door and bumped directly into his chest. "Sorry."

In the next instant he embraced her, his musky smell, encompassing heat, and sheltering strength overwhelming her.

"I'm not sorry." He tipped a finger beneath her chin, tilted her head upward and dipped his head.

Breath to breath, his lips slowly met hers.

Oh…she had heard of this phenomenon but had never experienced anything even close. Time stopped. Nothing mattered but his kiss. Any experience she had kissing men didn't matter in the least. This kiss. Soft delicious lips, demanding her to respond, yet surrendering to her when she did.

You are in big trouble, Summer.

A slight moan escaped her lips when the kiss ended.

"I wanted to do that all night," he rasped, his voice husky. "It was more than worth the wait."

He smiled riveting her gaze on sparkling, aqua eyes. The man was gorgeous, virile and absolutely tantalizing.

"Damn Carlucci. Where did you learn to kiss like that?" she teased, shaken to the core and not sure she wanted him to know how vulnerable she felt in that moment.

Summer slipped out of his arms and headed to the counter separating the dining room from the kitchen. "Would you like a glass of wine?" *I sure as hell need wine.*

She took a deep breath, uncorked a bottle of Longboard Maverick Cab and poured hefty portions into two crystal wine glasses.

"Let's sit in the living room." She grabbed the glasses and led him through the L-shaped space.

First taking a large gulp, she placed the goblets on the marble coffee table in front of a cream colored, leather sectional facing the wall of floor to ceiling windows. She sat down on the couch that afforded a dazzling, breathtaking view of the New York City skyline and fidgeted in her seat.

Vinnie sat on the sofa next to her and drew her close to his side setting off a new explosion of wanting him.

"Amazing view, right? It sold me on the place and I only previewed this property during the day, never after dark. I couldn't believe how beautiful the lights were the first night I stayed here," she babbled.

"Yep. The view *is* pretty spectacular." Vinnie gazed fixedly only at Summer and sipped his wine.

"Nice line, Carlucci."

How she wanted this man. He obviously wanted her. Why not?

Any opposing arguments disintegrated in his thrall. Twisting her torso, she faced him, raised her hands and gently cupped his face between her palms. She brought her lips to his, nipping and teasing until he drew her closer and devoured her mouth, their tongues intertwined. He hugged her closer still, her breasts pressed against his broad chest, and continued to kiss her until they had no choice but to release the lip-lock and breathe.

More. She crossed her arms, grabbed the hems of his borrowed sweatshirt and her underlying sweater, swept them both off over her head and tossed the shirts aside. Exposed, she shivered, a rill of anticipation flowing through her. He unhooked her black, lacey bra with one split second twist of his hand, and it fell between them.

"You are beautiful," he whispered.

His powerful hands cupped her breasts entirely, caressed gently, touched her sensitive skin feather light sending wave after wave of desire through her like molten lava at her core.

In one tiny corner of Summer's mind, a whispered warning: he was her client and she shouldn't let this continue.

She never wanted him to stop.

He eased backward flat out on the couch, sweeping her on top of him, and she knew she was lost. His chest felt like granite beneath her breasts - scalding hot granite. He threaded his hands through her hair and then fused her lips to his. Their tongues danced together sensually, and she tasted sweet wine. She kissed a trail down the side of his neck as his fingertips tattooed larger widening patterns on her bare back, slowly moving downward edging the waistband of her pants. Summer groaned when he plunged both his hands under the waist band and massaged her, the pressure fusing her pelvis tightly against his. Undulating wantonly, she thrilled at his arousal beneath her.

Her landline phone jangled, and she gave a start.

"Let it go," he growled.

She arched her back savoring the synchronized rise and fall of their bodies having no intention of answering a phone.

Silence. Thankfully.

Seconds later her cell phone rang. The ring tone was generic and not associated with any of her loved ones, so she almost disregarded that call, too. Until the memory of a stranger calling her cellphone when Bree was shot vividly reminded her that unknown callers frequently were the messengers of emergencies. Ironically, Vinnie was the stranger who called Summer that night.

"I have to get it. It might be family." In motion off

the couch, she swept his sweatshirt off the floor and tucked it under her armpits to cover her naked breasts. As she raced into the kitchen, she tied the sleeves of the shirt into a knot at the back of her neck. Frantic, she dipped her hand inside her purse on the kitchen counter while the ringtone, thankfully, still sounded, nabbed the phone and swiped to connect without checking caller ID.

"Hello," she gasped, breathless, reversing to backtrack toward the living room.

"Hey, Summer, you sound out of breath. Are you in your gym again?" came Jacob's hearty voice.

"Um… Sure, Jake," she said.

Striding into the living room, she continued, "I *was* in the middle of a workout."

She winked at Vinnie, now sitting ramrod straight on the sofa apparently ignoring her. Summer also realized that the man was fully clothed while she, on the other hand, wore a sweatshirt "drape".

"…Douglas case," Jake said.

Pacing aimlessly, she listened more attentively to her boss.

"They dropped the lawsuit. I couldn't wait to tell you, Summer."

"Wonderful. Congratulations." She drifted to the window and caught Vinnie's reflection in the glass. He hadn't moved a muscle.

"No, congratulations to *you*." He chuckled. "I needed to tell you."

"Needed to tell me?" In motion again, she furrowed her brow. "Why? I didn't do anything."

"Let me try to remember what that old blow hole Anderson said. Something along the lines of, '*After speaking with Ms. Layton, our client feels that dropping the lawsuit would be in his best interest.'* You nailed it once again." Jake belly laughed.

Summer burst out laughing, too, happy at her boss's obvious approval. Back in the kitchen, she leaned against the counter.

"And some other big news. Talked to my dad tonight. He wants to make it official. Levant and Layton. How does that sound?"

Gleeful, she wanted to yell, yippee!

"Hmm. Sounds okay…" she said deadpan. "But Layton and Levant sound much better." He hooted in her ear.

Smiling she added, "I'm kidding. I'm truly honored, Jake. Thank you."

"I know you're *not* kidding." He chuckled. "Dad even wants to come down from Massachusetts for a dinner or lunch."

She shoved away from the counter and circled back to the living room. "Either is fine with me. Just let me know. Thank you so much Jake. I better get back to my…workout."

Summer disconnected the call as she entered the living room. Empty. For a second, she thought Vinnie was exploring or perhaps visiting the restroom. Until she heard the front door latch click.

Conflicting emotions cascaded through her at his desertion…rudeness? What the hell? Was he seriously *jealous?* After what passed between them, he would just *leave?* She scrolled furiously through her contacts to call and to confront him. But she stopped scrolling when she caught her reflection in the window—bare shouldered and wearing his sweatshirt like a necklace curtaining her chest.

Maybe he just did them both a favor, stopping before they went too far. She probably had gone too far already. Their relationship had to remain professional. She needed to clear his name. She couldn't let emotions cloud those facts.

Not daring to examine the emotions that already clouded her feelings about Vinnie, she stomped into her bedroom and threw the sweatshirt into the clothes hamper. She changed into workout clothes and then trod to her gym. Summer ran full speed on the treadmill for over an hour until sweat poured off her.

Dialing down the speed to a leisurely walk, she cooled off, and felt more grounded. Running always cleared her head.

Summer gazed into the mirror wall in front of the treadmill. "I'll deal with you, Vincente Carlucci," she said to her reflection. She threw back her head and laughed. "And I'll enjoy doing it immensely."

Chapter 11

"I'll call you," Vin said to the air. The door to Summer's condo latched close behind him.

Vinnie was certain that she hadn't heard him and equally certain that she didn't notice that he had left. Whether or not Summer cared that he no longer waited on her sofa was a different story.

He trudged down the hallway, punched the down indicator button on the wall and tapped a foot noiselessly on the plush carpet waiting for the elevator doors to open. This is *not* how he envisioned the evening to end.

Doubts and misgivings plagued him. Vin wasn't happy with Summer's apparent delight at Jacob's attention, but he realistically didn't view the hotshot lawyer through the green lens of jealousy. He more than understood dedication to a career and the necessity to "answer" when the boss called. He wished mightily that his career dedication could be rechanneled into active duty and he, too, would have calls from the brass to answer. But throwing a switch like Summer had just done? Because Jacob wanted to chat or give her an Atta girl? What was that?

On the ground floor level, he strode toward the double-door exit beaming the pleasant doorman a smile he didn't feel. He met the man's repeated expression of gratitude for the bag of pastries with a nonchalant wave of his hand, think nothing of it. Behind the wheel of his Ford, he started the engine, popped in the cigarette lighter and tapped a Marlboro out of the pack while he waited for the lighter to heat.

Igniting the tip, he sucked in a lungful of fortifying, nicotine-laden smoke, exhaled and took another drag before putting the car in gear and steering out into the street. Smoking usually cleared his head. Not tonight. Summer dominated every thought, just like she had dominated the wildfire intimacy between them. He took a final drag and stubbed out the cigarette in the ashtray with force just short of denting the metal.

He brought his fingertips to his nose. Despite the overlay of pungent tobacco aroma, her delicate scent still lingered on his hands. Vinnie marveled at the memory of her satin skin beneath his hands, her perfect body… No woman had ever spun him around like she had. And no woman had ever shut down a moment quite like Summer. Wink, wink, *workout*?

Vinnie's emotions teeter-tottered between anger and guilt. *Maybe I'll call her to apologize for leaving abruptly.* Hell no. His pride stung over more than the halt to lovemaking. He had literally put his career in her hands and now…his heart.

He purposefully overshot the drive of his condo building not ready to close himself off in a quiet space. Vinnie itched to rejoin his action-packed world, use his brain, ensnare felons, work with his team, score for the Bureau. The dark cloud of false accusation hung overhead close enough to smother him. Summer's braking before the bedroom might have struck him as a challenge; persuade the lady next time…or the time after that if there were enough heat between them to keep them both interested. In his vulnerable state he could only feel diminished.

No matter how dependent he remained on Summer professionally, he refused to be anything but her equal privately. He wagged his head shaking free of the introspection. His autopilot driving had him approaching the Federal building.

His gaze traveled up the façade, unsurprised to note light-glow in some upper windows. 24/7/365, he thought. Was Muñoz up there? With Finelli, Morphy and Pouw? He ached to join his men, work an Op, toss back a few victory beers. How about Ashley? He narrowed his eyes and focused on the SAC's corner location on the upper floor. Maybe. Only if there's a critical Op in play. Was there?

"Ugh. This isn't helping," he said, a little more depressed by talking to himself.

Despite his outsider status, Vinnie felt drawn here. Rather than turning around and heading home, he gave in to his impulse and drove up the parking ramp. He recognized a few scattered cars as he pulled into a slot and cut the engine. Vin popped open the glove compartment and rummaged a hand inside, emerging with a laminated membership card to the Federal building's gym. Pocketing the card, he opened his door and slid out of the driver's seat.

Vinnie strode to the entrance, slipped the card out of his pocket and slapped it against the electronic reader. The flash of the green light indicator and satisfying metallic click of the door lock disengaging satisfied him. Grinning he swung open the door and entered the building. He bound down the flight of steps, opened the stairwell door and sauntered into the gym.

The heavy aromas of sanitizer, sweat and socks pinched his nostrils. Vinnie temporarily ignored the trio of men grunting through workouts at weight stations, whipped open the locker room door and strode inside.

Since his membership card still worked, he assumed his locker combination remained the same. He spun the dial clockwise, counterclockwise and then clockwise again and opened the door with ease. His gym bag was undisturbed.

After he changed clothes, he reentered the gym, paced over to the free weights rack and hoisted up a fifty-pound dumbbell in each hand. Alternating biceps curls, he peered into the wall of mirrors and identified his workout companions: Finelli, Morphy and a rookie in accounting and fraud whose name escaped him. The kid's specialty, however, piqued his interest and he debated how best to approach him, feel him out about his possible involvement in the investigation against him.

Finelli and Morphy didn't hesitate to connect with Vinnie.

"Hey, sir," Bob Finelli said, extending his hand.

Vinnie shifted the weight in his right hand to his left and shook Finelli's hand. "Good to see you, Bob."

He faced Morphy, his hand outstretched. "And you, too, John."

"Likewise," Morphy said giving Vinnie's hand a hearty shake. "For the record, sir, this whole thing with you is pure bullshit. As usual OPR has its head up its ass. Even Sally thinks so."

"My Carol, too," Finelli echoed.

Vin grinned shaking his head. "Thanks. But they're still pointing the finger at me. Can't *wait* until this is cleared up."

"Us, too," Finelli said. "Have you heard from Muñoz? He's getting real tired of holding the team together without you."

"Haven't heard from anyone on the Bureau since this whole thing came down."

Finelli nodded his head. "Yeah, we've been ordered not to contact you. I know Muñoz feels like shit about it."

Vinnie tilted his head toward the Rookie in the far corner of the gym. "Do you think the kid over there in Fraud could help me learn more about the investigation?"

His men glanced in the kid's direction and then shook their heads in unison.

"Nah," Morphy said. "He's too green. All this is high up and hush-hush."

"Got it," Vinnie said. "Thanks, guys. Maybe we can have a beer together sometime?"

"I wish," Morphy said. "We'd have to wear disguises and go undercover. Command is watching your team like a hawk. I'm surprised they didn't think about your gym card. Just goes to show that OPR doesn't know its ass from a hole in the ground."

Vin chuckled. "Right. Anyway. Be safe out there. With the help of God, I'll be back after the first of the year."

"That long?" Finelli asked.

"Yeah. The preliminary hearing is in mid-January."

"Sorry, sir. Good luck."

"Thanks again." His men drifted back to weight stations and Vinnie focused on pumping the dumbbells, and then wandering station to station, enjoying the exertion and mind-blanking physicality.

Vinnie remained behind after the gym emptied pushing his muscles to the limit. The hot shower spray afterward refreshed and loosened away tightness. Striding to his car in the brisk evening air, he felt more himself than he had since this whole shitstorm hit. The solidarity of his men buoyed his spirit and relief flooded him like a life-saving transfusion.

Mercifully, sleep came the instant he lay down on his bed. He awoke Sunday morning renewed and almost optimistic. Vinnie showered, shaved and dressed in gray slacks, a powder blue and white pinstriped shirt and a navy-blue V-neck sweater, and then zipped out the door headed to 7:30AM Mass at St. Mary Church.

****

Summer wrestled the bed covers all through the night as if swimming the shark-infested waters that surrounded Vinnie. The second time she experienced the vivid nightmare ended the same: Vinnie disappeared beneath the frothy, churning waves, lost to her forever.

Her mourning was unbearable, and in her dream state the truth was inescapable. Despite the pull-tug of their relationship, his cocksure ladies' man reputation and his unceremonious departure last night, she loved Vinnie. In the dream the intensity of her emotions robbed her breath.

Reality wasn't much different. The memory of his hands on her body, the electric jolt of every tiny sensation and the heady thrill of his muscles beneath her hands left her endlessly wanting more.

She awoke before dawn, at first shaken by a deep sense of impotence and loss. But when she opened her gritty eyes and her familiar surroundings registered, she was filled with gratitude that she hadn't lost Vinnie to the sharks. She called upon the Sacred Source and prayed that her powers might overcome the evil lies against him.

A remembered portent from the dream swelled within her mind as if haloed in light. *He knows the wrongdoer. Find him.*

More determined than ever to represent him, Summer flung back the bedcovers and rose to meet the day with new energy. She rarely sought out organized religion, but that Sunday she felt called to ceremonial worship. Dressed in an Armani emerald green, wool pantsuit and low-heeled pumps she hustled downstairs and asked Johnny to hail a cab to take her to the nearest church.

When she walked into the hushed narthex of St. Mary Church and spied Vinnie in a back-row pew on the left side of the nave, she thanked the Sacred Source for bringing her here.

Hesitating in the vestibule, she considered sitting next to him, but opted instead to seek a seat on the far right of the church, opposite his seat.

Summer enjoyed the service following along with the readings and the prayers in the small missal provided in the book rack mounted on the back of the pew in front of her. She closed her eyes letting the choir's sweet music wash over her, a Baptism for a shiny new day.

Shuffling amid the throng out of church at the end of Mass, she scanned the assembly searching for Vinnie. Outside a light snow fell, a gentle hush that seemed an extension of the peaceful hour spent in worship.

His familiar silhouette moved along the esplanade below her. Bounding down the stairs, she caught up with him heading toward the parking lot adjacent to the church, skidded to a halt behind him averting a fall with iffy traction in the snow dusting, and tapped him on the shoulder.

He pivoted at her touch. His widened blue eyes lit with delight before he narrowed those eyes, doused the warm reaction to her presence, and regarded her as if she had pulled a gun on him. "Hey," he said, his tone clipped.

"Hey yourself," she said lightly. "Fancy meeting you here."

"Uh huh," he said. "Why is that? You following me?"

Summer threw back her head and laughed. "Don't flatter yourself. Purely coincidental."

"Okay…um. About last night…"

Now it was her turn to narrow her eyes and pin him with an accusatory glare. "Yes, about that? What was with the disappearing act?"

His retaliating scowl had her itching to fight and she further narrowed her eyes to slits.

The slow, sexy upturn of his lips in a half smile had the challenge seeping out of her. This man undid her in too many ways to name. Feisty Summer had met her match in Vinnie.

"I was about to stop at an Italian bakery I like to pick up a few things," he said, completely ignoring her question. "Care to join me? We can watch the snow from my balcony."

Oh yes. "Sure," she said nonchalantly.

Summer slipped her hand around his bicep and walked with him to his car.

Chapter 12

Vinnie swung his car into a crowded parking lot and braked, waiting for a mini-van to reverse out of a parking space. The snowfall had stopped, leaving behind a powdered sugar dusting on tree limbs and bushes. Spears of sunrays pierced through iron colored clouds overhead.

Summer sat patiently in the passenger seat allowing Vinnie the chivalry of opening the door for her and providing her a handhold tow out of the car. He didn't unclasp her hand during the short walk to the shop's door. The pulse revving contact with his warm hand had her reliving the electrifying memory of that huge hand journeying all over her body last night.

Bells tinkled overhead as Vinnie opened the door at the entrance to *Antonio's*. Summer closed her eyes savoring the yeasty aromas of fresh baked bread, buttery cinnamon scents and the rich garlic, onion, and tomato redolence of Italian cooking. Summer had expected to find only corner bakery fare here. She was delighted how far the bustling deli exceeded her expectations.

"Oh Vin, this is amazing." Her eyes darted from one display case to another. Salamis hung from the wooden beams amid assorted sizes of pots and pans - all for sale. Clerks seemed in continual motion behind the counters helping customers.

Her growling stomach drew her to the display case of serious food first. A snow white haired, olive skinned, striking gentleman greeted her with a heavy Italian accent. "Hello beautiful lady. How may I be of service?"

"Everything looks so good; I can't decide." She peered through the glass at the pasta dishes, meatballs, sausage...

"Take your time. I will enjoy looking at your beauty."

Vinnie's deep-throated laugh sounded. "Calm down, Tony." He sauntered up behind her.

"Oh, *why* are all the gorgeous ladies taken?" Tony shook his head, his lips downturned. He winked at Summer.

Vinnie hooted. "Do I have to tell Connie that you're flirting with my lady?"

"No need to get nasty, Vinnie." Tony chuckled.

"What are you doing behind the counter anyway?" Vinnie said.

"Football season. My boys are going to the game as usual. How's your dad?"

"He's doing great. Thanks for asking."

"Tell him I said hello. And it's too long since we played golf. Now let me give my undivided attention to your lady. Looks like you don't feed her enough."

Rooted to the spot, Summer absorbed the highlights of the exchange. *Taken? This man obviously thinks we're a couple. And Vinnie not only didn't deny it, he set the stage. My lady?*

She blinked as the realization sank in that she liked his possessiveness—a lot.

"Is Connie your wife, Tony?" she said.

A broad smile that crinkled the corners of his eyes illuminated his handsome face. "My beloved of forty-five years."

"Connie is a lucky lady," Summer declared.

"Ah love, I'm the lucky one. Now, let me help you with your selections. The sausages and peppers are delicious today. Connie made them first thing this morning. Also, the meatballs. You'll not find any better than my love's homemade meatballs anywhere." He raised his right hand in sober testimony.

Summer took Tony at his word. "I'll take some of each please. Oh. And some of those stuffed shells… and a nice big square of that lasagna."

Tony handed the containers of food in succession to Vinnie, who loaded the basket he had hung over his arm.

"Since you're buying out the place, maybe I should get a carriage?" he teased.

"Nope. But you'll need another basket." She tossed a hunk of Swiss cheese and an oversized Genoa salami into the basket setting it swinging on Vinnie's arm.

He staggered theatrically as the flying salami hit home before heading back to the entrance to pick up another basket.

At the bakery counter Summer tugged a paper number fifty-seven out of the dispenser and glanced at the digital board to gauge her wait. Forty-nine. She eyed the selections growing hungrier by the minute. Vinnie approached. She didn't have to turn around to sense his nearness. His clean, shower soap scent and radiating heat enfolded her like a hug.

Summer leaned into his broad chest feeling supported and safe. She arched her neck and gazed up at his face, delighted with the tender softness she detected in his sky-blue eyes. Happy with him and this foodie treasure trove he had introduced, she said. "This place is just like Zabar's in the City. They have croissants and rugelach, too. Truly I'm in heaven." She stood on tip toes and kissed his cheek softly. "Thank you for bringing me here."

"My pleasure."

Summer's breath caught in her throat at his dazzling smile.

Weak-kneed she finished her purchases and trailed Vinnie to the cashier. She added cloth bags to the items on the conveyor belt, helped him stow the movable feast inside the bags and completed the transaction with her American Express card.

****

Vinnie finished jamming the last sack into his trunk and surveyed Summer's purchases askance. "Kind of extreme food shopping, don't you think?"

"Everything looked so delicious; I couldn't pass it up. Don't worry, it won't go to waste. I'll eat any leftovers all week like a queen."

She placed her hand on his as he began lowering the trunk door, her softness an unexpected sensual whiplash. "One sec," she said.

Her arm shot out and she nabbed a bag of rugelach grinning. "All set."

He slipped into the driver's seat. Her compelling floral scent and the tantalizing aromas of baked goods overlaid with tangy Mediterranean foods engaged his senses. Summer's eyes danced as she faced him, her cheeks bulging with pastry. Despite last night's frustrating behavior, he thoroughly appreciated everything about this unpredictable woman.

"Try this." She popped the cinnamon encrusted morsel into his mouth and smirked as he widened his eyes, delighted.

"This is amazing." He chewed slowly, savoring the butter laden pastry melting in his mouth. "I usually just buy some rolls from Tony after church. Didn't know what I was missing."

A car edged up and halted behind him. He threw the gear shift into reverse and relinquished the space.

"I'm glad I bought a couple pounds." Summer touched another rugelach to his lips. He opened his mouth to capture the treat, enjoying the pastry and the intimacy of her feeding him.

She folded the top of the bag a couple times and placed it on the floor by her feet. "If I don't stop, I'll eat the whole thing."

Fifteen minutes after they left *Antonio's* Vinnie stopped the car in front of his building. "Home sweet home."

Summer peered upward through the windshield craning her neck. "How many floors?"

He surveyed the red brick façade mentally comparing his home to Summer's sky spearing building on the Hudson. "Only seven. Not much of a view, but it serves my purpose."

"It looks great." She unfastened her seat, shoved open the passenger door and hopped out of the car, apparently eager to explore.

Vinnie pushed the button to unlatch the trunk and slipped out of his seat. As he strode to the back of the car, he noticed Summer checking her cell phone. He tried not to dwell on the possibility that Summer might repeat her fickle behavior alone with him again upstairs. *Jake* might want to share every stray thought. He shook off the negativity enjoying her company too much to hold a grudge.

"There's underground parking and I have a space, but it's not close to the elevator door." Vin pointedly regarded the bulging contents of the trunk. "Not ideal, but we'll have to go through the front."

"Let's see if you're complaining when you sink your teeth into some of that lasagna." She looped a bag over each arm and followed him into the lobby. "Which floor?"

"Seven," he said.

He rode the elevator enveloped in her intoxicating scent. Summer's simple presence seemed to emit gamma ray sensuality. Lasagna the last thing on his mind, Vinnie led her down the hall, juggled bags to use his key and then barricaded the open door with the toe of his boot.

She strolled past him swinging her slender hips. Falling in line behind her, Vinnie enjoyed the view. He set the grocery bags on his kitchen counter and then ambled over to Summer who had stopped circling his living room and stood in front of the sliding glass door. Following her gaze, he cringed at the folding chairs and cheap plastic table that comprised his balcony furniture.

"Here, let me take those." Vinnie gave a nod to the bags.

Compliant, she held out her arms. He unhooked the handles and plopped the sacks on the counter that divided the living room from the kitchen.

She drifted to the middle of the living room and fingered the beautiful rust and orange colored blanket

Tricia had knit for him draped over the back of his ancient brown leather couch. "Pretty."

Next, she wandered over to one of two cherry wood bookshelves that framed the sixty-inch flat screen TV that was a bitch to mount to the wall by himself. She studied the spines row by row before she moved in front of the second shelf. "You can tell a lot about a person from his bookshelf."

He grinned. "Oh yeah? What's the verdict about me, counselor?"

"Your collection is wonderful." She pointed to several novels in succession. "Read that. Read that. *Loved* that. Ooh, can I borrow that?" On a laugh she said, "You've uncovered my Achilles heel.

"I told you before that I don't like shopping, but that's not entirely true. I spend hours in Barnes and Noble. My to be read pile is out of control."

She squatted gazing at the bottom shelf. "Wimpy Kid, Goosebumps and all the Harry Potter books. Now that doesn't fit with Lee Child, Harlan Coben and Dennis Lehane."

"I bought those for Joey and Barry over the years. I guess I'm too sentimental to have donated them when I've moved. They're too old for them now, but they used to love to come to my place, grab a book and sit right down on the floor to read."

Summer knelt on the floor and pulled a book out. "No way! You have *Me Too Iguana*? My sisters and I had all the Sweet Pickles Books. This was Skye's favorite." She beamed him a smile.

He grinned back at her remembering his nephew's delight in the story. "That was Joey's favorite, too. Tricia deposited it on my bookshelf one day because she was sick of reading it to him over and over."

"Bree favored *Very Worried Walrus* and I loved *Nuts to Nightingale*. So many wonderful memories." She slipped the book back in place on the shelf and accepted Vin's outstretched hand.

"I could get lost looking at all your books."

"Feel free anytime." He flexed his bicep to tow her to her feet. "Except now. I'm starving. Ready to eat?"

As she rose from the floor the lapels of her suit jacket parted affording him a glimpse of black lace against creamy skin.

"Or…" he said.

She parted her lips provocatively. Her gaze was direct and dripping with feminine guile. "Or…what?"

"Dessert first." He cupped a hand at the nape of her neck and drew her into a soft kiss.

Summer necklaced her arms around his shoulders and fused her lips to his. He threaded his fingers through her silken cap of hair and deepened the kiss. Her taste, her smell, the touch of her breasts pressed against his chest were the most potent aphrodisiacs he'd ever known.

The misgivings he had suffered after their volcanic foreplay yesterday evaporated. He had never brought a woman to his home before preferring to accept his dates' invitations so that he had the freedom to leave in the evening—or the morning after.

Why had he made an exception with Summer? The passionate woman in his arms had left him no choice. He wanted to make love to her this first time in his bed.

He ended the kiss and gazed into her eyes, thrilled at the tenderness in their pine green depths. "The bedroom?"

She hesitated a second before nodding.

Vinnie led her by the hand down the hallway and into his room. Muted sunshine filtered through navy blue drapes dappling the solid navy bedspread with light.

Summer let go of his hand and slipped her jacket off her shoulders letting it fall to the floor. She wore a black, lace trimmed camisole—the material against her porcelain skin a cookies and cream contrast. The corners of her lips upturned in a slow, seductive smile.

He cupped her breasts through the silk, his thumbs teasing her nipples. Her chest heaved as her nipples hardened. She moaned and arched her neck. He kissed the vee of her cleavage trailing hot kisses up along her neck and up her chin until his mouth reached hers.

She wrapped her arms around his neck as she had before, but now she devoured his mouth, tangling her tongue with his. Desire swamped him. Still fused to her lips, he wrapped his arms around her, shuffled her backwards with him, sat on the edge of the bed and pulled her between his legs. He fingered the button at the waist of her slacks.

Summer stepped back just out of his reach. She bent at the waist and tugged his shirt out of his pants. The next dizzying second, she unbuttoned his pants and slowly unzipped his fly. She hooked the waistband of his boxers with the tip of her index finger and trailed the tip of her tongue down the path of the opening zipper and gaping underwear along the shaft of his penis. Every nerve ending fired as he reached for her on a moan.

Her teeth nipped his stomach. "Not yet," she said.

Summer brought her lips to his ear and whispered,

"Why don't you slip out of these—" She tugged on a belt loop. "—While I use your bathroom?"

Breathless and aching to make love with her, he said, "Sure. It's down the hall on the left."

She scooped her jacket up off the floor and sashayed seductively out of his room.

Rubbing his hand over his face, Vinnie rose from the bed, shed his pants and boxers and folded them neatly on a side chair. He stripped off his shirt and tossed it atop the folded clothes. With one swing of his arm he whipped the comforter off the bed, propped the two pillows against the oak headboard and climbed in under the crisp white sheet, happy that he had changed the linens that morning before leaving for church.

He propped against the pillow with his hands intertwined behind his head. When he awoke that morning encouraged by his team's support last night but still stinging from Summer's seeming rejection, he hadn't dreamed that he'd have another chance with her today.

The implications of wanting Summer in his bed were not lost on him. He was falling in love with her. Was he ready to tell her? He thought, yes.

The sound of his front door latching shut had him frowning. "Summer?"

No answer.

He threw off the sheet and paced down the hall naked. He ducked his head into the open bathroom door. As he suspected, the room was empty. He checked the kitchen and family room area, gazing out the sliding door on the offhand chance she had inexplicably drifted out onto the balcony. Nope. Vinnie backtracked to his bedroom—the only room in his condo with a window facing the street.

Vin stepped over to his bedroom window, parted the drapes and peered outside. He glimpsed a flash of green in the open door of the back seat of a cab. The cabbie slammed shut the trunk.

Vinnie hooted a laugh. "Well played, lady. Well played."

The passenger door closed, followed in quick succession by the driver's door, and the car accelerated away from the curb. Vinnie left the window and donned his clothes before heading to the kitchen.

She had placed a sheet of white paper on the countertop next to his bakery bag. On the stationery she left a lipstick kiss and the message, *Payback is a bitch.*

Smiling, he sat on a stool at the counter, her letter in hand. He had certainly met his match. No other woman was like her. There was only one Summer.

Chapter 13

Vinnie parked his car in the underground parking lot of his condo building and strode past the bank of elevators, too impatient to wait. He bounded up the stairs two at a time, breathing heavily by the time he reached his door. The freedom of physical exertion after spending the last twelve hours standing in the kitchen of his family's restaurant invigorated him and worked off some of the stiffness. How did Dad do that every day for decades?

He tossed his keys into the dish on the table near the door, hung his jacket in the hall closet, and strode into the kitchen switching on lights as he progressed. Vinnie had relaxing plans for the evening starting with a bracing, hot shower. But first, he set down the bag holding a Tupperware container of soup, hefted a five-quart pot out of the cabinet nearest the stove, popped off the Tupperware's plastic lid and filled the pot almost to the brim. He covered the pan, set the burner to simmer and hurried to the bathroom. Stripping off his clothes, he threw them in the hamper and then stepped into the shower. The hot water pounding against his back eased his aching muscles. The mirrors were blurred with steam when he stepped out of the shower and wrapped a soft, plush towel around his waist.

The spicy, comfort-food aroma of his mother's tomato rice soup had him bound for the kitchen after he donned fresh pressed jeans and a worn flannel shirt.

Vinnie ladled out a bowl of soup and broke off a hunk of Italian bread. Switching on the power on the TV remote, he navigated to a prime-time station, took a seat on his sofa and dug into his meal. That night he planned to watch the news while he ate and then begin reading the latest Lee Child novel.

Halfway through the broadcast his cell phone chirred.

Smiling at the caller ID readout on the screen he answered, "Brooklyn how the hell are you?"

"Hanging in there, Jersey. It's been too long," Dennis said.

At the student orientation at John Jay College of Criminal Justice, Vin, a grad student from New Jersey, had instantly hit it off with Dennis, an aspiring security pro from Brooklyn. The two were great buddies from that point forward, but after they had completed their studies, life took over and they didn't see each other often. However, they never missed holiday calls each year and the chance to catch each other up on their lives.

"How are Gina and the girls?" Vinnie smiled at the thought of Dennis's cute kids -all four of them.

"All good. But this is actually a work-related call, Vin. Are you interested in a job tonight?"

Adrenaline surged, and his prior aches and pains disappeared at the unexpected, and more than welcome, "call to duty". "Sure. What kind of job?"

"Security on the balloons. I know it's late, but Bobby just called on his way to the hospital with Marge. She went into labor and I'm a man down."

"Another baby? Geez don't they have five

already?" Vinnie laughed.

"Wrong. This is number seven. I'm catching up, though. Gina's pregnant again; still trying for our boy."

"Holy shit, that's great. Congratulations."

"Thanks. I think we're crazy. My mom thinks we're crazy. But Gina doesn't. Even though with our luck we'll have five girls."

"For the record, I think you're crazy." Vin grinned as Dennis's belly laugh sounded in his ear.

"About the job tonight." Vin hesitated. "I'd like to help you, but I'm not sure my credentials pass muster. I've been suspended."

"You and I both know the suspension is bullshit," he spat out. "Besides, you don't need to be *active* FBI to work the Parade."

"You knew?"

"Sure. Word gets around."

"And you're offering me plum security work anyway?"

"Let's not waste time discussing the bogus charges. I know you. That's all I'm going to say. Do you want to work tonight or not?"

"You bet I do."

"Great. Get your ass over to 78th street. That's where the RV is parked. See you there."

"Thanks, Brooklyn. I really appreciate it."

"I've offered you a job with my firm every year since I took the business over from my dad. The offer is still open if you want to tell those Fibbie bastards to stuff it. See you soon."

The line went dead. Vin pocketed his phone and wasted no time carrying his soup bowl into the kitchen and setting it down on the counter. He bent at the waist and rummaged inside a lower cabinet for two thermoses. First, he filled one with soup and then he primed his coffee maker to brew a pot for the second thermos. While the coffee machine sputtered and dripped, he loped down the hall into his bedroom.

Vinnie stuffed a thermal shirt, gloves and a woolen cap into a backpack. Back in the kitchen he poured coffee into the second thermos and stowed both beverage containers in the pack. He buttered a hunk of bread and munched it as he headed out the door of his condo.

Before he put his car in gear, he sent a text to Tricia: *Will be late to dinner tomorrow. Working the Parade this year. LU Vin.*

Traffic was light approaching the GW Bridge and into the city. He pulled in behind the RV after a half hour drive. He could hear the deep throated sound of male laughter through the RV's closed door. Grinning, he swung open the door and stepped inside. Dennis stood before the seated group of men conducting a briefing. Vinnie strode over and shook hands with Jeff, Ernie and John—former John Jay classmates, too.

"The band's back together again." Ernie slapped him on the back.

Vinnie knew a few of the other guys having worked the Parade for Dennis in the past and they greeted him warmly.

Dennis gave each an assignment and then Vinnie trouped out into the cold with the security force. Another rush of adrenaline coursed through his veins. Smiling, he realized that *this* was what he had missed since he was suspended. He needed the indescribable bond of fellow law enforcers and the excitement of working together. Vinnie had willingly accepted the danger and hardships of protecting and serving. That his motives and conduct continued to be in question was a hardship he would never accept. He had to get back on the job before he went crazy.

Dennis's security firm worked in conjunction with the New York City Police. The NYPD did an amazing job each year, but after 911 the department store that hosted the parade wanted to beef up security to the max—thus the contact with Dennis's father's company. Although the company had grown into an international security firm after Dennis took over, the Parade had held a special place in his dad's heart. Dennis continued to offer his company's services for the Thanksgiving Day Parade free of charge in memory of Dennis, Sr.

Vinnie was assigned the Wimpy Kid balloon. He checked his watch to make sure it wasn't too late before he sent a quick text to alert Tricia for Joey's benefit. Wimpy Kid books were Joey's favorite.

He guarded the balloon that night as a steady stream of children and adults roamed around the balloon staging area. Around midnight he hustled back to the RV to thaw out and doze until just before sunrise. Walking the Parade route with the balloon, his gaze constantly roved taking in every face and movement in the crowds. After guiding the balloon safely into Herald Square, Vinnie exhaled, satisfied. He grabbed a cab back to the RV to retrieve his car and thanked Dennis profusely for the work.

"Don't forget. I still want you to come to work with me and forget the Feds. If you can think of any way that I can help with your case let me know."

"Thanks. Means a lot."

Vinnie crossed the George Washington Bridge before Santa made his appearance in Herald Square, averting the traditional monster traffic jam after the Parade ended. He made a quick stop at home to shower and to change his clothes before setting out for his parents' house.

He took the wheel of the Ford feeling physically tired but enlivened in spirit. He had immensely enjoyed last night and that morning. Dennis's job offer didn't seem so out of the question, either. It at least deserved more consideration. Vinnie was FBI through and through—a fact that heightened the injustice of the false accusation against him. His honesty and loyalty were in question. Why should he remain loyal to the Bureau under the circumstances?

When he pulled into his parents' driveway, his confidence was buoyed by the faith in him that Dennis had displayed and almost had embraced the notion of a Plan B.

Vinnie opened his car door at the same time that Joey shot through the front door of the brick and cedar house. "Uncle Vinnie! I saw you on TV!" he hollered running to the car.

Vinnie slid out of his seat on a bead for Joey. He caught his nephew up in a bear hug. Then he let Joey loose and ducked back into the car to scoop up a bouquet of roses and a bottle of wine off the passenger seat.

Joey had waited patiently for his balloon guarding hero to shut the car door. He walk-jogged next to Vinnie trying to keep up with his uncle's long-legged strides. "The game is on. Panthers are winning. Bet Summer is happy. I thought she was coming with you.

Barry is rooting for the Panthers; I think he is just to make Grandpa mad. Grandpa wants the Bears to win. Why didn't Summer come?"

Vinnie hooted a laugh at the nonstop chatter and ruffled the boy's hair fondly. "Do you take a breath?" he teased. "She's with her family on the Outer Banks."

He opened the door and gestured for Joey to pass in front of him into his parents' home.

"She's so lucky. Dad went to Florida. We were supposed to go his apartment today. Barry is pissed. Mom told us Dad called last night and changed the plans," Joey said.

"Well his loss is our gain. I'm glad you're not with your dad today."

Relief swelled inside of Vinnie as his mother walked toward them from the kitchen saving him from commenting further. In his heart he hoped his ex-brother in law would rot in hell for what he was doing to his boys.

"You looked very handsome on TV, honey." Rose hugged him infusing Vinnie with warm acceptance and with gratitude that he had always had two parents who put him and Tricia first.

"Thanks, Ma. Sorry I missed the pumpkin bread, though."

"No worries. I saved you an end piece." She took the offered flowers and buried her nose in the bouquet. "Thank you. These are beautiful. Come into the kitchen while I put them in water."

He closed his eyes and breathed deeply. No place smelled as good as home on Thanksgiving.

Vinnie drifted into the kitchen and gave Tricia a warm hug. Leaning close to her ear, he whispered,

"Their father ditched the kids again?"

"Please don't say anything about it today. Barry is very upset. For some reason he blames me. Like it's my fault his father treats him like an afterthought. But I did text my new lawyer to let him know. I'm thankful for Summer this Thanksgiving. I'm going to keep the house."

"That's the best news I've had in a long time."

She squeezed his arm and then turned her attention to their mother. "I'll carry that into the dining room."

"What can I do to help?" Vinnie said as he lifted the lid off a pot on the stove.

"Nothing." Mom shooed him away with a couple sweeps of her arms. "Go keep your father company."

Vinnie obeyed his mother…only after he swirled his index finger in the pot of mashed potatoes and popped it into his mouth. Licking butter off his finger, he walked down the hallway into the den.

"Hey, Pops, how are the Bears doing?"

Vinnie's father rose from his seat in his mostly threadbare, upholstered recliner to embrace Vin. "Not bad. They're coming back after the half."

Vinnie took a seat on the sectional next to his nephew, Barry and squeezed his knee. "Glad you're here today. Someone has to root for the Panthers for Summer."

His mom bustled into the room toting a plate with a slice of her homemade pumpkin bread and a mug of aromatic coffee.

"Thanks, Mom. This will hold me until dinner." He beamed her a smile.

She smiled back at him. "You're welcome. What's Thanksgiving without my pumpkin bread?"

"You spoil the boy," his father groused, his half smile belying his complaint.

At a commercial break Dad faced him. "How are things going with your case? I don't like to bring it up at the restaurant. Too many people with big ears."

"Nothing new."

"Why not?"

"It takes time, Pops. The hearing isn't until January. I have to wait until then."

"Shouldn't you be more proactive? Are you sure she's doing everything she possibly can for you?"

Vinnie noticed his father's stressing the word, *she,* but he didn't take the bait.

"Yes. I'm positive she's doing everything possible."

"Dinner's on the table," Tricia called out.

The boys jumped up and raced out of the room. Vinnie and his dad rose from their seats in unison.

Dad lay his hand on Vinnie's arm.

"What, Pops?"

"Are you sure you have the right lawyer?"

"I know you have a problem for some reason with a female attorney defending me, but she is the best in her profession. Period." Vinnie's pulse raced from the insult of his father's questioning his judgment. Or did his heart always beat faster whenever he thought about Summer?

"You're falling for her, aren't you?" His father stared directly into Vinnie's eyes.

Refusing to break the stare, Vinnie said, "Dad. Really?"

"I see it in your eyes. Your career is in jeopardy. I'm worried about you. Keep it professional."

"I am, and I will."

Tears welled in the old man's eyes breaking Vinnie's heart. "Ah, Dad. Don't worry okay?"

He nodded as Vinnie swept his arm around his shoulders. "Let's go get some crescent rolls before those nephews of mine finish them all."

Vinnie waited a couple seconds watching Dad amble away from him. Trailing his father into the dining room, he mulled over Dad's parental wisdom. *He might be right.*

Was he crazy to fall in love with Summer now when he had everything to lose? Was he crazy to fall in love with a challenging and unpredictable woman like Summer at any time? She was intoxicating…but… How did she feel about him? She had never discouraged his making it personal. She had also never given him the slightest indication that she was interested in a serious relationship. *God knows we've been very good at frustrating each other.*

Maybe he'd cool things off until after he was back on the job.

He joined his family at the head of the table opposite Dad, linked hands with Tricia and Joey and thanked God for the delicious-smelling food on the table and for his loved ones gathered around him. When his phone vibrated against his hip, he slipped his hand in his pocket, slid out the phone and checked the screen for caller ID below the level of the tabletop. He slipped the phone back in his pocket ignoring Summer's call.

Chapter 14

Summer recorded, "Happy Thanksgiving," on Vinnie's voicemail and then left her room at The Inn of the Three Butterflies. Descending the back stairs leading to the inn's sunny kitchen, she smiled, remembering the text Vinnie had sent her minutes after she had spirited away in a cab the Sunday before Thanksgiving.

Touché Lady. Next time NOBODY leaves until…

Summer floated through the kitchen into the dining room thinking about what would come after the word, "until" in his message, and took her seat at the table. She grinned across the feast-laden tabletop at Bree, like looking in the mirror a year ago when Summer, too, had a mane of below the shoulder, fiery auburn hair like her identical triplet. Linking hands with her father, Mike to her left at the head of the table, and her sister, Skye seated to her right, she said, "Amen," at the conclusion of her father's Thanksgiving blessing.

The whole house had filled with mouth-watering aromas all day. Her mom, Kay, had started her family's holiday with from scratch cranberry bread and hot chocolate swimming with tiny marshmallows. Summer had joined her sisters and extended family in front of the television, chomping on the sweet bread and watching the annual *Thanksgiving Day Parade*. Summer was stunned when she thought she spied

Vinnie walking the route near the Wimpy Kid balloon.

"Wait," she said popping out of her seat and approaching the flat screen mounted on the family room's wall. "Did you guys just see Vinnie Carlucci in the parade?"

Nobody could confirm the sighting—which was nothing more than a momentary flash on the screen anyway. Summer returned to her seat convinced that she had imagined the incident since she had Vinnie Carlucci constantly on her mind.

Ella, Bree's soon-to-be stepdaughter, squealed in glee as Santa Claus glided into Herald Square on his reindeer-drawn sleigh float.

"I want to go to that parade someday, Daddy," Ella had declared.

Jack Tremonti had responded to his daughter with the parents' universal mantra, "We'll see…"

No amount of prior gym workouts the past few days could compensate for the meal on the table in front of her that Summer intended to thoroughly enjoy. She planned to take advantage of the near seventy degree temps the next several days and rack up hours of jogging along the beach while at home on the shores of the Outer Banks. Her future held plenty of mega-calories burns.

Her future. She gazed at Bree and her fiancé, Jack, seated shoulder to shoulder across from her. Ella chatted with Skye, her sweet voice adding to the cheerful chorus of family conversations. Jack's unscheduled visit to the inn seven months ago and his and Ella's unwitting involvement in Vinnie's FBI investigation had changed the course of Bree's future. Her Christmas wedding at the inn was anticipated with elation on both sides of the families. Had Vin's stay here changed the course of Summer's life, too?

Doubtless her immediate attraction to Vinnie when he had barged into that very room seven months ago while the family entertained Jack and Ella at breakfast was overwhelming, and unprecedented. Even more surprising, his sexual appeal to her grew with every encounter. She grinned, bowed over her plate of food, thinking about their recent, intimate roller coaster rides.

After she had read Vinnie's text during her cab ride her cell phone had trilled.

Summer had accepted Vinnie's call prepared to take substantial heat for leaving him, most likely naked in his bed, and...in dire need of a cold shower. Instead his hearty laughter boomed in her ear.

"You read my text?" he had said.

"I did. I take it I've made my point?"

"Crystal clear. We're even."

"Good," she had replied. "Then I won't bother to apologize."

"Nah. Me, neither. When can I see you again?"

The prospect had set her every nerve ending aflame. She hadn't really thought that her retaliation would leave him cold enough to cut off their personal relationship. But she had taken a risk. Summer was relieved that Vinnie was man enough to stand up to her...self-confident enough to take a joke.

She loved contemplating seeing him again. And again. The next time that she seduced him, or he seduced her, would *not* end in anything but fulfilled passion.

"After Thanksgiving?" she had suggested. "I'm leaving for North Carolina on Tuesday."

"Deal. Wish a happy thanksgiving to your family for me."

"I will. And from me to yours."

"Sure. I'll miss you, Summer. Can't wait to see you."

He'll miss me. She hung on the sentiment long after she had hung up the phone.

Since then her head had spun and her heart had leaped at the mere thought of Vinnie Carlucci. In retrospect she had done a good deal of missing him, too.

The bridesmaids' and wedding dress fittings yesterday had left Summer fantasizing about her own wedding someday—a scenario she had never even vaguely envisioned before. When Bree had swept into the dressing room and stepped up onto the platform in front of the mirrors wearing her wedding gown and veil, tears had welled in Summer's eyes while her heart had melted.

Skye had passed Summer a box of tissues. Dabbing her eyes, Summer had exclaimed, "Oh, Bree. You're gorgeous."

Bree had smoothed her hands down the sides of her hips. "Yes? You like the dress?"

"Like it? I *love* it."

"It couldn't be more perfect," Skye had said. "Jack will *flip* when he sees you."

Bree had given her sisters a dreamy smile gazing at her reflection in the mirror. "Thanks, guys. Mom, what do you think?"

Kay waved a hand in front of her face, her eyes streaming.

Bree hooted a laugh. "I'll take that as you agree

143

with Skye and Summer."

Her mother nodded assent, a wonderstruck expression on her lovely face. Summer's heart swelled. Their magical mother had entrusted them with everything she knew about their legacy from generations of identical triplets before them and their connection to the Sacred Source. She hadn't needed to teach them to shapeshift. The ability had come naturally to Skye who had linked with her and Bree's toddler hands and empowered them to flutter and soar and skim the ocean waves transformed into the marine creatures that Skye adored. Kay had never succeeded in passing on her visionary skills to her daughters. Sure, the triplets' intuitive connection with each other bordered on extra-sensory. But their mom's skill in "seeing" events surpassed her daughters.

Bree and Skye drifted over to their weeping mother and encircled her shoulders with their arms.

"Oh Bree," Kay blubbered. "I'm so happy for you."

Bree chuckled. "I know, Mom."

When Ella had skipped into the dressing room, a raven-haired, princess clad in her pine green velvet gown, all four women reached for fresh tissues. Ten-year-old Ella would serve as Bree's Maid of Honor.

The seamstress had fluttered around Bree, pinching the cream-colored satin material at her waist and then stooping to fold the hem while plucking pins out of her mouth and affixing them to the delicate material.

What kind of gown would Summer choose for her wedding day? Sleek and fitted. Probably strapless. Silk? That she had even toyed with the daydream had her widening her eyes and shaking the idea straight out of her head.

"Can you try your dresses on?" Bree had requested. "I can't wait to see you in them. All of us on my wedding day. It's a dream come true."

Bree would have her fairy tale. Judging from the hang the moon expression in Jack Tremonti's eyes whenever he regarded his bride to be, the groom would have his fairy tale, too.

Summer sighed and forked up a mouth full of turkey stuffing. She savored the butter saturated bread, calories be damned. Sheer pleasure at the tasty meal and the warmth of her family surrounding her filled Summer.

"How are things going with Vinnie? Making progress?" Kay asked.

"Huh?" Summer vehemently hoped that her mom hadn't "seen" any of her recent interactions with Vinnie.

"His defense. Are you getting closer to proving his innocence?"

"Oh. No. Well maybe." Flustered, Summer trained her thoughts on her professional relationship with Vin. "I've hired a computer expert. Finding the money is key."

"Makes sense," Jack said.

"Right. I'm sure it won't be long," Summer said. "Mom, this meal is delicious." Switching subjects might not necessarily divert her mother from delving into her recent past with Vinnie. No one could control Mom's visions.

But as far as Summer knew, Mom had never invaded her girls' privacy.

Summer placed her fork and knife on her empty

plate and leaned back in her chair. "I better stop now. I'm sure you've baked your specialties for dessert, Mom."

Kay rose, her plate in hand. Clad in gray slacks and a peach cashmere sweater, her mother glowed with obvious contentment having her family home for the holiday. She began gathering empty dishes from around the table. "Yes, I have baked a few things."

Mike winked at his wife. "There are pecan, pumpkin, mince and apple pies fresh from the oven early this morning. I might have peeled a few—hundred apples helping out."

"That reminds me," Kay said. "Thank you again, Summer, for the apples you picked in New Jersey. They're absolutely perfect for pie filling."

Remembering the apple orchard had Vinnie foremost in Summer's thoughts once again. His sweet company. His lovely family. His irresistible smile. His huge hand warming hers; and his embrace shielding her from the chilly breeze. Dinner at Via Lucci afterward. Her intense, consuming pleasure at his touch...

Disturbed by the frequency he came to mind; Summer was glad for the distraction of this family gathering and a little distance from Vinnie's overpowering personality.

After too much pie, and who could resist fresh whipped cream topping, Summer seized upon Bree's proposal of a sister walk on the beach after they helped Mom with the dishes. Even with three of them drying the plates, flatware, glasses and pots that Mom washed by hand after the dishwasher overloaded, dealing with the dirty dishes' aftermath of the family Thanksgiving meal was at least an hour proposition for them.

At last released from KP, Bree, Skye and Summer dashed to the screen porch and exchanged sandals for running shoes. Together they slogged through shifting sand until gaining firm footing on the packed sand at the water's edge. Sandwiched between her sisters, Summer basked in the mild breeze and remnants of lemony rays from the lowering sun.

The familiar incessant roar of sea breeze and rhythmic waves breaking against the shore filled her ears. All her senses engaged caught up in the eye widening spectacle of sunset hues streaking the huge dome overhead, the briny aroma of the sea and the cold jolt of lapping waves over her feet.

She sighed, sated with food and the mind cleansing freedom that walking this beach always afforded her. "Honestly, I don't know how I stand living near the big city. Every time I come home it's like I'm born again."

"I feel the same way," Bree said. "But I do love my life in Chicago." She beamed Summer a smile. "Especially, now that Jack and Ella are in my life."

"I can imagine," Skye said. "I envy you, Bree."

"Get real, Skye," Summer said. "You would hate living anywhere but here."

"True. What I meant is that I envy the Jack part. He's your soul mate, Bree. I knew it from the beginning."

"Speaking of..." Bree clasped Summer's hand. "Something you want to tell us, Summer?"

Summer pulled up short narrowing her eyes. "I'm not sure what you..."

"About Vinnie?" Bree interjected.

"Well, I thought I brought you up to speed on that at dinner."

"I'm not talking about working as his lawyer," Bree said, her smile amused.

"Hm. Well. We have spent some time together socially." Summer warmed to the subject. "I love his parents, although I had a shaky start with his dad. A bit of anti-feminism with Vin's choice of me as his attorney at the outset. But I've won him over for sure. I've totally fallen in love with his sister, Tricia and her boys. Hard not to…"

"And…?" Bree said.

"I don't like where this is going." Skye spun on her heel. "See you back home."

"Skye, wait," Summer said to her sister's back.

"It's okay, Summer." Bree touched Summer's arm softly. "Skye has yet to forgive Vin for my injury on that case with him."

"I know. But he really wasn't to blame. And you're all healed now, right?"

"I am. I never thought he was to blame. Neither does Skye, deep down. But you know how we hurt for each other? Skye can't seem to forget how that bullet wound felt. Hurt like a bitch."

"I know." Summer shuddered, remembering. Neither she nor Skye had to be notified when Bree was shot. They felt the wound the instant it happened.

"So? You were saying," Bree prompted.

"Actually. I'm sort of glad to talk with you alone. About Vinnie."

"Okay. What do you have on your mind?"

"I'm thinking of asking him to be my plus one at your wedding. Do you have a problem with that?"

"Of course not! Why would you think you'd have to ask my permission in the first place?" Bree beamed her a smile.

"Well. You do have a history and everything."

"Oh that. It was forever ago. You know we were never…we didn't." Bree huffed a laugh. "I was never a notch on his bedpost."

Neither am I. But I'm working on it. "What about Jack? I'm pretty sure he hated Vinnie on sight. Plus, he was pretty bent out of shape every time he referred to you as, 'my girl'."

Bree reared back her head and belly laughed. "So true. But that seems forever ago, too. Jack knows Vinnie is nothing more than a friend to me. He's very secure with me now."

Bree's penetrating emerald eyes bored into Summer's. "Of course. I already knew you planned on inviting Vinnie to my wedding."

"All right…" Summer shrugged. "I guess I should have realized that."

"Uh huh. How could I not know when my sister has fallen in love?"

"Wait. What?" Summer sputtered. "I never said…"

"Didn't have to." Bree winked. "Come on. Let's catch up to Skye."

Chapter 15

Rambling along the sand next to Bree, Summer tried to absorb that her sister believed that she was in love with Vinnie.

Summer shivered. *That's ridiculous. I've never been in love with anyone.*

But…her feelings for Vinnie *were* rare—sweet, downright gooey, and then there was overpowering lust, and yearning. How could she have let this happen? Didn't loving someone require utter surrender?

Fiercely independent with a high need for control, Summer had no experience surrendering her heart. She had never had the slightest desire to relinquish that much control to a man.

But the visions of the women in her family were always dead on target. Bree must be right.

Regardless, Summer couldn't afford to allow her emotions to cloud her professional obligation to Vinnie. *First be his advocate. Deal with the rest after he's proven innocent.*

The rest. Summer missed him. An admission she'd never make to Vinnie or her family. She hardly recognized herself in her deepest truth - a woman who secretly longed for him remembering every touch. Every caress. His overwhelming sexual power over her. She wanted to surrender. Could she?

Increasingly she couldn't ignore the tender

emotions for him that had taken root in her heart. But how would she clear his name to give them both the freedom to…love each other? Did he love her, too?

She wagged her head and twisted her lips frustrated that she couldn't see a clear professional or personal path with Vinnie.

Summer had never called upon the Sacred Source to win a case for the Prosecution or for the Defense. She had solely relied on her professional acumen and her encyclopedic knowledge of legal case history.

Everything about Vinnie's case felt different—intimate and critical to win. Of course, she cared strongly about every client—the State in her former job, and currently each Defendant that entrusted her to be his or her advocate since joining forces with Jacob Levant. But Vinnie…this man…

Lost in thought, Summer emerged from her reverie when Bree veered off from the shoreline to slog through the sand fronting the inn. Catching up with her, she and Bree mounted the deck stairs and entered the screen porch.

Bending to untie her running shoes, Summer gazed up at her sister. "Bree, has Mom seen anything?"

"Not that she's said. I can't imagine that she'd withhold it if she had."

"Right." Summer kicked off her shoes and then balanced on each leg. She bent her opposite knees sideways and angled her calves upward so that she could reach each foot to slip off her sandy, athletic ankle socks. "But I've never asked her to look into any of my cases. I think I want to make an exception with Vinnie's defense."

"I understand. Let's go find her."

Buoyed by the possibility that her mother's gift might give her the edge in defending him, she trailed Bree into the inn. Nothing smelled better than Thanksgiving dinner. The homey aromas of herb roasted turkey, cinnamon, butter, baked apples and nutmeg lingered in the kitchen. Skye sat at the table with outstretched legs, her feet propped on a ladder-back chair, sipping from a mug and thumbing through a magazine. "Hi. What's up?"

"We're going to ask Mom to look into my case. Want to come?"

Skye narrowed her eyes. "As in the case defending Carlucci?"

"That's the one."

"Hmm."

Bree huffed, "Oh, Skye. Give the man a chance. The whole gunshot thing is ancient history. He needs us to support him. *All* of us."

One by one Skye unfurled her long, slender legs and rose from her seat. "Oh, all right." She beamed Summer a smile. "Might be fun seeing Mom in action."

The trio left the kitchen and went in search of their mother. Kay was seated on the loveseat in the parlor, her long legs tucked beneath her. Her head rested on Dad's shoulder within the crescent of his muscular arm. A mental image of nestling within the shelter of Vinnie's embrace flashed vividly in Summer's mind.

Would evenings like this be in store for her if she opened her heart to Vinnie? Kay's eyes had always danced, and she had grinned from ear to ear every time she had regaled her girls with her true love story. Dad, a newly discharged Navy Seal, had taken up house painting. The inn had represented his first major job.

Mom had known the second she met him that she would marry handsome and very mortal Michael Layton. Dad hadn't known the whole of his wife's special "talents" experiencing love at first sight. When Mom had revealed her true nature to Dad after several increasingly hot dates, his delight in her had soared to wonderment. They made an amazing couple and had set the relationships bar in the stratosphere for their daughters. Summer had never strained to reach that bar. With Vinnie, she might not have to strain at all.

Mom didn't budge from her cozy position as Summer entered the parlor trailed by Bree and Skye. The triplets plopped down on the heirloom Aubusson rug in front of the loveseat, one of the few of their grandmother's possessions that had survived the fire that had destroyed the original Inn of the Three Butterflies.

Shifting from her position, Mom planted both feet on the floor and regarded Summer. "You need me to look."

Summer nodded without offering further clarification of why she had sought out her mother. Without doubt, Mom already knew.

"All right." Mom closed her eyes slackening her arms at her sides.

Summer tracked the tennis tournament, side to side movements beneath her mother's eyelids. Seconds passed before Mom's soft voice sounded. "A laptop with white space around it. Let me see."

Mom's head bowed. "It's open….

"Ah. The fingers of two hands arched over the keyboard. Man's hands. Fingernails cut to the nubs. A clunky ring on the left hand. Burnished gold."

Summer held her breath. A wedding ring maybe? If Mom could describe it, that might solidify Muñoz's guilt. Vinnie never wore jewelry. Not that the fact figured into her belief in his innocence in light of this information. Still. It might provide her first solid lead.

She didn't probe. Summer knew that Mom wouldn't fail to omit the tiniest detail.

Kay raised her head and slowly opened her eyes. She sat a few seconds, silent, as if dazed. And then she riveted her gaze on Summer, intent, her green eyes sparkling. "That's all I saw, darling. But I also had the strongest sense that Vinnie knows this man. Well. He's a friend."

Not the least surprised at the information, Summer nodded. "You said the ring was clunky. Could it be a wedding band?"

Kay shook her head. "I don't think so. More like a signet ring. *If* it was a wedding band, it would be a very unusual one."

Summer's shoulders sagged. She had had high hopes that she'd solve her case "magically".

"Thanks for helping, Mom. You definitely confirmed it's an insider job. That's something."

"If I see anything else, do you want to know?"

"Yes, of course." Summer unwound her legs from a lotus position and rose from the floor. "I'm going to change into my pajamas and go watch some football."

"Me, too."

"Me, three," chimed in her sisters.

****

Summer had wisely booked a return flight to Newark for the Monday after Thanksgiving. The foresight had spared her from the largest crush of fliers during the holiday weekend *and* she had missed the rash of flight cancellations due to a snowstorm in the mid-Atlantic two days earlier. She had TSA Precheck clearance and she sped through the security lanes at Norfolk International Airport unimpeded. Her luck held when her flight boarded on time, taxied to the runway and accelerated to takeoff five minutes ahead of schedule.

Seated in a solo first-class seat on the port side of the narrow express jet bound for Newark Airport, Summer debated taking a nap. The brutally early 6:45 AM departure had her up at 3:00 AM, tiptoeing through the room she had shared with her sisters, brushing her teeth, throwing on clothes and finger combing her spiky hair before slipping out of the quiet inn into the briny scented ocean breeze, inky darkness and predawn chill. She had intended to make it an early night yesterday, but the Packers and Vikings faced off on Sunday night football and she had to wager that the Vikings would win just to gall her sister Skye, who never missed an opportunity to root for her "beloved Pack" from preseason until playoffs—and occasionally, if the stars were in her favor, during the Super Bowl. She had driven them crazy gloating when Green Bay had won the Super Bowl.

As little kids, Summer and Bree actually joined Skye as fellow Packers Backers and their dad bet against them - $1 each—to keep the girls in the game. He schooled them on each play, each penalty. Green Bay won way more games than they lost, so the girls were *really* involved in the stakes. Those memories solidified their love of football and they tried to catch all the televised games of their favorite teams during the season. When they were in grammar school the NFL created a brand-new team on home turf. Bree and Summer instantly became avid Panthers fans. Since college, Bree also enjoyed watching the Chicago Bears play; even more now that her fiancé, like most native Chicagoans, loved da Bears. Summer occasionally rooted for the New England Patriots since law school. But Skye hadn't turned her back on Green Bay—even this season when her sisters gleefully cashed in on most bets.

Last night the trio hung in until the final whistle and the Packers only lost by seven points. But they lost to Skye's dismay. The fun and laughter were worth the lack of sleep. Summer and Bree were each five dollars richer, also.

The triplets were feminine women but growing up they were unapologetic tomboys which delighted their parents. Each sister had played at least one sport through high school. Bree and Summer had played in college, too. Bree was a killer tennis player. Summer might have sought out a pro golf career after college graduation if the law hadn't fascinated her. Skye might not have played beyond high school, but she could still rocket pitch a soft ball.

She smiled thinking about her sisters who meant everything to Summer. They were virtual carbon copies physically, and like most identical siblings, they shared a powerful psychic connection. The trio also had genius IQs. Their personalities, however, widely differed. Skye channeled her keen intelligence and superior connection to the Sacred Source through creativity. She was firmly rooted on the Outer Banks, calmer, more ethereal and considerably more powerful than her sisters. Her marine life paintings had put her on the International Art world's short list of contemporary masters. Perhaps she was able to achieve the unparalleled realism that differentiated her art because she could live and breathe in her subjects' skin.

Bree and Summer had gravitated to the challenging fields of medicine and the law, leaving the nest on Outer Banks and thriving in urban environments. Bree had cultivated the ability to shapeshift entirely without Skye's assistance. Summer, aside from tinkering with partial shapeshifting; for example, the gorilla arm that had made her a recurring arm-wrestling champ, had been gifted with prophetic dreams.

If she napped now, would Mom's vision present to Summer in her dreams? She rejected the thought knowing she couldn't force the power, even in calling upon the Sacred Source. With the sisters of the legend the power just…was.

Summer clamped her feet around her briefcase underneath the seat in front of her and dragged the bag forward toward her. She bent down and hoisted the satchel onto her lap, unbuckled the leather straps and raised the flap. She fingered the folders inside and selected Vinnie's file. She stowed her briefcase on the floor to the left of her feet, opened the tray table and spread open the case file.

Her earlier inclination to nap forgotten, she immersed in the paperwork, her mind ticking off actions that hopefully would lead to the truth and his exoneration. She peered at her cellphone's screen, tapped settings and connected to Wi-Fi. Typing rapid-fire with both thumbs, she composed an email to Barbara asking her to set appointments with the four men in Senior Special Agent Carlucci's unit who had volunteered as character witnesses for the Defense.

Summer particularly looked forward to meeting with Special Agent Muñoz.

Chapter 16

Summer disconnected the call and slouched in her office chair, her phone in hand. Mike Haws had just given her his first report after spending time at the Newark Field Office. The Bureau's tech wizards had walked Mike through the basis of the embezzlement charge against Vin. Undeniably the trail began with an online transaction removing funds from the Informant Account and depositing the exact sum missing into his checking account. Then the funds were electronically withdrawn from Vin's account and went ping-ponging in cyberspace to a complex web of cloaked IP addresses with an undetectable endpoint—so far.

"I don't know Vincente Carlucci," Mike had said. "I suppose he could have withdrawn from the Informants Account by his own authority routinely. But if he orchestrated these other transactions, he's an advanced hacker to say the *least*. They didn't let me touch the computer. Evidence and all that. Can you petition for remote access for me? They can backup, clone, whatever, to safeguard the evidence. I need access to the original data."

"I'll put that in motion the second we hang up," Summer said. "Do you think you can find the money, Mike?" Summer had held her breath, utterly clueless how she'd proceed if Mike answered, no.

"Maybe. Next step I want to see how his computer

was hacked. My theory is that all this was done remotely with hacked passwords, etc."

"All right. I'll notify you when you can take that step. Thanks Mike."

"No problem, Ms. Layton."

Summer sat dangling the phone in her hand. She needed to dictate to Barbara the verbiage for the petition and then fast track the document through the approval process. She needed to schedule defense witness interviews. She needed to hire an investigator to background check Paul Muñoz. Where did he get the money to finance an expensive vacation when he claimed to be perennially strapped? The timing of the vacation *was* suspicious.

She wished that her instincts homed in stronger on Vinnie's partner's guilt. Truthfully, it didn't add up. Why would a father desperate enough to steal from the FBI blow the money on Disney World? Was Paul a closet super hacker?

Summer could answer yes to both questions in the realm of possibility. But in reality?

Of course, she'd upturn every rock and follow any investigative trail. She sighed and straightened in her seat, ready to tick off the list of tasks in handling Vin's case and a multitude of others to deal with her workload. But, she couldn't concentrate.

Why hadn't he called since before Thanksgiving? *Is he still mad at me for leaving him in his bedroom?*

Despite a tiny twinge of guilt about her payback, she grinned remembering his text. *Next time NOBODY leaves until…*

Summer was so ready for "next time". And "until…" There was a handy excuse to contact him today. She wanted to invite him to Radio City with Bree and Jack and Ella. And, also to ask him to come to Bree's wedding with her. She decided to draft the petition and hire the investigator first.

When she had cleared her plate enough to feel free to make the personal call, Summer selected Vinnie's cell number from Contacts and connected.

He answered on the third ring. "Summer. Did you have a nice holiday?"

"I did. And you?"

"Really good. I worked security on one of the parade balloons in the morning and then had dinner with the family."

"Holy shit! Wimpy Kid?"

"Yeah. Joey got a big kick out it."

"We saw you on TV! I thought I was hallucinating." *I thought I was seeing you in every handsome face since I missed you so much.*

"Nope. That was me."

She smiled, impressed that she had improbably picked him out of the crowd. A few beats of silence hung between them.

"You still there?" he said.

"Um…yeah." She hesitated.

"Uh. You called me?"

"I did. I thought…maybe…"

****

If Summer were wearing her Counselor hat, she wouldn't hesitate a second to explain the reason for her call. Despite his dad's warning to keep it professional with her, he missed her and hadn't stopped thinking about her throughout their brief time apart. "Have dinner with me."

161

"Um…sure, yes. Where would you like to go?"

"I'll surprise you. Pick you up at your place at seven?"

"All right."

"Good."

"Vinnie, wait."

"Uh huh?"

"Make it my office. I have a lot of work to catch up on today."

"See you at seven."

****

Vinnie texted Summer that he was out in front of her office building. He relaxed in his warm car idling at the curb, satisfied that he had finally found a mechanic who had fixed his ailing heater. He lit a Marlboro with the car lighter, rolled down his window and dangled his arm out the window, holding the smoking cigarette between his thumb and index finger. After each drag, he exhaled the smoke out the window.

Summer emerged through the glass doors about five minutes after he had finished smoking. She looked sensational in a fitted red wool coat and black high heeled boots. The passenger door swung open and she slipped in beside him bringing a blast of perfume-scented cold air with her. Springtime in winter.

"Hi," she said rubbing her leather gloved hands together. "It's freezing out there."

"Yep. It was even colder when you were away. You're lucky you missed the storm."

"That's what I hear. Hey. You got your heater fixed."

"I did. Can't have you freezing your pretty ass off."

She gave him a light punch in his right arm. "Glad

you think it's pretty."

He stopped at a red light and faced her. "From what I've seen so far."

Her jade eyes smoldered as she gave him a feline smile. If the lady was willing, tonight would be the furthest thing from professional.

"Where are we going for dinner?" she asked as Vinnie merged onto the turnpike.

"You'll see." He turned on the radio that he had pre-tuned to the all Christmas channel. "You like Christmas music?"

"Addicted. This is perfect."

They made small talk and mostly listened to music during the twenty-minute drive. She sang the refrain, "Gloria, to Angels We Have Heard on High," a pretty soprano right on key that made his heart swell. There was so much to this woman he'd yet to discover. Everything he did know about her pointed to two undeniable facts. He had never met anyone like her. And he had never felt this way about anyone.

He pulled up to the curb and switched off the engine.

She glanced through her window and then turned toward him furrowing her brow. "Via Lucci?"

"Yep." He opened his door and paused, his hand on the handle. "Hold up. I'll get your door."

Vinnie shut the driver's door and skirted the front bumper striding to her side of the car. He held out his hand to her after he swung open the passenger door. The touch of her small hand against his palm and her allowing his helping her out of the car satisfied his desire to pamper and protect her and filled him with pleasure.

She peered at the façade of the restaurant. "It doesn't look like it's open."

He bent his arm and wrapped her hand around his bicep as they navigated the icy sidewalk toward the awning covered entrance. "Technically it isn't open. Tuesdays are my parents' only day off except for certain holidays."

They reached the door and Vinnie fished in his pocket for the keyring. He unlocked and opened the door and ushered her inside the dimly lit barroom. "Hold on," he said.

Ducking behind the bar, he flipped a couple switches illuminating the lights over the bar and in the upper level, main restaurant. She shrugged out of her jacket, hung it on the coat tree near the door and then sat on a bar stool watching him, a half smile on her lovely face. He surveyed the array of wine bottles and selected a red blend that he thought she'd like.

After he supplied her with an ample pour, he ambled over to a window table, set the wine bottle on the table and lit the votive candle in a glass holder in the center of the table for four. He removed two place settings and set them on a neighboring table. Then he gathered candles from the five other tables in the bar area, grouped them in a cluster at the center of the window table and lit each in succession.

He pulled out a chair facing the street that afforded a pretty view of the sparkling Christmas decorations on the city block. At his nod, Summer strolled toward him, her wine glass in hand. He held the seat for her and then nudged her closer to the table, his head bent over her shining cap of flame colored hair.

Vinnie couldn't resist kissing the crown of her

head. She angled her neck and gazed up at him, her eyes soft.

"I won't take long in the kitchen," he said. "I'll have a nice dinner for us in less than half hour. I'll bring you some bruschetta right away."

"Sounds wonderful."

He scurried up two steps, through the main dining room and into the kitchen, a world that had become all-encompassing for Vinnie since his suspension. He flicked on lights and hurried over to the fridge to select ingredients for her appetizer and dinner. After he sliced several ovals of bread from the baguette shaped loaf, he wielded the knife to dice a fresh tomato. He coated a sauté pan with olive oil, added the tomatoes, fresh basil, minced garlic and a pinch of red pepper and heated the mixture until the vegetables were tender. Vinnie heated the grill and toasted the bread lightly. Carefully spooning the vegetables onto bread, he placed the bruschetta on a plate. After he put a pot of water on the burner over a high flame, he served the appetizer to Summer.

Back in the kitchen he prepared the meal, *gemelli* pasta with a red sauce and sautéed swordfish, and toted two artistically arranged dinner plates to the window table. He placed her plate before her and took the seat opposite Summer, his back to the window. She had poured him a glass of wine and he raised it gazing into her jade eyes that radiated candlelight. "I'd like to drink to how beautiful you look tonight."

She hesitated before she raised her glass and lightly clinked it against his goblet. "And how handsome you look tonight."

Summer set her glass down after taking a sip of

wine. She leaned over her plate and inhaled deeply. "This smells delicious."

"Hope you like it. I made up the recipe recently. Dad said it was pretty popular."

Chewing delicately her eyes widened. "God, this is fantastic. Can you teach me to cook like this?"

"Sure."

"Thanks." She took another bite. And then she dug in with appetite.

He ate his dinner quietly observing her animated eating.

She emptied her plate and then leaned back in her seat. "I'm serious. I want you to teach me."

"Happy to. I can teach you a lot of things," he quipped.

Nothing slow about Summer Layton. "Or maybe I can teach you."

"I'm a willing student."

Whether they outdared each other or not, he wasn't about to miss this opportunity. "Would you like to try a visit to my place again?"

"Yes." Her smoldering gaze set him motion.

"I'll clean up the dishes as fast as I can." He lifted their plates off the table.

"Let me help," she said picking up the wine glasses. "It will go faster."

****

In Vinnie's bedroom a ribbon of moonlight shone on her porcelain skin. He took her in his arms, aching for completion, stunned by her beauty. Her silken skin brushed against his chest as he tightened the embrace and pressed her naked body close to his heart. The contours of every inch of her fit to him, skin to skin.

"I want you. All of you," he whispered.

She arched her neck and parted her lips, an invitation he did not hesitate to take.

His mouth fused with hers, maybe too roughly, but he couldn't hold back. Engulfed in the taste, the smell, the unbearably sensual feel of her he couldn't turn back.

Vinnie swept her up into a fireman's carry and in two broad steps, brought her to his bed. She lay on her back, her eyes closed, her legs parted, quivering in passion. He straddled her slim body caressing her breasts, lightly thumbing her nipples into hard nubs. He had to taste her, everywhere, all of her.

As if drinking from a desert oasis after nearly dying of thirst, he and Summer took their fill of each other. Enflamed to mindlessness when Summer opened to him, Vinnie held back until her body gathered and tightened around him.

He voiced with her a duet. "Oh God NOW." And then Vinnie experienced the most cyclonic orgasm of his life.

He was grateful that she hadn't immediately fled afterward, but curled up in his arms, her head resting over his heart. "Sounds like a whole percussion session in there," she said.

"Not surprised."

"That was amazing."

"Yep. Not bad for the first time."

"Lord. Sign me up for the second." She chuckled.

"What's so funny?"

Summer shifted in his arms to lay her head on his shoulder. She looked him in the eye. "This evening was so unexpected. Want to know why I really called you today?"

"Yeah. Sure."

"To ask you if you wanted to go with me and Bree, Jack and Ella to Radio City Music Hall to see the Christmas show."

"Sounds like fun. When?"

"Saturday."

"Sure."

"Oh. And if you would like to go to Bree's wedding with me."

"Really? Is Jack good with that?"

"Oh yeah. You'll see Saturday. He's not the least bit insecure about Bree now."

"When is the wedding?"

"Christmas Day. But we'd have to arrive on Christmas Eve."

"I think my folks might be disappointed if I'm away Christmas, but I'll celebrate early with them to make it up to them. I accept."

"Okay." She nestled her head on his chest again. "Thank you. And I also called because I missed you like crazy during the Thanksgiving weekend."

In the next instant, she softly snored.

Chapter 17

Summer paced back and forth in front of the arrivals' corridor at Newark International Airport, craning her neck hoping to glimpse Bree, Jack and Ella heading her way. So far, two delays of the outbound Chicago flight had added a couple hours to her vigil. She lightly gripped the shoulder strap of the briefcase that swung with her movements and bumped against her hip.

After she had noticed the first hour's delay on the arrivals board, Summer had strolled into the nearby Starbucks café, purchased a Venti Caramel Brulée Latte and had claimed an empty table where she could spread out a couple files to pour over.

She had enjoyed the delicious drink, but now the caffeine had her even more jittery anticipating her sister's arrival. Unable to concentrate on her work, Summer had thought of nothing else besides the fun things she had planned for Bree's visit.

The iced snowman cookie she had bought for Ella in one hand, and her cell phone in the other, poised to receive a "Landed!" text that *should* come in five minutes, Summer positioned herself at attention at the mouth of the long hallway.

Her ringtone sounded, and her phone vibrated against her palm. Identifying the caller, Michael Haws, she answered immediately.

"Hi Mike. Hope you have some good news for me."

"Sorry, Ms. Layton. Not really good or bad news, just more information about that expensive trip Vincente Carlucci's partner took recently that you were concerned about. I did a little digging into Paul Muñoz's finances working with your lady investigator, Lisa."

Summer arched her eyebrows. *"Lady* investigator?"

"Female. Whichever you prefer. She's real sharp, by the way. She'll be contacting you and following up with a written report."

"All right. What can you share now?" Summer gazed forward. A group of people had moved in front of her blocking her view. She stepped to her right for a better vantage point.

"What we uncovered is for your ears only."

"Of course, Mike, that goes without saying."

"Last month large deposits were made into Muñoz's checking and savings accounts. First to the checking account. $125,000. Three days later I found two more transactions. Transfer of $100,000 from checking to savings and a simultaneous withdrawal from the checking account of $25,000. Roughly a month before these transactions, I found a record of a loan application for a second mortgage on his house for $125,000. The lien for the second mortgage was recorded the day after the checking account deposit was made. Taken together these transactions point toward a cashier check issued in the amount of the second mortgage which was deposited initially into the checking account.

Lisa tailed mister and missus for a few days while I checked out his bank records. Paul Muñoz drove his wife to Cancer Care Center, parked the car and accompanied her inside. Lisa asked me if I could access her medical chart on a hunch that she might be a cancer patient. And I did insofar as to confirm if that hunch was accurate. It was. Teresa Muñoz was diagnosed with stage 4 breast cancer four months ago. I don't know what treatment she's undergoing, if any. I'd rather not invade her privacy any further. But, Ms. Layton, I would guess that Muñoz mortgaged the house to afford the expensive trip with his family that might have been the last time they vacation together."

"Oh, that's so sad. Now I feel terrible for suspecting him."

"Can I check him off our list now?"

"Yes."

"Great. I'll keep you informed."

"Thanks, Mike." She disconnected the call and bowed her head, tears welling for the young mother and her babies.

"Bad news?" Bree touched Summer's arm gently.

Summer squealed and threw her arms around her sister. "I've been standing staring down this hallway for two hours and the one time I glanced away you appear. I'm *so* happy you're here."

She squeezed Bree in a warm hug and then stooped down to Ella's eye level. The little girl wore a navy-blue tailored coat with matching hat and gloves and looked like a living doll.

"Oh Ella! You look so pretty; like a little princess."

Ella beamed her a smile and launched into Summer's outstretched arms. Embracing her, Summer arched over Ella's crown, drinking in the shampoo sweet smell or her soft, raven hair.

Releasing her, Summer stood smiling down on Ella.

"Aunt Summer, it's so fun to finally be here. We've been sitting on the plane forever." She rolled her eyes.

Summer laughed at Ella's melodrama.

"Well, I hope the long trip was worth the wait. I think we're going to have so much fun together. Let's go get your luggage." She clasped Ella's hand.

"What does a guy have to do to get a hug around here?" Jack boomed, drawing Summer's attention. He plopped down Ella's unicorn backpack near Summer's feet and opened wide his arms.

Laughing Summer drew Ella with her into the circle of Jack's embrace. Arching her neck, she gazed up at him. "I'm so glad you're here, too."

Linking hands two by two, Summer and Ella, Bree and Jack rode the escalator down to the ground level of the airport.

"Just to assure you, Summer, we're not moving here," Jack joked as he lugged the third huge suitcase off the conveyer belt.

Summer grinned at him and then directed her guests out double doors where a stretch limo she had hired idled at the curb. Comfortably seated in the back seat of the car, Summer poured Ella a glass of lemonade and offered champagne to Bree and Jack.

"Are you sure you want us to stay with you?" Bree said. "Will we be cramped in your apartment?"

"I have plenty of room, no worries. Anyway, I want to spend as much time together with all of you as possible. I'd hate it if you stayed in a hotel."

Bree placed her hand over hers, a warm touch that sparked a surge of carefree elation inside Summer. Nothing compared to her powerful connection with her triplets.

Along the way, Ella chattered about her school projects, the books she had read and the movies she had seen. She peppered Summer with questions about the sights: Which building is that? Is that one the Empire State Building? The new World Trade Center? Can we go to the top of the Empire State Building? On a boat ride on the Hudson River? Which bridge is that? Did you know that people call that bottom part of the bridge the Martha Washington?

Bree and Jack seemed to sit on the edge of their seats, poised to stop Ella from monopolizing the conversation. Summer smiled and subtly shook her head. She was delighted with Ella's curiosity, innocence and overall excitement. That was kind of the point of the whole weekend that Summer had planned.

The driver unloaded the suitcases at the curb in front of Summer's building. Johnny flew through the doors and raced up to the car.

"We've got this," Jack said pleasantly.

Each adult extended one of the three suitcase handles and rolled the baggage into the lobby while Johnny held open the door. Summer herded the trio into the elevator.

On her floor, Summer unlocked her front door, held it open to let her guests enter in front of her, and then wheeled a suitcase into the foyer.

Ella raced straight ahead toward the windows in Summer's living room and gasped. "We're up *so* high,

Aunt Summer. I feel like I'm flying."

Jack drifted into the room behind Ella and whistled. "What a great view. It reminds me of Bree's condo. The Layton girls like their vistas."

Bree joined her fiancé, circled her arm around Jack's waist and gazed downward at the wide expanse of the Hudson. "No matter where we are, we need a view of water. For me it's the Chicago River and here Summer overlooks the Hudson River. Skye's got the whole Atlantic in her backyard. Guess in our hearts the three of us are always near the OBX. Where it's usually a *lot* warmer than here or Chicago. Skye said it was in the high sixties today."

Summer plopped her purse and briefcase on the kitchen counter and ambled nearer to her sister. "But we're so lucky this weekend. The weather is supposed to be unusually warm tomorrow for this time of year."

"That's great news."

Her text tone chimed, and Summer strolled over to the counter, foraged in her purse for her phone and read the text. "Wow. Jacob has extra tickets for the show tomorrow. Do you mind if I invite Vinnie's sister and nephews?"

"Of course not. The more the merrier," Bree said.

Before she responded to the text, Summer consulted Jack. "Are you really okay with Vinnie coming tomorrow? If you're uncomfortable with him, I can retract the invitation. Considering your history, I don't think he'd be surprised."

Jack boomed a laugh. "Honestly, I have no problem with Carlucci." He kissed Bree's lips softly. "I got the girl."

Bree gave Jack the dreamiest, heart melting smile.

The strong desire to have that kind of connection, too, swept through Summer. Vincent Carlucci's face flashed in her mind larger than life—perhaps the fulfillment of that desire.

Summer sent the text accepting Jacob's offer and then slipped her phone into the pocket of her jeans.

"If you ladies won't miss me too much, I have a few phone calls to make before dinner," Jack said.

"Go right ahead." Summer pointed to the hallway leading to the three bedrooms. "Your room is the first doorway on the right. Ella's room connects to the Jack and Jill bathroom off your room."

He planted a kiss on Ella's crown, retrieved two suitcases from the foyer, rolled them down the hallway and strode into the guest room.

Summer ushered Ella and Bree into the master suite. She had folded three matching nightgowns on her bed.

"Oh Summer." Bree beamed at her. "Just like when we were little.

"When we were small, we came every year to the Big City with Nana and Pop to see the Rockettes," Bree explained to Ella. "Nana always packed brand-new matching pajamas for me, Aunt Summer and Aunt Skye."

"I can't wait to put it on." Ella touched the Christmas plaid gown. "Ooh, it's so soft."

"Why don't we start our jammie party early? Since we're ordering pizza delivery for dinner, we can ask your daddy to answer the door. Want to put our nightgowns on right now?"

"Yes!"

"You won't hear me object," Bree said. "Come on

Ella. Let's get you settled in your room and you can change."

The delicious pizza pig-out watching National Lampoon's Christmas Vacation on Netflix and snuggling together on Summer's sectional proved the perfect start to the weekend. Ella conked out halfway through the movie and when the credits rolled on the screen, Jack carried his little girl into her room.

Summer slipped into her bed luxuriating beneath the warm, down comforter. She composed a text to Vinnie extending the invitation to Trish, Barry and Joey, laid her phone down on the bedside table and switched off the lamp.

She was asleep before she received a reply.

****

New York City during the holidays dazzled visitors. Huge lighted bows adorned office buildings. Lights sparkled everywhere adding a shimmering luster to trees that lined the sidewalks and to buildings' facades.

Ella's apparent delight with all the glittering decorations was contagious. Summer felt like a kid bounding out of the limo in front of Radio City Music Hall. Her breath caught in her throat when she spied Vinnie standing on the corner, his back toward her. There was nothing childlike and innocent about the rush of desire sizzling through her at the sight of him. *Damn the man wears the shit out of those tight black jeans.*

A crimson turtleneck peeked above the collar of the black leather jacket he wore, a vivid touch of Christmas color. *Red definitely is his color.* Joey and Barry flanked him—mini versions of their uncle.

"Hey good looking," she called out.

He turned and shot her a grin. "Hey, pretty lady."

The boys in tow, he ambled over to her and wrapped her in a hug. The lovely sensation Summer experienced in the brief embrace struck her as exactly *right*. Dreamily, heart meltingly right.

Jack stepped up and shook Vinnie's hand. "Good to see you."

Vinnie arched an eyebrow and beamed him a smile. "You sound like you actually mean that, Jack."

Jack matched Vin's smile. His grin lit his face. "I always mean what I say."

"Yeah, I get that." Vinnie brushed a kiss on Bree's cheek keeping one eye on Jack. "Guys, these are my nephews, Barry and Joey. My sister couldn't join us today."

Greetings were exchanged and then the ladies joined the two alpha males and the boys on the ticket holders' line.

While they waited, Ella held court with the boys who seemingly hung on her every word. The group shuffled in the queue until reaching the lobby. Although the weather was mild, Summer appreciated the radiating warmth inside. After another wait, they boarded an elevator and exited on the first mezzanine level.

The kids hooted gleefully when the usher escorted them to front row seats.

"We're early," Summer said. "Want to go downstairs and visit Santa?"

"Yes!" from Ella.

"Sure," from Joey.

Followed by, "Whatever," from Barry.

They deposited their coats on their seats, retraced

their steps back to the elevator, boarded after a large group vacated the car, and road to the bottom floor where Santa sat on a red, velvet throne.

"Would you like your picture with Santa?" Bree asked Ella.

"If Barry and Joey will come with me."

"Would you mind, boys?" Summer said.

"No problem, the boys don't mind at all," Vinnie interjected.

Barry scowled at his uncle, but when he turned toward Ella, his eyes softened with his half smile. Ella's innocent charm had both boys entranced.

Summer and Bree waited on the line with the kids, and the men volunteered to purchase snacks and souvenirs. After the Santa photo session, and after spending the most money possible for the largest photo package, Summer led her charges to meet Jack and Vinnie at the elevator.

They returned to their seats five minutes before two men sat at huge, identical pipe organs on either side of the stage. Christmas music swelled and soared from the instruments filling the expansive chamber of the largest indoor theater in the world. The glorious sounds reverberated through Summer kick-starting her Christmas spirit.

Ella sat between Barry and Joey grasping her Rockette statuette firmly in her fist. Whenever she pushed a button on the back of the statue, the Rockette's skirt illuminated and twirled. The kids devoured popcorn and cotton candy, washing the treats down with Coke - at nine AM. The trio appeared absolutely elated at the lack of diet control on the part of the adults.

Bree and Jack, Summer and Vinnie bookended the row. Vinnie stretched his arm around Summer's shoulder and edged her closer to him. "What great seats. Thank you for inviting the boys." He leaned forward gazing down the aisle at his nephews. "They're having the time of their lives."

"I'm so glad they came. They're being so nice to Ella."

The lights dimmed. Vinnie withdrew his arm and clasped Summer's handing entwining his fingers with hers. The edge of his ring dug into Summer's finger.

She knit her brow unable to remember his wearing jewelry.

Ella blurted out, "It's Santa!" She pointed downward.

Santa ambled down the aisle showered with applause and exclamations of delight from the large faction of kids in the audience.

The spectacle of the annual Christmas show caught Summer up, enthralled, a reaction that hadn't diminished year to year. She loved the Rockettes' synchronized dancing—her father's all-time favorite entertainment. Ultimately, the beauty of the living nativity had tears welling in Summer's eyes. She leaned forward and trained her gaze on Bree, smiling at the tears brimming in her sister's eyes, too.

The lights came back up. Summer shrugged into her coat and slipped a shopping bag out of her purse. She gathered the collectable popcorn and drink containers from the kids and stowed them in the bag.

Bree giggled. "Just like mom used to do, Summer. Gosh, this was fun."

Vinnie relieved Summer of the shopping bag as

they filed out of the aisle. Opting for the stairs instead of waiting for a downward elevator, they clambered out of the theater and regrouped outside on the sidewalk.

"Listen. We want partners walking in the city. Who wants to hold my hand?" Summer said.

Without a word, Barry clasped first Ella's hand and next his brothers.

"Well, okay," Summer said.

"I'll hold your hand," quipped Vinnie.

"Sounds good," she said on a laugh.

She and Vinnie took the lead walking to Rockefeller Center, followed by the kids and then Bree and Jack. The impressive sight of the seventy-two-foot-high, glittering tree came into view.

A wonderstruck expression on her face, Ella said, "*Wow*."

Summer used her phone to take photos with the Christmas tree as backdrop of Ella, Joey and Barry together, then Ella, Bree and Jack, and then Vinnie with his nephews. Bree commandeered Summer's phone to take a picture of Vinnie and Summer together. And then she asked a passerby if they would take a picture of all of them together.

Regrouping with walking partners, they headed to the triplet's historic favorite New York restaurant, Bill's Burgers, a couple blocks away. They huddled in line outside the small restaurant chatting about the performance at Radio City Music Hall. Filing inside at lunch opening time, Summer snagged an enviable booth on the lower floor.

"Are you going to order a milkshake?" Bree asked Summer.

"Of course. Are you?"

"No. I have to fit into my wedding gown."

"Oh, come on, Bree. You have to have one. When was the last time we were here?"

"About ten years, I guess."

"Exactly! It will probably be another ten years before we come again."

"Oh, no it won't," Ella chimed in. "I think we should make a tradition, and all come every year."

Joey and Barry bobbed their heads in agreement.

"Sign me up," Jack said.

"It's unanimous," Vinnie said.

Next year with Vinnie, Summer thought. Would there be next year with Vinnie for her?

"In that case, I'll skip the milk shake," Bree said.

Summer frowned wagging her head. "Uh-uh. How about a compromise? Want to split an Oreo shake?"

Bree chuckled. "Deal."

Summer placed the order for the table, put down the menu and caught Vinnie's penetrating gaze. "What?" she asked, even though she interpreted the glint in his eyes and sexy half smile easily enough. Memories of awakening in his arms a few days ago and being met with his *exact* same expression quickened her pulse. Despite the sheer fun she had with his and her family up to then, she half wished they were alone.

Vinnie broadened his smile. "Just like looking at your beautiful face, that's all."

"I'm with you, Vin," Jack said. "I could gaze at Bree all day."

"Ew," Ella said.

"Yeah, ew," Barry added.

Summer pointed her finger and waved it back and forth between the two men seated across the table.

"Since when are you two chummy?"

Jack snorted. "Guess we found common ground loving Layton sisters."

Summer's heart skipped a beat at Jack's supposition.

"Yeah. Two lucky SOB's."

Vinnie's reply had her heart soaring.

The waitress brought the food to the table and the hungry horde dove in.

Summer sat back in her chair. "I'm stuffed. Everybody finished with their lunch?" She gazed around the table observing nodding heads.

Jack grabbed the check and refused to split the bill with anyone while Summer texted the car service.

Outside on the pavement Ella's eyes brimmed with tears. "Bye, Joey. Bye, Barry."

"Ah, don't cry." Barry placed his hand on Ella's shoulder. "Let's not say goodbye at all. Instead, how about see you next year?"

Ella beamed him a smile. "See you next year, Barry, Joey and Uncle Vinnie."

Uncle Vinnie. How easily kids dubbed a loving adult family. Summer's heart melted at Ella's innocence.

Vinnie drew Summer close to him and kissed her lips lightly. He cast his gaze around the group and smiled. "Thank you all for including us today. We had a great time. Summer? I'll see you soon?"

"Um. You're welcome. And yes. Call me."

He clasped each of his nephews' hands as the limo pulled up to the curb.

"Wait. Would you like a ride to Port Authority?"

"Nah. It's a good day for a walk."

Summer locked her gaze on Vinnie's broad back until he turned the corner. And then she joined her family in the car.

"He's a good guy, Summer," Bree said.

Her heart swelled as she mentally ticked off the myriad of sweet times they had enjoyed since Vinnie's predicament had brought them together. "Yes. He is."

Chapter 18

Summer stripped off the sheets in the guest room, bent into a downward dog position and swept the pillow slips and sheets into a pile on the hardwood floor. She rolled the bed linens into a ball, scooped them up into her arms and headed toward the laundry closet. Thank goodness she'd see Bree again in a few weeks at her wedding, or else Summer would probably spend the rest of that day crying and feeling sorry for herself.

The Newark Airport bound Town Car had picked up Bree, Jack and Ella at 4:30 AM. Summer had hugged Bree goodbye, tears streaming, while her sister's shoulders quaked with her equal emotions. The Layton girls *always* cried at the end of sister time. And each parting seemed harder as they aged.

She swung open the bifold closet doors, stuffed the sheets into the stacked washer, tossed in a detergent pod and set the cycle to cotton/sturdy. Wandering into the kitchen, she poured a second cup of coffee. Mug in one hand and cell phone in the other, Summer drifted into the living room and sank down onto the sectional, crossing her ankles and propping her feet on the coffee table. Feeling hollow and sad, she gazed out the windows at the crimson streaked, sunrise panorama, sipping her coffee and missing her family. Time had flown the last few days.

She set her mug down on the coffee table, turned

her attention to her phone's screen, opened the photos app and scrolled through the recent images, focusing on the shots in front of the Rockefeller Center tree. Backtracking she viewed those photos again marking her favorites intending to print and frame them as Christmas gifts. Summer depressed the home button until the virtual assistant chime sounded. "Order prints. Buy frames."

Summer dropped her phone into her lap and sat staring at the lightening sky, Jack's questions the night before repeating in her mind.

"So. Have you told him about the legend?"

"Are you referring to Vinnie?"

Jack had rolled his eyes.

"Well, no. Why would I do that?"

"In case you missed it today, he essentially said he's in love with you."

"Uh…no. Um. I did get that. But we're not *serious* or anything."

"Take it from me." Smiling, Jack had clasped Bree's hand. "Tell him sooner rather than later. You'll skip a lot of misunderstanding."

Should she take Jack's advice? Summer had never revealed her inherited abilities to *any* man. Because she hadn't come close to a forever love. Maybe until Vinnie.

Her phone jangled in her lap and she looked down at the screen, smiling for the first time that day at the serendipitous appearance of his number on the screen. "Good morning, Vin. You're up early."

"I figured you'd be awake. Jack mentioned they had an early flight this morning."

"Yes. And I couldn't go back to sleep after saying

goodbye. I have too much to do today anyway." She rose from the sofa and paced around the living room.

"It's Sunday. Are you going in to your office?"

"No, but I kind of wish I was. I'm dreading today."

"Why? Do you have a problem? Can I help?"

An open-ended offer to help. She smiled again as his grip on her heart tightened. "Thank you, but no. It's nothing really. I have to start my Christmas shopping at the mall. Yuck."

Vinnie's laughter boomed in her ear. "You're the only woman I have ever met who hates shopping. I thought the malls were closed on Sundays anyway."

"The malls *are* closed in Bergen County. But— they're open in Nanuet, so I'm heading up to the Palisades Center. Pray for me."

He huffed a laugh. "Instead of prayers how about some company?"

"You mean it?"

"Sure. I don't have anything to do today. And I should buy some Christmas gifts, too."

"Fair warning. There's a huge Barnes and Noble at this mall and I'm treating myself to book shopping as a reward for crossing everything off my Christmas gifts list. I can happily spend *hours* browsing in a bookstore."

"No problem. Let me treat you to dinner afterwards and it's a deal."

"Perfect." Now Summer actually looked forward to dealing with the crowded mall. "This day just got a whole lot better."

"What time should I pick you up?"

"It opens at eleven."

"I'll pick you up at ten if that works for you."

"See you then."

****

Summer waited outside with her large tote bag slung over shoulder watching Vinnie's Ford approach. She jumped into the car as soon as he parked at the curb, plopping her bag into her lap. Vinnie outstretched his arm toward her, took hold of the handles and lifted the bag off her legs.

"This is pretty heavy." He grunted swinging the tote into the back seat. "What's in it?"

"A clipboard with my Christmas list, bottles of water, my purse, the newspaper with the store ads, and some protein bars for when I start to get hangry, an extra pair of sunglasses and a bunch of extra pens."

"Hangry?"

"You know. You're so hungry it makes you angry." She grinned at him.

Vinnie snorted. "You are something. You do realize that you can buy water and food at a mall?" He patted her leg and then steered away from the curb.

"Sure. But I like to be prepared anyway."

Vinnie wagged his head a half smile dimpling his cheek. A shimmer of exhilarating attraction radiated within Summer. Damn, she was happy just being with the man.

"Thanks again for inviting the boys yesterday," he said. "They had a great time. I knew Joey would have fun, but Barry really shocked me. He actually talked about what he would order for lunch next year on the way home."

Summer gazed at Vinnie's profile overtaken with a sense of rightness, of completeness in his company. With him even doing everyday things seemed as special as yesterday. "Ella couldn't stop talking about Barry and Joey last night. I think she has a crush on both of them. She fully expects for us all to go to the show next year, too."

"We're game." He merged onto the Garden State Parkway after expertly navigating the zooming Route 17 traffic around Paramus.

Summer was game, too, for repeating the Christmas tradition with Vinnie next year...and every year. The realization gelled into certainty; equally parts joyful and terrifying. Her parents were the standard bearers for true love and Summer never really believed that she'd encounter the man who'd hit that bar with her. Now? As unsettled and strange as it made her feel, Summer inwardly acknowledged that he was her true love.

"Where do you like to park, Summer?"

"If you follow the frontage road around back, you'll find spaces outside the Barnes & Noble store."

Vinnie switched off the engine and Summer twisted her torso to reach into the backseat for her bag.

"I'll get it." Vinnie opened his door.

She followed suit, swung shut her door and met him on the other side of the car. He leaned into the back seat and emerged with her purse and the clipboard.

"Wait. I need my other stuff."

"Nope." He thumbed the key fob. A double beep sounded, and the door locks clicked shut. "I promise if you get hangry, I'll feed you." Chuckling he grasped her hand and led her toward the store entrance.

Two hours later Summer was pleased with her progress and checked off another loved one from her list. Vinnie carried the shopping bags bound for the parking lot to stow the first round of purchases.

"Let's take a break and get something to eat at the food court." He slammed shut the trunk.

"Great idea. I'm starving."

A tray in hand, Summer followed Vinnie navigating the crowded labyrinth of tables trying not to slosh water on her pizza slice.

"Hey handsome! Come sit with me," called some female.

Summer frowned, indignant and decidedly territorial. *Who the hell is that?*

Equal parts relief and sheepishness struck her when she recognized Tricia seated at a table ahead, waving.

****

"Christmas shopping, sis?" He set his tray down on Tricia's table and kissed her cheek.

Summer slid her tray onto the tabletop taking the seat next to Tricia and then giving her a hug. "It's so good to see you."

"Good to see both of you, too. The boys are upstairs in the theatre. A transformer movie about a bumblebee or something. Works great to Christmas shop solo. They have zero patience in the mall."

She nudged her bags under the table with the toe of her boot. "I've done so much I have time for a cup of coffee." She yawned. "Sorry. Shopping is exhausting."

"Tell me about it." Summer gave a laugh. "Honestly I would rather work out on a treadmill than shop."

"Oh, not me. I love shopping. I just haven't been able to shop…Barry leaving and all. But I have great news. I checked our joint savings account yesterday just to see if there was *anything* left for the boys' Christmas.

I almost dropped dead. Chuck must have worked miracles forcing Barry to do the right thing. I definitely have enough to keep our house with some to spare. I can't thank you enough Summer. Chuck Roberts is a magician."

"That's terrific. Happy that I thought of him after learning about your situation." Summer glanced at her clipboard. "I'm glad we ran into you. I need suggestions for the boys for Christmas."

"I ordered Switches for both of them. That's all they were talking about on Thanksgiving," Vinnie chimed in.

Tricia arched her eyebrows. "Oh Vin, that's way too much money."

"I like spoiling my nephews." He turned toward Summer. "I know a few games they mentioned they wanted - if that works for you."

"That would be great." She put her list down and took a huge bite of her pizza.

"I better get going." Tricia looked at her phone's screen. "The boys should be done in a few minutes. We'll hit the bookstore for my fix and then head home. Take care." She pecked a kiss on Summer's cheek and then half rose leaning over the table to kiss Vin.

Toting her paper coffee cup, she headed toward the escalator.

Vinnie reached across the table and squeezed Summer's hand. "Thank you for all you did to help Tricia with the divorce."

"It's all Chuck's doing. I just put them together."

"I appreciate you anyway." He lifted her hand, rotating it as he brought it to his lips, and kissed her palm. He grinned at her shiver thinking about the end of a pleasant day and the hopeful invitation up to her place after dinner together.

He tenderly let loose her hand and then picked up his second slice of pizza, folding it in half before taking a generous bite.

She crumpled up her napkin and tossed it lightly onto her tray. "We need to find a video game store next. I think Tricia will love the book series I have in mind for her. I want to find the perfect sweater for my dad and anything girlie for Ella. I love picking out clothes for that little girl." Summer took a dainty sip of water fixating Vin's gaze on her lips. "Thanks Vinnie."

"For what?"

"For coming with me. You actually made shopping bearable."

"No problem. I like spending time with you." The hand to God truth. Despite the fact that her position as his lawyer was a constant reminder of the cloud hanging over his head and his estrangement from the Bureau, Summer was a bright spot in his days. And a ball of flame in his nights.

He finished eating and shoved his chair away from the table. "Let's knock off the rest of your list."

Summer followed him to the trash can. He dealt with the garbage on their trays and then clasped her hand. Her soft, tiny hand in his, they walked toward GameStop in search of video games for Joey and Barry.

"Vin-man what are you doing here? Damn you always get the pretty ones, don't you?" came the irritating, familiar voice.

Last person he wanted to see that day. Vinnie leaned toward Summer to whisper in her ear. "Shit.

"Hey kid, how are you?" Vinnie said.

"Doing great, buddy. You look like you're doing pretty great yourself. Are you going to introduce me to this little beauty?"

He suppressed a smile as Summer shivered in apparent revulsion at the description of her. "Summer this is Tyler. Tyler this is Summer."

Tyler adjusted the shopping bags he carried into one hand. He extended his free hand to Summer. "Tyler Cornelius Wellington at your service."

Summer shook his hand with two fingers, her eyes slits. "Charmed."

No missing the sarcasm in that one single word. Unless you were clueless like Tyler. The kid would be single forever if that was his "charming" best with a lady.

She withdrew her hand with purpose as if any further contact with the guy required liberal hand sanitizer.

Vin gave a nod at the numerous shopping bags Tyler held. "Christmas shopping?"

"Haven't even started. I picked up a few things for me."

"I'd say more than a few." She glanced at her watch.

"What can I say? I deserve a treat." He gave her a toothy grin. "What store are you headed to? I'll tag along."

Summer caught Vinnie's eye. "Actually, we have to get going."

"We do. Sorry," Vinnie said.

"No problem. Good seeing you."

Vinnie clapped a hand on Tyler's shoulder and then circled his arm around Summer. "Merry

Christmas, kid."

He propelled her forward as Tyler responded, "To you, too."

Summer fixated on the shop window. "He's just standing there watching us. Who *is* he to you? My dipshit meter was on tilt."

"He's the HRIS geek who told me about Paul's expensive vacation."

"Oh…I'd never guess that he's FBI. Don't Fibbies have to be strong, fit…"

"Like me," he teased.

She gave him a crooked grin. "*That* guy gave me the creeps."

"Really? Nah. He's harmless. He wants to piss with the big dogs, but he'll never make it into the field no matter how much ass-kissing he does. He doesn't have the right disposition. The guys don't like him."

"Huh. I thought you liked him."

"More like I feel sorry for him. I get the feeling that Tyler is always trying to prove himself to his dad. He got drunk one night and I let him sleep it off on my couch. He said a few things about his father. It was the drink talking. I ignored it. His dad is some CEO or something. They live in Franklin Lakes in some huge mansion."

"That explains the shopping bags from luxe stores then."

"Let's not let the kid ruin our day." Vinnie halted in front of the game store.

"Oh, he couldn't if he tried. I've already forgotten him." She stood on tiptoes and kissed his cheek.

Chapter 19

They never made it to dinner that evening unless the eggs "Bagicaloop" that he stirred in her frying pan counted.

Summer leaned over his shoulder gazing into the pan. "Mmm. I didn't think I had anything in the fridge that could smell that good."

"Eggs Bagicaloop is a vintage family recipe." Vinnie swiveled his head to peck her on the cheek. She smelled like a Spring garden and radiated the heat of recent lovemaking. He resisted burrowing his nose into her soft neck and kissing his way down through the folds of her velour bathrobe, deferring to the sizzling fry pan.

"You're such a chef, you put me to shame."

"Nah. The so-called recipe is eggs, milk and anything reasonably complementary that you have on hand. Throw it in a buttered pan and stir the whole mess together. In this case, some parmesan cheese, cheddar cheese, cherry tomatoes and mushrooms." He switched off the gas and plated two portions of eggs. "Where do you want to eat?"

She waggled her eyebrows. "I'd say bed, but honestly. Sustenance first." She hooted a laugh.

Beaming at her, the memory of devouring her inch by inch earlier spooled in his mind. Vinnie wanted nothing more than to repeat the intimacy. But okay.

Sustenance first.

He toted the plates over to the countertop and set them down. Pivoting toward the stove, he opened and shut a couple drawers until he hit on the silverware and took out two forks. Threading his fingers around the saltshaker and peppermill, he scooped them up, rounded the counter, and joined her on a neighboring bar stool.

Summer eagerly took a fork out of his hand and tucked into the meal. She bumped her shoulder against his and emitted a groan. "Oh, Vin," she rhapsodized, her mouth full. "I never tasted anything so good."

He huffed a laugh. "You're just starving from all that shopping and…sex."

"Hell yeah." She focused on the food like the eggs would morph into chicks and run off if she didn't down them first.

Unlike his lady, Vinnie took his time eating, already fully sated. Lovemaking with Summer defied description. Her tenderness one second and wantonness the next kept him unbalanced; challenged to stoke her desire and keep his raging desire in check so that he could take her and surrender to her, transporting him to a height of completion he'd never known.

He had whispered, "I love you," in her ear as they clung together panting.

Had he imagined her muffled response? "I love you, too."

The woman had but to crook her finger. He'd give her anything.

Vinnie had long ago surrendered his defense into her capable hands. With each minute spent since she had entered his life, he surrendered more of his heart to

Summer. Fresh from the hot shower they had taken together, running his hands over her soap slick body and contorting his large frame in the stall to fit their bodies together to make love again, he knew that this woman represented *all* he'd ever want in a lover.

Her fork clanged onto her plate. She leaned back crossing her arms over her breasts. "Yum. Thank you, Vin. You're such a terrific cook. I think you should tell Ashley to stuff it when I get you reinstated and open Via Lucci Segundo. Maybe in the city. I swear, you'd be an instant success."

There was that feline smile again, her eyes sparkling, emerald green. "Besides. You'd look so handsome on camera doing cooking segments: the *Today Show, Good Morning America*... What female could possibly resist you? You'd have a waiting list for reservations."

Vinnie huffed a laugh. "Yeah right." The compliment coupled with her ear to ear grin had a rush of pure happiness zipping through him. Vinnie wrapped his arm around the back of her chair, possessive and deeply grateful that this amazing woman seemed to think that he was capable despite his demoralized state from the undeserved wresting away from him of his hard-won status at the Bureau.

He had no intention of becoming a restaurateur. Sure, Vinnie would always help his folks if they needed him. And he looked forward to cooking countless meals for Summer...and their kids. He only hoped that she could accept the dangerous nature of his work when he was back on the job. Vinnie was certain of two facts: he had no job plan B if he wasn't exonerated, and he had no personal plan B if Summer didn't want him as much as he wanted her.

She hopped down off her stool and collected their empty plates. "Only fair that I do KP. Thanks for the meal. It was so good."

He relaxed in his seat watching her rinse the plates and utensils and loading the dishwasher. Her short hair had partially dried into maroon and strawberry spikes framing her heart shaped face. Her delicate features struck him as perfect. He really had it bad for Summer Layton. Vinnie couldn't stop staring.

As if she felt the heat of his gaze, she peered at him through her long eyelashes. "What?"

"Just enjoy looking at you."

Her cheeks blushed a pretty pink. God, he loved this woman.

A bell chime sounded.

"My email indicator," she said. "Can you do me a favor? Bring my laptop in here? It's on the coffee table in the living room."

"Sure." He retrieved the slim MacBook Pro and placed it on the counter in front of the stool Summer had vacated.

****

"Thanks." Summer dried her hands on a dish towel and then returned to her seat next to Vinnie.

She flipped open her laptop, moved the cursor to the Outlook icon and opened her mail inbox. Summer scanned the list of messages: junk, spam, save for later and one that immediately piqued her interest from the sender, Skye.

Double clicking on the email from her sister, she read the narrative noting the paper clip attachment symbol. Rapidly digesting the information, Summer, for that moment, was glad that her screen was angled away from Vinnie. "Hey, sis. Mom and I sat down after you left, and she described her vision to me in detail. Attached is a rendering of her glimpse of the ring on the man's right hand. The inlay on the side is pretty unique. I hope it helps you identify the guy who framed Vinnie. Mom says to tell you that if she sees *anything* more that can help, she'll call you right away. Love you always, Skye."

A thrill of excitement skittered through Summer. She double-clicked on the attachment and studied the image in Preview. A circular inlay on the side of the ring encompassed the image of an eagle with wings unfurled, standing on a striped shield. The talons of one leg gripped an olive branch, the other a spray of arrows.

She angled the laptop so that Vinnie had a clear view of the screen. "Does this image mean anything to you?"

Vinnie turned his attention toward her computer. In a split second, he said, "Sure. It's the FBI NA class ring. Quantico National Academy. I have one. Why do you ask?"

His response jolted her. She flipped shut the laptop like springing the jaws of a mousetrap. "Uh. I thought maybe it would help with your case… It's not important."

He frowned, clouds in his powder blue eyes. She sure had knocked the earlier happy grin right off his face. Disappointed that she was no further ahead with his defense than before, she struggled with now having to reveal her family's truth. Summer rued that she had shown him the go-nowhere photo in the first place.

"Anything with my case is important to me. What

the hell does an Academy ring have to do with it?"

Summer regrouped determined to put the up until then, outstanding evening back on track. She slid the computer away from her along the countertop, symbolically discounting its importance, and then dismounted the bar stool. Positioning directly in front of him, she threaded her fingers in his soft, black chest hair and eyed the bath towel wrapped around his waist.

Smiling, she hoped seductively, she glued her eyes to the towel. One good yank.

He tipped a finger under her chin, and she raised her eyes to meet his. "Summer?"

Her mind raced to concoct an explanation. She simply wasn't ready for the big reveal. "I kind of figured it was a dead end. My computer expert sent this photo to me. He apparently…found a google search of this image on your laptop. Big zero, right?"

Vinnie knit his brows. "Doesn't make sense. Why would I google the class ring? I graduated ten years ago. Didn't even own the laptop then."

"See? Zero." She hooked her index finger inside the towel at his waist leaning in to fuse her lips with his.

He loosened the belt around her waist and then slid her bathrobe off her shoulders to puddle on the floor.

She executed the one yank maneuver and unwrapped his towel stepping in between his legs. He folded her into his embrace, her breasts flattened against the hard planes of his chest, his heart thrumming a drumbeat on her skin.

"The bedroom?" he said, his voice thick with arousal.

She nodded. *Oh yes.*

He slipped off the stool and swept her up into his arms.

Hours later she awakened at his soft kiss and blinked her eyes in the gloom.

"Don't wake up," he said. "I'm leaving so you can sleep a while longer before work. I'll call you this afternoon."

"Okay," she mumbled. She rolled over and instantly slept.

In her dream Vinnie drowned again. No matter how hard she swam, he disappeared in the sharks' midst with his arm outstretched toward her in desperate pleading. This time, however, he wore a chunky ring on his right hand.

When she woke that morning, she couldn't shake the nightmare. What the hell was the Sacred Source trying to tell her? The original unedited dream had prompted noble action, as was always intended, from Summer's gifts from the Sacred Source. The import was easy to grasp. Vinnie was in trouble of some kind. Summer was meant to do something about it: mount his legal defense.

But now? Had Summer superimposed the image of the ring on her vision? She clearly remembered his wearing a solid ring when he held her hand in Radio City Music Hall.

Summer closed her eyes. *I sat to his right.* She blinked her eyes open. Yep. He wore the ring on his right hand.

She couldn't accept that since Vinnie possessed "the" ring, he wasn't innocent. Right?

Of course, he was innocent. Of course.

But he hadn't worn a ring last night. Actually...

except for Radio City she hadn't noticed his wearing any jewelry. What's the deal with that? Why a ring one time? And then never again?

She shook her head determined to clear all doubt of him from her mind. Tossing off the covers, Summer swung her legs over the side of the bed and rose to face the day.

Pacing into the kitchen bound for her scheduled brew coffee pot, a dreamy smile touched her lips at the sensation of soreness between her legs. Thinking about his prowess as a lover left her weak-kneed and yearning.

She would *not* doubt him, having singular pride in her bullshit detector. A handsome face or a hunky bod would *never* sway Summer. Vinnie was so much more than a pretty face. He was smart and fierce and brave. She couldn't deny his tenderness with his nephews and her niece. The man was unfailingly kind. And funny. Bree loved him. As a friend, but still. Bree was nobody's fool. Like her, her sister had unfailing intuition. Like all three sisters of the legend.

She sighed. *He loves me. And I told him that I love him. I do.*

Summer was not wrong about Vinnie.

Mom had the clear sense after her vision that Vinnie knew who framed him. It was completely reasonable that whoever was guilty also went to the FBI Academy. And had a ring to prove it. Like Vinnie. No question that's the explanation. No more doubts.

But back to square one.

Chapter 20

Summer checked her briefcase for her passport and boarding pass, snapped the buckle shut, shrugged the leather strap over her shoulder and wheeled her carryon down the hallway of her foyer. She locked the door behind her and ambled to the elevator bank.

When the elevator doors swished opened on the lobby, she glimpsed the shiny black limo idling at the curb through the glass, the back door gaping open. Summer strode outside, surrendered her suitcase to the driver, dipped her head and slipped inside the car.

Her doorman leaned against the door frame. "Thank you for your generous gift. Merry Christmas, Ms. Layton. I hope you have a safe, wonderful trip."

"You're welcome. Merry Christmas, Johnny."

Nestled in the comfortable, leather seat, Summer's mind wandered. She usually preferred to drive home to the Outer Banks for longer stays, but Bree had insisted that she fly this time for the wedding to avoid any possibility of delays. Last week's ice storm in Virginia had sealed the deal.

Jack had paid airfares for all the out of town guests despite Summer's adamant protest. He declared that it was his prerogative and that if she wanted to return the favor when she married, he'd graciously accept. *Wow, when I marry.* She shook her head at the enormity of the notion. But she delighted at the fairy tale image of

Vinnie in black tie waiting at the altar that flashed in her mind.

Excitement coursed through her. *Bree is getting married!*

She loved Jack and already considered him her brother. They were a perfect match. But Bree *married!*

The car veered to the curb at First Class check-in at Newark International Airport. Summer swept through the glass doors into the bustling terminal. She and Vinnie had agreed to meet at the TSA precheck area. In an instant she spotted him leaning against a wall across from the check-in line. His tall frame, even leaning sideways, towered above the crowd. His imposing physicality: snug jeans hugging muscular thighs, a dark green turtleneck above the collar of a fitted, black leather, bomber jacket emphasizing his broad chest; had the heads of female passersby snapping in his direction. Vinnie scanned the area oblivious to the attention.

Looking for me. Delight swelled inside Summer.

A broad smile bloomed on his face when his gaze lit on her. Her heart fluttered and she returned the smile.

"Hey pretty lady." Vinnie slipped the strap of her briefcase off her shoulder and clasped the handle with his huge hand. "Did you check your luggage already?"

"I only have this little carry-on."

His eyes widened. "You're kidding. I checked a suit bag. I figured you'd have at least two suitcases to my one."

"Nope. This is it." Didn't count that she had shipped to the inn four huge boxes of clothes and Christmas presents last week.

His penetrating, turquoise eyes held hers. "You truly are the perfect woman." He drew her toward him, his hand at the small of her back. Instinctively she arched her neck as he leaned down and kissed her lightly on the lips. He tasted like peppermint and smelled of woodsy aftershave. A familiar shiver ran up her spine even at the brief intimacy.

Summer grinned up at him. "Can I get into my briefcase for a sec?" He held the satchel toward her. She unbuckled the case, foraged inside for her passport and boarding pass and then refastened the buckle. "Thanks."

She stepped toward the TSA checkpoint, Vinnie in tow. Clearing the entry, she shuffled on the snaking line, presented her documents at the podium and then queued at the end of the conveyer belt, hoisted up her suitcase and breezed through the magnetometer.

Vinnie joined her after his scanning process, and they strolled together to the Admiral's Club near the security clearance area.

"They're predicting a major snowstorm to hit the East coast later today." Vinnie fixated on the TV monitor hanging on the wall. "Looks like we're lucky to be on the first flight out."

Summer sipped tea with lemon raising her eyes to the TV screen. "Good thing Bree insisted that I fly rather than drive."

She keyed in to the meteorologist reporting the rapid movement of the storm. "I'll be relieved once we're airborne."

As if on cue, their flight's boarding process was announced. She and Vinnie gathered their things, left the Club headed for the gate, and waltzed aboard the airplane to their first-class seats.

Vinnie's right arm usurped the armrest. Summer

delighted in his physical closeness.

He raised her left hand to his lips and gently kissed her knuckles one by one. "Thanks for asking me to be your plus one."

Her delight with this trip and his nearness ratcheted up a notch. "I'm so glad you accepted. And thank you for giving up Christmas with your family."

In forty minutes, the flight began the descent into Norfolk. Gazing through the porthole at the toy-sized tankers chugging in the Chesapeake Bay, Summer felt giddy with anticipation. The sight of the familiar landmarks around the airport reminded her of how much she missed home.

The flight arrived at the gate less than an hour after takeoff. A bell tone sounded, and Vinnie unfurled from his seat into the aisle, his head bent in the limited ceiling space. He opened the overhead compartment and hauled out their carry-ons. Passengers seated in front of them filed out of the plane. Summer scooted out of their row in front of Vinnie and briskly led the way into the terminal toward baggage claim.

****

"I didn't know your mom was meeting us at the airport," Vinnie said as they walked past security.

"She's not."

"Then who's that woman who looks exactly like her waving at us?"

"Aunt *Kamille*?" Summer opened her arms wide and broke into a run. She launched straight into her aunt's arms at the end of the hallway.

Vinnie caught up smiling at the pair.

"Mom didn't tell me you were coming. It's so *good* to see you. Vinnie, this is my Aunt Kamille, mom's sister."

He chuckled extending his hand. "I think I could have figured that out for myself."

Kamille ignored his outstretched arm and hugged him instead. "Well, of course you could, honey."

She winked at Summer. "Yes, he is as handsome in person as I saw him in my mind."

Vin furrowed his brow. "In your…"

"Aunt Kamille, you look wonderful," Summer cut in. "I love your scarf."

"Thank you, darling." Kamille tugged on the black scarf dotted with Santa Claus heads around her neck. "Just a bit of whimsy."

"Were you waiting for us for a ride to Nags Head? We reserved a rental car."

"So kind of you to offer, but…" Kamille closed her eyes. A couple seconds passed.

Vinnie was about to tap her on the shoulder to see if she was all right when she blinked open her eyes grinning. "Your Aunt Karol's plane just landed. We're going to rent a car. She wants to make a quick stop at a gallery in Norfolk before we head to the inn."

Summer shook her head smiling. "I can't believe Bree didn't tell me you were coming. She usually can't keep a secret."

"Oh, she doesn't know we're coming. I talked to Kay on the phone the other night and the wedding sounded like such fun that I decided to invite myself. And you know your Aunt Karol. God forbid I have any fun without her." Kamille rolled her sparkling green eyes.

Summer huffed a laugh. "I've missed you."

"I've missed you girls so much." Kamille swept

Summer into another bear hug.

"I hope you have a hug for me, too, Summer." Another carbon copy of Summer's mom breezed by Vinnie and wrapped her arms around Summer and Kamille.

Karol held her sister at arm's length eyeing the exact Santa scarf that she wore. "Of course, we wore the same scarf." She smiled broadly turning her attention to Summer. "I bet your mom has one, too."

Vinnie cleared his throat. Three pairs of identical pine green eyes locked on him in unison. What are the odds of that kind of genetics? Add in Kay, Bree and Summer Layton and he'd have an army of lithe, porcelain skinned, red headed, jade-eyed angels.

"Join us, handsome. I'm Aunt Karol. You must be Vinnie."

He gladly joined in the group hug. The fact that Summer's aunts seemed to know a great deal about him both surprised and delighted him. Maybe he was more than a convenient plus one to Summer. He sure as hell hoped so.

Summer hooked arms with her aunts and ambled down the long hallway leading to the rental car counters in the baggage claim area. Vinnie followed behind rolling and carrying luggage and totes for the ladies.

The group separated after receiving keys to their rental cars. Vinnie moved the driver's seat all the way back in the Lexus sedan, fiddled with the mirror settings and then backed the car out of the space and out of the parking garage.

"I'm so excited my aunts are here. My sisters are going to go crazy." Summer bounced in her seat.

"Amazing how much they look like your mom.

Bree never told me your mom was a triplet, too. Wow. Two generations of identical triplets."

"At least… Um. Stay to the right here," she said.

He accelerated onto highway 64 and joined the flow of traffic. "There's something I can't put a finger on about your aunts. Intriguing. Tell me about them."

"Aunt Karol is the baby, by five minutes, and she never lets her sisters forget that as they've aged."

"They look pretty ageless to me."

Summer giggled. "I think so, too. Karol's an incredible artist."

"That's interesting. Skye is the youngest in your family, right?"

"Uh huh."

"And isn't she an artist?"

"Exactly. Skye specializes in painting marine life. Aunt Karol is famous for her cityscapes. They're so realistic you'd think they were photographs. She travels all over the world."

"Where does she live?"

"In the most gorgeous house in La Jolla, California. It's right on the water."

"Sounds pricey."

"That's an understatement. When I said she was famous, I meant it. She lives there alone with her four Boston terriers and her full-time housekeeper or butler, whatever his title. He's got a British accent and everything."

"She never married?"

"No. She's always been a free spirit. But don't worry; she has *never* lacked male attention."

Vinnie arched his eyebrows. "I'll bet."

"Aunt Kamille is happily married. She has two

boys, my cousins, Jimmy and Martin. Have you ever heard of Mariposa bakeries?"

"Who hasn't? My dad orders all the cookies for the restaurant from them."

"That's Aunt Kamille. She started baking cookies in her kitchen when the boys were little and sold them to local stores. Uncle Brian and the boys run the company with her now. They're based out of Boston but distribute nationally."

"I thought I smelled vanilla and chocolate when I hugged her."

"I'm sure you did. Come to think of it, me, too. Odds are she brought cookies in her tote bag. I hope so. They're so good."

****

Vinnie stretched his stiff legs in the parking lot of The Inn of the Three Butterflies inhaling the tangy scented ocean air. "Is it always this warm in December?"

Summer closed her eyes and lifted her face toward the dazzling sun in the Carolina blue sky. "Sometimes. This day is just perfect. I hope the weather holds for the wedding."

She sighed, gifted him with a sweet smile and clasped his hand.

Mike Layton bounded down the porch steps. "I thought I heard a car pull in."

Her dad enveloped Summer in a hug and then he extended his hand to Vinnie. "Welcome back Vinnie. So glad you could come."

Vinnie shook Mike's hand. "Thank you, sir, it's great to be back."

"What a relief you decided to fly. I just heard on

the news that the storm is hitting New York and New Jersey. Delays are starting at the airports. So glad you got the early flight out."

"I have Bree and Jack to thank for convincing me not to drive." Summer leaned into the back seat of the Lexus and tugged out her briefcase by the handle.

Vinnie opened the trunk and unloaded the luggage. Mike hoisted up one of the suitcases and led Vinnie and Summer into the front parlor.

"Leave the bags there. We can take them up to your rooms later. Mom made up the room for you girls, Summer. And Vin, you're in the guest room you stayed in last visit," Mike said. "Everyone is out on the back deck. I came inside to get a couple of bottles of champagne when I heard your car engine."

Mike waved a beckoning hand. "Come on into the kitchen. Now that you're here we can officially start the pre-rehearsal dinner party."

Vinnie fisted the necks of two chilled bottles of champagne and followed Mike, who carried a tray of champagne flutes.

"Honey, can you please grab that glass I fixed for Ella?" Mike tossed out over his shoulder.

"Aw, Vin. Look at this." Summer held out a champagne glass filled with pink liquid and Maraschino cherries, complete with a tiny umbrella. "Dad always made the best *cocktails* for us at the inn's parties when we were kids."

Grinning, Summer turned to follow Vinnie outside.

Bree jumped up when Vinnie and Summer stepped through the sliding glass door. "Summer, you made it!"

Summer handed the champagne flute to Ella and then embraced Bree closing her eyes tightly.

Bree gazed at Vinnie over Summer's shoulder. "You, too, Vin."

He beamed Bree a smile.

"I think we left just in time," Summer said.

She shivered. "I don't even want to think about missing your wedding."

Bree twisted her lips, her expression somber. "Jack just got off the phone with his college roommate, EB."

"EB?" Summer said.

"Edwin Beauregard. EB was his decided preference," Jack quipped.

Vin and Summer nodded their heads in unison.

"Understandable," Vin said.

"EB's flight is cancelled," Bree continued. "They aren't offering rebooking until the day *after* Christmas. There's no possible way for him to be here for the wedding." She cast Jack a doleful gaze touching his arm. "So, Jack doesn't have a Best Man."

"You should ask Uncle Vinnie, Daddy," Ella said. "I think he is a best man."

She trained her huge blue eyes on Vinnie. "How are my boys?"

Vinnie knelt down to Ella's eye level. "They're doing good. They had a great time with you at the Christmas show. I mentioned that I'd see you at the wedding and the boys said to tell you hello."

"I can't wait to see them again next year." She scampered over to the chaise lounge where Skye was seated, plopped down and wiggled her way into sharing the chair next to Summer's sister. "Are you going to ask Uncle Vinnie to be the best man, Daddy?"

Vinnie cleared his throat glancing sideways at Bree. The last time together with Jack in New York

City had *seemed* to clear the air between them, but historically the closeness of Jack and Vinnie's relationship would better be described as lock horns than best man.

"I think that's a great idea, Gabriella," Jack said.

Vinnie did a doubletake and met Jack's gaze.

"Vin, would you be my Best Man?"

"Uh…"

Jack held out his hand, palm upturned. "Bree will vouch for me that this was my idea. We discussed this after the call from EB. I asked if she had any objections."

"We both want you to be part of our wedding, Vinnie." Bree slipped an arm around Vinnie's back.

Mike sent a cork skyward with a resonant pop. Vinnie scanned the faces of Summer's family assembled on the deck as Mike filled the champagne glasses. His gaze was met only by smiles—even from Skye.

"I'm honored, Jack, yes." Vin winked at Summer and held up his glass. "I would like to propose a toast to Bree and Jack."

The family raised their glasses.

"May your joys be as deep as the ocean and your troubles be as light as the foam."

Chapter 21

Summer was the first triplet wide awake pre-dawn on Christmas morning, as if sheer anticipation of the day ahead had jolted her out of slumber. She lay on her back in the twin bed, overheated beneath the light blanket. Tossing off the covers, she outstretched her arm and plucked her phone off the nightstand at her bedside.

She turned her pillow over and nestled her head into the downy softness, the crisp cotton pillowslip cooling her neck. Her phone in front of her face, she activated the home button and opened the weather app. Seventy degrees already!

Rolling onto her side facing Skye's bed, she deposited the phone back down on the night table. "Are you awake?" she whispered.

Skye rolled over and faced Summer. "Uh huh. Man, it's hot in here."

"I know. It's seventy degrees and the sun isn't even up."

"Awesome. Let's put on our suits under our workout gear and wake up the little bride."

Summer shifted position to peer through the gloom at Bree's bed. Her sister's chest rose and fell with each soft snore. "How can she sleep so calmly?" She swung her legs over the side of the bed and stood upright. "I'm all tingly and it's not even my wedding."

"Come on." Skye drifted over to the bed and arched over Bree. She crooned the first stanza of the wedding chapel song into Bree's ear.

Summer belted out the second stanza.

A huge smile bloomed on Bree's face and she blinked open her eyes. "Good morning you idiots."

"Morning little bride," Summer said. "It's warm outside. Want to go for a swim after we jog the beach? I figure we have time before hair and makeup."

"Sure." Bree sat up in bed.

Skye bounded up onto Summer's bed and bounced up and down. *"Come on and marry me Jaaack,"* she sang on the top of her lungs.

Summer accepted Skye's handhold and jumped up onto the bed, too. She held both of Skye's hands, bounced on the mattress like a five-year old, and sang along with her sister.

Bree leaned back against the headboard and regarded her siblings with a wry arch of her eyebrow. "You're gonna break something if you keep bouncing like that. Mom would have a cow if she walked in here right now."

Three raps on the door sounded snapping Summer and Skye to attention. Their mother's gifts were legion. She probably saw her errant kids acting like...errant kids.

"Uh oh." Summer clamored down off the bed, Skye in tow. "Come in," she called out.

The bedroom door swung open. Instead of their chastising mom, Aunt Kamille and Aunt Karol, wearing identical seersucker robes and bunny slippers, paraded into the room, apparently bearing gifts.

Kamille, her long auburn hair wrapped in assorted

sizes of pink, sponge curlers, toted a tray. She placed it at the foot of Bree's bed. "Breakfast cookies, girls."

Each triplet wasted no time in nabbing a cookie and devouring huge bites. "Mmm," Summer said, her mouth full. "What are breakfast cookies?"

"Chocolate chip, coconut, macadamia. Eaten at breakfast time."

Summer belly laughed. "Okay, then." She reached for another.

Karol set a sixteen by twenty-inch canvas on the floor at the side of Bree's bed, propping it upright against her thighs. "Yours and Jack's wedding gift from me, darling."

Bree exhaled, her hand over her heart. "This is the *exact* view that I love so much from Jack's condo. The Lake, the Pier...my gosh. It's *perfect*. Thank you *so* much," she marveled. "How on earth did you know this?"

Karol patted her chignon and then waved a hand in dismissal. "I have my ways...I'm glad you like it."

"Like it?" Bree sprang out of bed and threw her arms around her aunt. "I *love* it."

She released Karol and then embraced Kamille. "Thank you so much for the breakfast treats. I love you both. I'm so glad you're here."

Summer and Skye stood back grinning...and relishing cookies. Swallowing the last bite, Summer said, "We thought we'd go for a jog and a swim. Want to join us?"

Her aunts shook their heads in unison.

"You girls go," said Kamille.

Karol nodded agreement. "Yes. Have fun. We're going to see what your mom wants us to do. There are people *everywhere* here. Delightful. But a *multitude*. I think even Kay has her hands full feeding everyone."

"So, Jack's family has arrived?" Bree gazed at Karol. "They all took late flights last night and planned on caravanning here after meeting up at the airport in Norfolk."

"Yes. I was introduced to Jack's parents and two of his brothers while I was baking in the kitchen this morning. I suppose we're putting pressure on Kay by coming here without an invitation," Kamille said.

"Nonsense," Karol retorted. "We're only two more."

Bree chuckled. "Mom's in her glory. I can't *believe* I get to marry Jack today."

"Yep." Summer struck up another chorus of the wedding chapel song.

On a laugh, Bree held out a hand, stop. "Let's go out on the beach. But before we do, I want to stop by Jack and Ella's room and wish them Merry Christmas. Wasn't Ella adorable opening Christmas presents last night? She was so excited about every single gift."

"Love that kid," Skye said.

"Me, too." Summer held up her hand. "But hold up, Bree. You can't see Jack all day. Not until the wedding."

"But…"

Skye and Summer shook their heads. "No buts," Summer said. "Straight to the beach."

Summer stood on the expansive deck drinking in the seaside panorama while she waited for her sisters to don running shoes and smear on sunscreen. The pewter colored ocean swelled in lazy waves glistening fluorescent along the horizon with the impending sunrise. The breeze ruffled her hair as she closed her eyes and upturned her face toward the lightening sky, savoring the smell and feel of home. She heard voices in the distance and scanned the beach to locate their source. Surely some of Bree's wedding guests took advantage of the lovely weather.

Skye sidled up next to Summer followed by Bree. In unspoken unison, the sisters descended the wooden steps and trudged through shifting sand until they reached the packed sand near the fringe of lapping surf.

Turning northward, the southerly breeze fanned them from behind. When they returned, the wind in their faces would cool them delightfully.

"Are you nervous?" Summer asked Bree.

"Not really. The ceremony will be exactly what we want. Just immediate family."

Skye hooted a laugh. "Yeah like hordes of immediate family. Do you think Dad feels left out that his bajillion sibs aren't here? Now that Aunt Karol and Aunt Kamille showed up?"

"Nah." Bree wagged her head. "Honestly, Daddy only cares that the three of us are here together."

A wave of exhilaration swept through Summer. "The three of us together! Wow, do I miss the three of us together. Do you think Jack will be okay with occasional just sister time after today?"

"Of course. Kind of terms of matrimony for me."

Skye nodded her head. "Yeah, me, too."

"Me three." Summer cast her sisters a wry smile. "*If* I ever get married…"

Bree pulled up short tapping Summer on the shoulder to signal her to stop. "Whoa. What do mean if? I think Vinnie is really close to popping the question."

Summer rolled her eyes. "I haven't given that a single thought."

Bree hooted a laugh. "Bullshit." She tugged off her T-shirt over her head, and then gazed directly at Skye, her eyes gleaming impish. "Want to go for a swim Skye?"

Skye and Summer intuitively caught Bree's drift. Without a word, the pair swept off their shirts and stepped out of their shorts. Bree stripped off her shorts and then linked her right hand with Skye's left. Summer took her place at Skye's right side and the trio sloshed into the water.

The swells lapped over Summer's ankles, then knees, then thighs. When they waded into the rolling surf up past their waists, they hopped up and over a cresting wave. On a downward dive, Summer surrendered to the electric surge Skye's power cascaded through her body. When the blast of metamorphosis subsided, a triplet of dolphins leaped and surfed the waves.

****

Vinnie unhooked the suit bag hanging in the back seat and slammed shut the door of Mike Layton's ebony, 4-Runner. He waited for Summer's dad to round the bumper. Vinnie fell into pace with the burly man and strolled companionably toward the front entrance having enjoyed their light conversation driving to and from Kill Devil Hills on their quest for a tuxedo rental. He had discovered that he had a lot in common with Summer's dad. They both had served in the military, he as a Special Ops Marine and Mike as a SEAL. And although they hadn't discussed it, they both loved

Summer.

Mike gave a nod toward the suit bag. "This is a great thing you're doing for my Bree."

"Are you kidding? I'm honored. And glad that Jack and I can be friendly."

"I thought you two would come to blows in May."

"Yeah. Well, the thought crossed my mind." Vinnie dragged his fingers through his hair. "But only out of concern for Bree. I didn't want anybody messing with her."

"I get that. I won't permit anyone's messing with my daughter. But as we both know; my Breeze has a mind of her own."

Vinnie chuckled. "Oh yeah."

"All *three* of my daughters have minds of their own. But that doesn't mean I won't figure out how to protect them."

Well aware of the underlying fatherly warning Mike conveyed, Vinnie simply said, "Yes, sir."

Mike reached the porch door first. He paused, his calloused mitt on the door handle. His penetrating gaze and coiled stance screamed, explain your intentions with my daughter.

"You don't have to worry about Summer, sir. Not with me."

He opened the door for Vinnie and waited for him to pass by before stepping into the parlor and facing him. "What do you mean by I don't have to worry about her with you?"

"The truth is…" Vinnie hesitated, determined to take what he viewed as an opportunity with Summer's father. "I'm in an uncertain position right now. I feel like the tables are turned with me and Summer. I want to protect her—as you might expect, sir. But right now, it's more like she's protecting me."

Vinnie huffed a breath. "When I'm reinstated in my job," he stated with conviction, unwilling to think otherwise, "I'd like a future with her. I'm in love with her, sir."

"I see."

"Do you have any objections?"

Mike leveled powder blue eyes on Vinnie, an unflinching power gaze that bored right through him. The eye lock persisted a couple beats and then Mike's gaze softened with a smile. "Not if she doesn't." He sidled through the parlor toward the back of the house.

Vinnie trailed him into the kitchen and followed his lead to pour a mug of coffee from the urn on the sprawling kitchen counter.

Mike sat down at the kitchen table and stirred his coffee with a spoon, a pensive expression on his chiseled face. Vinnie took a seat across from him.

"Not that long ago, I believe you claimed you loved Bree."

"Yeah. I still do."

He sipped from his mug and then set it down on the table. "Then I'm confused. You love both my daughters?"

"Yes. In different ways. How could you not love Bree? She's a sweet, kind woman. But Summer?" He shook his head smiling while hosts of impressions flitted through his mind. Her fierce talent as a lawyer, her feisty independence, her delicate features belying her inexplicable arm-wrestling skills, her silken body next to his, her humor, her razor-sharp intelligence, her perfection as a lover... "I can't tell you enough how special Summer is to me."

"Okay. Good." Mike nodded his head apparently mulling over Vinnie's assertion. He glanced at his watch. "We have plenty of time before we have to shower and dress. Feel like going for a run on the beach?"

"Sure. If you have shoes that fit me. I didn't pack smart."

"What size do you wear?"

"Fifteen."

"You're in luck. Me, too."

****

Approaching the water's edge alongside of Mike, Vinnie reveled in the balmy weather; a rarity in December having just left below freezing temperatures and soot colored clots of winter snow in New Jersey. "It's so warm. It's hard to believe this is Christmas Day."

"Actually, some Christmases we've had temps in the eighties here. Christmas has kind of taken second place to the wedding this year."

"I don't think so. It was really nice last night watching Ella open up gifts. I think she's delighted with spending Christmas here."

"She's a doll, that's for sure." Mike broke into a jog, running at an even pace.

Vinnie fell into step. To his left, he spied frenzied movement. A cadre of florists weaved garlands of white roses around a three-legged pergola situated near a copse of towering palm trees at the back of the inn. The palms were dotted with twinkling, fairy lights and the air carried a sweet floral scent. A red silk butterfly perched on top of each of the three posts of the wedding canopy.

"Father of the bride," Vinnie said. "You must be bursting with pride."

"I am. A little melancholy, too. I hope the whole bit about, 'you're not losing your daughter, you're gaining a son,' applies."

"Oh yeah. Jack's a good guy. A family man. I don't think you have any worries there."

"Seems so. I liked him from the first meeting. Are you a family man, Vinnie?"

"All the way. I'm really close to my parents and my sister and her two boys. I think you'd like them."

"I know I would."

Mike picked up the pace. Vinnie was exhilarated by the endorphin rush he experienced. What was it about the beach that untethered worries and set them sailing like the gulls and pelicans swooping over the whitecaps? Professing his love for Summer to Mike and receiving her father's blessing of sorts had made his legal problems seem inconsequential compared to the promise loving her represented. The brisk breeze and the clean air filling his lungs were like a Baptism of freedom and light heartedness. Vinnie agreed with Bree's long held belief that the Outer Banks were magical. The whole seascape had him entranced.

Adding to the magic, he thought he glimpsed a dorsal fin above the sea's surface. And then another. And another in sequence. He halted, shading his eyes with his right hand and gazing out over the water. "Did you sight dolphins offshore?"

Mike pulled up at his side. "Maybe."

Vinnie concentrated on the area of the last sighting. He gasped as three reddish-silver dolphins appeared on top of the crest of a breaker and surfed the wave into the shallows about a hundred yards ahead of him and Mike. "Wow, did you…"

He swallowed the rest of the sentence and his jaw hung open. Summer, Bree and Skye, clad in pine green bikinis, their maroon hair of varying lengths slicked back off their porcelain faces, cavorted in the shallows *exactly* at the end of the dolphins' ride.

Chapter 22

Vinnie rooted to the spot, gaping at the lovely women sloshing out of the water like sea nymphs, their laughter tinkling on the sea breeze. On shore, they stooped to pick up clothing scattered on the sand and slipped on shorts and T-shirts over their bathing suits. And then they linked arms and took off at an easy jog down the beach.

He scanned the beach behind him hoping he'd spy corroborating witnesses. The beach was deserted, except for Mike who stood next to him in silence, his face blank.

"What the hell?" Vinnie exhaled roughly. "You saw three dolphins, right?"

Mike nodded his head.

"Then they disappeared and were…replaced by your daughters?"

Mike gazed at him evenly but gave no response.

"What was in that eggnog last night?" Vinnie rubbed his eyes, the detective in him at odds with the sheer irrationality at what he had positively witnessed.

"Just rum." Mike chuckled.

"Then something is seriously wrong with me. I'm hallucinating."

"There's nothing wrong with you." Mike clapped a hand on Vinnie's shoulder. "All I can say is, it's not my story to tell."

"Story? What the hell, Mike?"

"Come on. Let's go back. I have something for you to read and then I think you'll want to talk to Summer."

Still reeling, Vinnie trailed Mike, entering the inn through the bustling kitchen. Kay and her sisters huddled over the stove, spoons in hand, sampling something out of a giant pot. A group of presumably Jack's relatives sat around the table drinking coffee and devouring Mariposa Bakery cookies.

"Vinnie, you're just the person we need to taste this sauce." Karol beckoned him over to the stove. "I think it needs more garlic. Kamille thinks more onion. What's your professional opinion?"

Kay ladled out a generous mouthful of meat sauce with a wooden spoon and handed it to him.

Vinnie sniffed the sauce. "Smells wonderful."

He bit off half of the serving from the spoon and chewed, delighted with the balance of flavors. "Don't add a thing. It's perfect just the way it is."

Vinnie popped the spoon in his mouth and finished the sample. "Delicious."

Kay beamed him a smile and then faced her sisters, a triumphant expression on her face. "I told you." She shooed Karol and Kamille away with a wave of her hand. "Now let me finish cooking without you two hovering over my stove."

Mike arched his eyebrows and gave a nod toward the hallway.

Picking up on the cue, he followed Mike to the reception desk in the front parlor. "Aren't there any caterers around here?"

"Sure. We have a wonderful caterer handling the wedding."

"Then why is Kay cooking all that food?"

"She wants the fridge stocked in case someone is still hungry after the reception. That's my darling Kay. No stomach should ever be empty at her inn." He gave Vinnie a crooked grin and then checked his watch. "In fact, the caterer should arrive shortly. The tent, tables and chairs were delivered while we were out jogging. I better get out back to help set up."

"Do you need me to pitch in?"

"Thanks for the offer, but Jack's brothers have it covered. They probably don't even need my two cents, but I need something to keep busy."

He selected a pamphlet off the desktop and handed it to Vinnie. "Read this brochure and then talk to Summer." He patted Vinnie's shoulder and headed back to the kitchen leaving him clueless in the wake of Mike's mysterious behavior and earlier hallucinations of dolphins changing into gorgeous women.

The brochure in his right hand, Vinnie bounded up the stairs two at a time. He opened the door and entered his cheerful, sun drenched room, the walls painted lemon yellow and the gauzy white curtains framing a turquoise seascape. He kicked off his shoes and tossed the pamphlet onto the bed. Stripping off his clothes along the way, he drifted into the bathroom and turned the shower on full blast. The hot water pummeled his back and he stood beneath the spray a few extra minutes, the shower working magic on his tight muscles.

He dried off with a plush bath towel and then shrugged into the inn's signature, terry cloth robe. The stack of gifts on the desk drew a smile. Summer had included him in the family's Christmas gift exchange last night. Thankfully, he had brought small gifts for everyone.

The Sweet Pickles books were a big hit with the three sisters. Summer had shot him the most beautiful smile after opening the gift, apparently delighted that he had remembered that the series was their childhood favorites. Ella had seemed entranced as Summer, Skye and Bree took turns reading the stories out loud, and he planned to check eBay when he returned home to buy her a full set of the books. The Nintendo Switch he bought Ella was the biggest hit of the evening, especially after he told her that he bought the same gift for "her" boys.

Kay and Mike had exclaimed delight with the homemade pastas from Via Lucci and his mom's coveted recipe for braciole.

He had received a tin of Garretts mixed caramel/cheddar cheese popcorn from Bree, touched that she had remembered it was his favorite during their college days, and a beautiful painting of his parent's restaurant from Skye. Summer must have given Skye a current photo of the restaurant because she had captured every detail, even the Christmas wreath hanging on the door. His favorite gifts were from Summer: a black, cashmere turtleneck and a framed picture of him and Summer in front of the Rockefeller Center Christmas tree.

Vinnie stepped over to the luggage rack in front of his bed and dug a hand inside the zipper pocket of his suitcase, emerging with a narrow, rectangular box wrapped with candy cane paper. He had decided not to give Summer her "real" gift in front of her family. The emerald bracelet was special to him and he wanted a more private setting to give her the gift. His grandmother had given it to him before she had passed away, telling him that she hoped he might give it to his special love someday. He had found his someday in Summer. After taking the piece to the jewelers for cleaning, he was pleased that the finished result made the bracelet look brand new. Nana would approve of Summer.

He placed the box on the bedside table, sat down on the edge of the bed and picked up the pamphlet that Mike had given to him. The title read, *The Legend of the Three Butterflies.*

Vinnie perused the narrative about Sarah and her husband and their ship's attack by Blackbeard.

Raising his head, he stared out through the sliding glass doors. "What does this have to do with Summer?"

Why would Mike direct him to read this fable and then talk with his daughter? *Sacred Source? Triplets? Three butterflies?*

"Whoa." Vinnie reread part one of the Legend. Did the babies turn into butterflies? He continued reading as the pieces started to click into place in his mind. The line, *as preteens they were all about dolphins* struck him like a club to the head. Dolphins, butterflies...triplets. Summer's mother was an identical triplet, too.

He closed his eyes and replayed the night of the Op when he and his team had apprehended Randy Wyatt for drug smuggling. Wyatt had kidnapped Ella. Bree had somehow knocked out Wyatt on the deck of his fishing boat and then collapsed. When Vinnie had questioned Bree about how she had slipped past his surveillance, she had responded that she and Skye had turned into pelicans, stormed the boat and while Bree dealt with Wyatt, Skye had turned into a dolphin to spirit Ella to shore. Of course, he had laughed the explanation off as absurd.

But…

Vinnie realized now that Bree's whimsical tale was fact, not fiction. Whatever the Sacred Source was, Summer and her sisters had it. He wasn't crazy or hallucinating that morning. The woman he loved had literally changed into a dolphin and back again.

He scooped up his phone off the bedside table, opened the text message app and typed, *Are you free to come to my room?* Vinnie tapped the send arrow and a whoosh sounded.

Undoing the belt and slipping out of the sleeves, he tossed his robe on the bed and dressed in sweatpants and a sweatshirt. A few minutes later the notifier tone sounded, and he checked his phone for her response. *On my way, but only have a few minutes before I have to get ready for the wedding.*

He bounded across the room, swung open the door and waited for her to appear.

****

Summer traversed the hallway, approaching Vinnie's room and caught sight of him standing in the doorway. Concern prompted her to quicken her pace. "What's up? Is everything okay?"

His broad smile reassured her. She stood on tiptoe returning his soft kiss on her lips.

"Everything is great. Come into my room a minute?"

She preceded him through the threshold, and he closed the door behind him.

"First, Merry Christmas." He kissed her again, lingering, passionate, as she melted into his arms.

Vinnie released her gently and held her at arms' length. "Second, I have another present to give you."

"Oh, no need. The book last night was so thoughtful; and I really loved it. Thank you for listening to my childhood stories. I'm flattered that you remembered."

The wrapped box on the desk sparked her interest. *Jewelry?* "Is that the gift?"

He followed her gaze and nodded.

Summer held out her hand, grinning. "Well, if you insist."

Vinnie belly laughed. He strode to the desk, picked up the box and then placed it in her palm.

She ripped off the paper in two tugs and took the lid off the box. Her hand froze in midair at the sight of the glittering emerald and diamond bracelet. "Oh," she gasped. "It's beautiful. But…"

It must have cost a fortune.

Vinnie furrowed his brow. "But, what?"

"It's *way* too much. I've never seen anything like it."

"It's one of a kind." He took the delicate bracelet out of the box and clasped it on Summer's wrist.

"It looks like it was made just for you." He kissed her pulse point.

"It's so beautiful." She twisted her wrist back and forth, dazzled by the glittering gems.

"Just like you."

"Oh Vinnie, I love it, but you spent way too much money."

"Let me worry about that."

"Thank you so much. I'm never taking it off." She stood on tiptoes and kissed him.

He raked his fingers through her hair and cupped her face with his palms. She moaned softly, lost in the singular oblivion kissing Vinnie stirred. Reluctantly, she pushed against his chest and he drew away.

"I'll have to thank you properly later…" She waggled her eyebrows insinuating the passion to come. "Bree will kill me if I'm late for hair and make-up."

"I'm looking forward to that thank you." He winked and then stepped over to the door and swung it open.

Summer moved forward pulling up short as he blocked her exit.

"You said you'll never take the bracelet off?"

"And I meant it." She ducked under his arm and faced him out in the hallway, smiling.

"I'm just wondering what happens when you turn into a dolphin? Do you take it off then?"

The implication pierced her; and she could literally feel the blood draining from her face. "Um… What are you talking about?" She shoved him gently back into the room and closed the door behind them with a bang.

"I ran on the beach this morning with your dad."

"I know he told me."

"I saw you and Bree and Skye swimming."

"Okay." Her mind spun. *Did he see us…before?*

"I thought I was hallucinating dolphins disappearing and then you and your sisters magically appearing in the waves exactly where I had sighted the dolphins."

She held her breath not daring to say a single word.

"I asked your dad if he saw the same thing."

"What did he say?"

"He said it wasn't his story to tell. He gave me this pamphlet." Vinnie moved to the bed and scooped up a copy of the *Legend* brochure and waved it in hand. "He said I should read it and then talk with you."

Hot tears welled. She had never imagined this confrontation. *If* a man were important enough to her to reveal her family's secrets, she always thought she'd decide the timing…the careful, well thought out explanation. That moment wasn't the perfect time. But Vinnie was that important man.

"Maybe you should sit down."

His eyes gleaming, he sat on the edge of the bed.

"I've never told anyone this before and you need to know that it's a closely guarded secret."

She expelled a breath gathering her courage. How would he react? Like Jack's rejection with Bree? Summer had no choice. He had seen. She had to tell him her truth. "I'm not going to ask you if I can trust you. I know I can." She closed her eyes and was silent.

"You can trust me with your life."

Summer sat next to him. "I really am trusting you with my life here."

She closed her eyes insulating herself from what she predicted would be his appalled shock. "My sisters and I are descendants of those triplets who escaped Blackbeard by changing into butterflies. In every generation since, identical triplets are born to the first triplet to conceive and those babies inherit the power emanating from the Sacred Source."

"What is the Sacred Source?"

"It's hard to explain, but it's the Source of unique gifts. This morning you witnessed the gift that Skye has perfected."

"Changing into animals."

"Yes. That." His soft eyes and knowing smile utterly confused Summer. *How could he be unfazed?*

"I've witnessed it before, only I didn't realize it. Bree told me that she and Skye had turned into pelicans. And then Skye, a dolphin. But I thought she was bullshitting me."

"She wanted you to think she was joking. Jack saw her change the night she rescued Ella. They broke up that night. He couldn't handle it."

"Kind of asinine if you ask me."

"Not really. It's hard to accept," she whispered.

"Nah. Not if he really loved her. There shouldn't have been any hesitation on his part."

Her heart leaped. "Are you telling me that you're not freaked out about this? That you won't run for the hills the minute you escape The Inn of the Three Butterflies?"

"Freaked out? Blown away is more like it. To think that your ancestors survived an attack by Blackbeard by literally flying away. And they were only babies. Wow."

She sat in stunned silence, awed by his reaction. Summer had dreamed that she'd find a man like her dad; a man who would adore her without reservation, like Dad adored Mom.

"I love you Summer. Warts and all. Wait. Do you have warts?" He guffawed.

"Very funny." She punched him on the arm. "I'm not a witch."

"Oh yes you are. You have me under your spell." He wrapped his arms around her. "And I don't want to be set free."

She nestled against him exulting in the perfect shelter he gave her.

He tipped a finger under her chin and gazed into her eyes. "As much as I would love to ravish you this minute..." Vinnie fingered the belt of her robe. "We better get dressed for the wedding."

Smiling at him, she rose. "Thank you for... I love you."

She strode to the door, swung it open and scurried out into the hallway.

"Save the first dance for me," he hollered after her.

Summer twisted around to face him. "I'll save every dance for you." She blew him a kiss, spun on her heel and disappeared around a bend in the hallway.

Chapter 23

Summer floated down the hall and shoved open the door of her parents' suite. Her infinite elation that Vinnie loved her—all of her—without reservation fueled her broad grin. How strange she felt now that her secret since birth wasn't secret any longer. She practically levitated into the room where she encountered her sisters and mother in varying stages of readiness for the wedding.

Kay, seated in a chair for her hair styling, observed Summer's reflection in the mirror. "You look positively glowing, Summer."

"I do?" An ear to ear blush heated her cheeks as three Layton women pinned her with their piercing green eyes.

"You sure do," Bree remarked with a smile. "Any special reason?"

She debated sharing her momentous news. On the plus side, Summer knew that her family would celebrate with her. And would welcome Vinnie into their...unusual fold. But the minus that Jack's reaction to Bree's revelation had been less than perfect convinced her to withhold the information on her sister's wedding day. Today was all Bree's and Jack's.

"Of course, there's a special reason," Summer said drifting over to Bree's seat in front of the mirror next to Kay.

She placed a hand on Bree's shoulder, her robe's terry cloth soft beneath her palm. "I'm so happy for you."

Bree laid her hand over Summer's. "I know you are. And we're so happy for *you*. Vinnie couldn't have reacted more perfectly."

Kay, Skye and Bree gifted her with dazzling smiles. She should have known that her mom or one of her sisters...or all of them would "see". Summer beamed them a smile as she plopped down onto the edge of the bed to wait her turn in the hair and makeup chair.

She shook her head still awed that he loved her— even when she was a dolphin, or whatever. "I'm really happy."

"Me, too," Bree said rising from her chair. "How do I look?"

Bree's long auburn hair was pinned in soft curls at the nape of her neck. An heirloom comb of dainty pearls woven around three alabaster butterflies fastened a long bridal illusion veil to her hair. Her lipstick and blush were the palest rosebud pink. Individual false eyelashes accentuated her emerald eyes. Jack would flip when he caught sight of his bride.

"Gorgeous." Kay's eyes glistened. "Like I dreamed you would look on your wedding day." She relinquished her chair to Skye and then strolled to the dress rack to put on her green velvet, long sleeved gown which was identical to Summer's and Skye's dresses except for tiny crystals ringing the neck and sleeves.

Tears welled in Summer's eyes. "You've never looked more beautiful."

"Yes," Skye concurred teary-eyed.

Summer rose from the bed and paced over to Bree. She kissed her cheek lightly and then sat in Bree's vacant chair.

Kira stood behind Summer eyeing her short-cropped hair. "How do you want your hair done?"

"Hmm." Summer gazed at her reflection. "Probably not much you can do with it, right?"

She fluffed Summer's spiky, bobbed hair with her fingers. "I can do some curls all around your face and put in some pretty pearl tipped bobby pins. What do you think?"

Summer looked over at Skye. Kira's mother, Donna wielded a curling iron methodically creating sausage curls. Her sister's long mane cascaded over her shoulders partially in a myriad of spirals, held back from her face with pearl bobby pins.

The pearls added just the right touch. Summer gave a nod to Kira. "That sounds perfect."

Kira set to work. Summer watched Bree's and Mom's movements reflected in the mirror.

Kay zipped up Bree's gown fastening the hook and eye at her mid-back. Bree pivoted facing Summer and Skye smoothing her hands over her waist down the sides of the cream-colored satin that hugged her figure in a slim column. Antique lace sleeves tapered to a circle of diamond beads around her wrists. The fitted bodice and the classic elegance of her wedding gown reflected Bree's taste and personality perfectly.

Summer inhaled on a gasp. "Oh, Bree." She covered her mouth with her hand as hot tears filled her eyes.

Weepiness apparently was contagious. Kay, Skye

and Bree caught up in the emotion, too.

Skye fanned her face blinking back tears. "My makeup will be gone the minute you put it on, Donna."

Kay bit her lower lip. "I *refuse* to cry."

Bree threw back her head and snickered. "Really, Mom?"

She gave her daughter a sheepish grin. "At least where you might notice, sweetheart. I'm pretty sure I'll dissolve in tears when you and your father walk down the aisle."

"Did I hear the word father?" boomed Mike's voice as three raps on the door sounded.

"Hi, Daddy," Bree said.

Mike strode into the room and halted abruptly; his blue eyes fixated on the bride. The women gaped back at him resplendent in a black tuxedo. Summer observed the swarm of emotions mirrored in her father's eyes, as if she saw his memories replaying: holding his infant Bree in his arms, letting go of her hand as she walked through the doors of elementary school bound for kindergarten, climbing the bleachers and watching her cheer at a high school football game, whistling from the audience at her college graduation, to that moment when he beheld her as a fairy princess bride.

He brought his fist to his lips and cleared his throat. "My Breeze," he said, his voice thick with emotion. "You look beyond beautiful. You remind me of your mother on our wedding day."

Bree's face illuminated with her smile. She paced over to him holding a red rose boutonnière between her fingers. Trembling she pinned the flower to his lapel. "You look so handsome, Daddy."

Mike stood a little straighter at the compliment.

"Thank you, darlin'." He winked. "You know you've always been my favorite."

At that comment, Summer and Skye burst out laughing.

"You tell me the same thing every chance you get," Summer said.

"Ditto." Skye left her chair, carefully slipped her gown off the hanger, hung it over her arm and stepped into the bathroom, closing the door behind her.

Mike ambled over to Kay and kissed her cheek softly. "My love, you look gorgeous."

Kay grinned at him. "You look pretty gorgeous yourself."

"The photographer said she's ready for some family photos before the wedding."

"Skye and I will be right there, Daddy," Summer said.

Mike, Kay and Bree left the suite. Summer closed her eyes at Kira's direction and surrendered to the soft brush strokes of eye shadow application, the pressure of the pencil lining each eyelid and feathery application of individual lashes. When she raised her eyes to gaze into mirror, she hardly recognized her own image. "Wow, Kira. Thanks."

"You do look amazing if I say so myself." Kira collected cosmetics and stowed them in a black, official looking carrying case.

Summer scooted out of the chair and headed to the rack where a single green velvet gown hung. She shed her robe, took the dress off the hanger, stepped into the central opening, shimmied the material up over her hips and plunged each arm into a sleeve. Skye opened the bathroom door and Summer presented her back to her.

"Zip me up?"

"Sure."

The slider rasped up the teeth in the zipper and then Skye's cool fingers worked the hook and eye at the back of Summer's neck. She spun on her heel and faced Skye. "You're all zipped up?"

"Yep with a few contortions. Come on. Let's do this thing."

Kay had designated the front parlor as the bride's private sanctum. When Summer entered the room with Skye in tow, Mike, Kay, Bree and Ella stood together, her sister a luminescent, beaming candle in their midst.

Mike squatted down to Ella's eye level. "You look like a real-life princess today. I can't believe my luck. Your daddy is becoming my son and you're my very first grandchild!"

Ella did look like a princess, or a porcelain doll, in her ankle length, green velvet, high-waisted, crinoline puffed skirt. Her naturally curly, below the shoulders, raven hair, held back off her face with Kira's and Donna's signature pearl bobby pins, gleamed in the sunlight streaming through the parlor's windows.

The little girl hugged her new grandpa, eyes closed, and then hovered near the bride training adoring eyes on Bree.

Bree smiled at Ella. "Okay, my Maid of Honor. You stand right here." She pointed to a spot on the carpet directly in front of her.

"Skye, you're in front of Ella. And Summer, right there in front of Skye. Mom, you're first in line."

Mike strode to the door, swung it outward and engaged the sliding clasp to prop the door open. He took his position at Bree's left side and extended his elbow. Bree slipped her hand into the crook of his arm holding her bouquet of scarlet tea roses in her right hand.

Strains of cello and keyboard music, *A Thousand Years*, drifted on the ocean breeze. Vinnie rounded the corner and Summer's breath caught in her throat at the sight of him clad in a groom-like tuxedo. Fantasies of walking down the aisle to meet him in front of the preacher spun dreamlike in her mind. Jack had asked Vinnie to escort Kay down the aisle and then stand to the side of the minister with him at the start of the wedding procession.

He placed a foot, his polished, black, cap toe shoe gleaming, on the bottom step of the stoop and gazed up at Kay smiling. "That's our cue, Kay."

Holding up the material of her gown, Kay gracefully descended the three porch steps and linked arms with Vinnie. He spirited her away, her mother's lithe figure next to his towering, muscular brawn an attractive contrast. *That's how we look together.*

Summer shuffled forward and then descended the steps pausing just short of the corner of the inn waiting for the beginning of the refrain that would trigger her processing along the rose petals strewn pathway to the wedding pergola. Her heart swelled listening to the romantic music promising that Bree and Jack would love each other for a thousand years.

In step with the music Summer moved forward. The sunlight that filtered through the palm trees warmed her skin and the balmy breeze that gently ruffled her hair carried the sweet scent of the long-stemmed red rose that she clasped between both hands. At the head of the aisle she took in the small group of guests on white folding chairs to her left and right. She winked at her aunts and Mom and then faced forward. Her eyes were drawn directly to Vinnie's face.

Magnetized, she glided forward, unaware of her feet touching the ground or the faces of anyone else's but his. The loving expression on his face melted her heart and had her openly grinning at him. Behind her in a few moments, Bree would walk toward her everything. Summer in that moment felt that she did the same thing.

She reached the position in front of the preacher where she turned left and took her position waiting for Skye and Ella to file into place next to her. She tore her gaze away from Vinnie's twinkling eyes and gazed down the aisle watching Skye's procession toward her. Ella came into view wearing her joy and pride in the occasion like a crown. Her broad smile in place, she solemnly walked down the aisle in a foot forward, two feet together cadence.

And then Bree and Dad rounded the corner. The guests surged to their feet at the first notes of Pachelbel in D. Kay sniffled as her daughter and husband came fully into view. Summer paid no attention to tears puddling in her eyes, fixating on the vision of her beloved sister's ecstatic face. She wanted to cement that vision in her memory forever among the many treasures living with her sisters of the Legend had brought to her life.

Mike ceremonially gave Bree's hand to her groom drawing Summer's attention to Jack's face. Her soon to be brother-in-law seemed utterly gob smacked with love. Perfect. Bree and Jack were a perfect match. Summer sneaked a glance at Vinnie feeling the heat of his gaze on her. He smiled and she grinned back at him feeling blessed that at this celebration of love, she was in love with her perfect match.

The ceremony concluded, a blur from start to finish for Summer. The duo played the recessional music, and the bridal party swept up the aisle in reverse order. Summer followed the flow laughing when Ella hopped up and down in excitement. The little girl had a new mother and Summer and Skye had a new niece.

Champagne flowed and the din of conversations swirled around her. Vinnie sauntered over to her and clinked the champagne flute in his hand against hers. "To a thousand years of love."

He leaned down to whisper in her ear. "You ladies don't live for a thousand years, do you?"

Summer clapped a hand over her abdomen and burst out laughing. "Good Lord, no."

"Good." He slipped his arm around her shoulders. "Then I get to love you for all our lives."

Chapter 24

Summer outstretched her arms straight up, yawned and squinted against the bright sunshine streaming through the bedroom window. She rolled over on to her right side. Skye's bed was empty. Switching to her left side, she checked Ella's bed and found her niece gone, too. A glance at the clock sprung her sitting up in bed, the soft sheets pooling at her waist. Ten AM!

She launched out of bed and hurried in to the bathroom. The thought of seeing Vinnie that morning propelled her into and out of the shower in five minutes. They had danced every dance under the stars last night as if they were the only couple on the beach. The dreamy memory of the shelter of his arms and his repeated pronouncements of love had her pleasantly spinning. Summer couldn't believe her good fortune. Slipping on sweats, she raced downstairs.

Grabbing an extra-large mug from the kitchen cabinet, she filled it with steaming coffee that smelled one step from heaven, and took a seat at the table joining Bree, Jack and her parents.

"Good morning, honey." Kay started to rise from her chair. "What can I make you for breakfast?"

"Sit Mom. I'm still stuffed from last night. The food was delicious."

"Everything was delicious." Bree beamed at her new husband.

"Where is everybody?" Summer plucked a biscuit from a platter on the table.

"Skye and Ella are hunting for shells. Kamille and Karol are packing." Kay took a sip of tea.

"What about Vinnie?"

"Oh. He left," Mike said.

Alarm and confusion sped up Summer's heartrate. "Left? Where did he go?"

"I guess you could say he ran for the hills." Mike chuckled. "He took your rental car. Seems like he couldn't get out of here fast enough."

Summer suddenly felt dizzy.

Kay placed her hand gently over Summer's hand. "Oh, don't be upset, honey. We all know he was no good."

"And guilty as sin," Jack sneered.

Summer gasped. "What are you talking about? I love him and he loves me."

"No, he doesn't. You're better off without him." Mike dismissed any rebuttal from Summer with a wave of his hand. "And I thought you learned in law school not to mix business with pleasure."

Skye walked into the kitchen with Ella in tow. "He was only using you, Summer. He knows what a kick ass lawyer you are. He played you. As soon as you got him off, he would have left anyway."

"You're all wrong. He loves me and I love him; and he is not guilty," Summer shouted.

"What is that buzzing sound?" Kay's gaze scanned the kitchen. "For god sake, Summer, answer your phone."

Her phone's vibrations jolted Summer awake. She sprang up sitting in bed, the soft sheets pooling around her waist. Taking a few deep breaths, she tried to calm her racing heart. "Just a bad dream." *But it felt so real.*

Her hand trembled as she snagged the phone and accepted the call. "Hello," she barked, her voice hoarse.

"Good morning, Ms. Layton. I sincerely hope I'm not interrupting anything." Mike Haws' clipped voice sounded in her ear. She had stopped asking him to call her by her first name, much like her assistant Barbara, finding his innate formality too deeply ingrained. He was a Rain Man in his field and had *always* exceeded Jacob's expectations in the past. That was all Summer cared about.

"Good morning, Mike. Merry Christmas. I hope you had a nice holiday."

Her greeting was met with a few beats of silence.

"Uh, thank you. It was satisfactory," he mumbled.

"That's great." She smiled at his obvious social discomfort.

"I have distressing news for you." His tone was crisp and assertive - back in control. "I've traced the EFT's. I'm afraid my findings will not help your case."

"Damn." She swung her legs over the side of the bed and sat ramrod straight, ready to take his punch. "Okay. Hit me with it."

"Most of the money, $390,000.00 to be exact, is currently deposited in a money market account. The deposit transaction occurred the same day as the withdrawal from Vincente Carlucci's checking account. It's a joint account held by Barry S. and Patricia K. Warner."

"Oh wow." She slumped her shoulders, defeated by the damning development.

"I believe that Patricia Warner is your client's

sister. Several transfers from Vincente Carlucci's account to his sister's accounts have occurred monthly during the past year."

Summer surged to her feet as if movement would allow her to absorb the information that she vehemently did not want to accept. "Yes, she is. Do you know who transferred the money into the account?" She drifted over to the sliding glass door gazing vacantly at the surging waves.

"Not yet. I've narrowed it down to a proxy server. I'll work on that next. I figured you'd wanted this information as soon as I found it."

"You're right, Mike. Thank you."

"It's my job, Ms. Layton. Goodbye."

White noise sounded in her ear at his abrupt disconnection.

She leaned her head against the cool glass, the phone still pressed to her ear. Was the dream a warning? Sun beams set the emeralds encircling her wrist glittering. *All those expensive Christmas gifts he bought.*

Summer hated the doubt invading her thoughts, but she refused to play the fool. She had to confront him.

Icy determination spurred her to toss the phone down on the mattress, strip off her pajamas and finish showering in five minutes. She donned soft jeans and an ancient OBX sweatshirt and headed downstairs.

Summer halted in the kitchen doorway observing Vinnie and her family. He sat at the table with her parents, Bree, Jack and Ella, the remnants of Mom's sausage, egg and cheese casserole on the plates in front of them. Skye stood next to the windows leading out to the deck.

Vinnie tugged a shopping bag out from under the table. He dangled the bag in front of Ella, picked up a fork and spoke into the improvised microphone. "Mr. and Mrs. Jack Tremonti and Miss Ella, you just got married, what are you going to do now?"

"We are going to Disneyland!" Ella said, drawing applause and cheers from the family.

"Well then. I think you might need what's in the bag."

Ella accepted the mystery bag from Vinnie. Digging under the tissue paper she revealed Mickey Mouse ears with a top hat, Minnie Mouse ears with a veil and another pair of Minnie Mouse ears with a pointy princess hat.

She handed out the "bride and groom" ears to Bree and Jack, donned her princess ears, jumped up and threw her arms around Vinnie. "Oh, Uncle Vinnie! I *love* this. Thank you so much."

"Gee, thanks so much Vin." Jack's tone dripped sarcasm. He put on his ears, a chagrined expression on his face.

"You look very handsome, Jack." Summer laughed as she strolled into the kitchen over to the coffee urn.

Mom started to rise from her seat. "Let me warm up some casserole for you."

"Don't bother Mom. I'm not hungry."

Vinnie scooted over on the bench making room for Summer. "There's my girl." He draped his arm over her shoulders and bussed her cheek. His one-hundred-watt smile muddled her thoughts further.

Her head ached from confusion. She couldn't accept that he was guilty. There had to be another explanation for the large sum in Tricia's account.

She rested, leaning against him, and sipped her coffee, her thoughts tangled.

Mike glanced at his watch. "What time do you have to leave, Bree?"

"We have about an hour or so. I guess we better finish packing." Bree slid off the bench and hugged first Mike, and then Kay.

"Thank you again for everything, Mom and Dad. The day was just perfect. Just liked I dreamed my wedding would be when I was a little girl." Tears brimmed in Bree's eyes.

Kay sniffled. "Don't start me crying again."

Mike coughed into his fist, apparently choked up, too. "Mom and I will help you organize. I can box anything you don't want to take with you and ship it to you."

"That's great. Thank you." Bree kissed Mom's cheek.

Ella stood and brought her plate over to the sink and then returned to clear Jack's plate.

"Thank you, sweetheart." Kay beamed her new granddaughter a smile. "You guys go ahead. I'll straighten up here and be up to help in a minute."

"No, you go, too, Mom. Vinnie and I will take care of cleanup," Summer offered.

Vinnie toted some dishes over to the sink and began rinsing and stacking the dishwasher. "Is everything okay?" He angled his head to gaze at Summer, his brow furrowed.

"Why do you ask?" She averted her eyes busying herself with clearing the table.

"I don't know. Something feels off."

"I didn't sleep well last night."

"Don't worry. You're not losing your sister but gaining a brother. You, Skye and Bree have an unbreakable bond. No mere man could affect that." Hands dripping with soapy water he reached out and towed her into a hug.

His magnetism compelled her; and she wanted to melt in his arms. But ugly doubts plagued her and colored her feelings for Vinnie. "I'm not worried about changes to our sisterhood now that Bree's married."

"Then what's the problem? Did *I* do something?"

"Let's finish up here and go for a walk on the beach." Summer ducked out of his embrace and strode back to the table to collect the remaining dishes and silverware.

Vinnie silently finished loading the dishwasher. He dried his hands on a yellow, terry cloth dishtowel, clasped her hand and led her out to the beach.

Summer kicked off her sandals. "Ah…" She reveled in the soft, southern breeze ruffling her hair and the warm, sugary sand between her toes. Cauliflower clouds lined the horizon.

"Can you believe this weather? I talked to my mom this morning and it's in the 20's with snow flurries. It's going to be hard to leave this tomorrow." Vinnie swept his free hand in front of him and gave her hand a squeeze.

She fell into an easy stroll with him along the water's edge, the cool water lapping against her ankles and sucking at her toes at each wave's ebb.

"It's always hard for me to leave here. Skye is so lucky." She stooped and picked up a tiny whelk.

She stood upright and he clasped both her hands gazing deeply into her eyes. Enthralled, she accepted his gentle kiss on her lips. Her breath hitched in her throat and she swayed on wobbly legs.

If only Mike Haws hadn't called that morning and broken her blissful bubble at the wedding with Vinnie. Last night Summer had fantasized about marrying him. Yesterday she had told him that she trusted him with her life.

But did she trust in his innocence? Did he take the money to help his sister? If he were guilty, she almost understood that powerful motivation. He was so close with Tricia, Barry and Joey, and his brother-in-law's shoddy treatment of his family hurt Vinnie deeply. She knew him so well. He would do anything to protect those he loved.

Vinnie's penetrating gaze unnerved her. "I know something is wrong. Tell me."

Summer took a deep breath. "Mike Haws called this morning."

"Really? The guy works during the holidays? I'm impressed."

His gaze searched her eyes. "Damn, from the look on your face I guess he didn't find anything helpful."

"He did find something."

"That's great news! Then, why do you look so bent out of shape?"

"He told me he found the money."

Vinnie scowled. "Where is it? Who did this to me?"

"Three-hundred ninety-thousand dollars was deposited in your sister's savings account the same day four-hundred thousand left your checking account."

Unmistakable shock dawned on his face. He couldn't fake the reaction. Was he shocked that he had been found out? Or was he shocked that his sister might be involved?

"That's not possible," he growled. "Haws made a terrible mistake."

"Haws doesn't make mistakes."

"Well, how the hell did the money wind up in Tricia's account?" he bellowed.

"You tell me." She remained impassive, unintimidated by his yelling.

He stared at her, his full lips a grim line. A muscle in his jaw twitched.

She raked a hand through her hair hating the necessity to continue probing. "You've spent a lot of money lately."

Vinnie glared at her remaining stubbornly mute.

"The game systems for the kids. And this amazing bracelet." She twirled her wrist. "Really expensive."

Summer left the ball in his court, hoping...praying for him to refute the evidence.

Her frustration mounted. "Say something," she pleaded.

"What exactly do want to hear?"

"Tell me you didn't put the money in your sister's account. Or, that you had no hand in helping her steal the money," she demanded.

His expression told her that she had utterly crushed him.

"You've already found me guilty, Counselor. We're done here." He turned his back on her and stalked away.

Summer stood and watched his retreat, too mad to cry.

Chapter 25

Summer lazed, propped against the cushions on the daybed in the corner of Skye's sundrenched studio, watching her sister sweep fluid brushstrokes on the canvas. A lace curtain fluttered in the breeze through an open window.

"You can talk to me, you know," Skye said without taking her eyes from her work.

"I know I can. It's just so peaceful and relaxing sitting here with you. I'm jealous that you still live here. I wish I could stay forever." *And hide from nagging doubts and how pissed I am that he left, refusing to explain.*

"Oh, come on," Skye turned away from the easel facing Summer. "You'd go stir crazy after one day of living my life. You're just feeling sorry for yourself." She wiped her hands on a towel hanging off the corner of her easel and then cleaned her brushes.

"I guess you're right. But if I had your talent then I really would be jealous." Summer smiled.

"Aw gee." Skye gave her a crooked grin, her eyes twinkling. "Can you get my phone?" she asked seconds before the cell phone on the coffee table in front of Summer vibrated.

Summer glanced at the screen before answering. "Caller ID reads, MMSN." She handed the phone to Skye.

253

Skye cocked her head and listened to the recording from the Marine Mammal Stranding Network. She disconnected and gazed at Summer. "That was K.C. the MMSN coordinator. There's a seal on the beach near Nags Head Pier. Want to respond?"

"Sure, we have plenty of time before we have to leave for the airport."

In their shared bedroom, Skye took two T-shirts and two baseball caps sporting MMSN logos out of the bureau. Clad in "official gear", Summer and Skye pounded down the stairs, raced through the first floor out the front door and hopped into Skye's jeep. The car was perpetually packed with a tote containing sighting forms, binoculars and a camera.

At the reported site, Summer helped carry the poles and signs used to set up a perimeter around the seal to keep any curious bystanders a safe distance away.

An older couple stood by the beach access. "Are you here to help the seal? We called it in," the woman called out. "We made sure no one went near him. Is he going to be okay?"

Skye approached the couple and Summer followed her. "Thank you so much for calling us. We'll evaluate his condition. Most likely he's on the beach to rest. Seals from Canada and New England migrate to our waters to feed. Once they've filled their stomachs, they rest for the return trip."

"We've been coming to this beach for forty years to celebrate our anniversary and have never seen a seal." The husband grinned at Skye. "It's so cool."

"It *is* very special to see one of these little ones up close," Summer said. She fell into step with Skye drawing nearer to the animal.

From that distance the seal could be mistaken for a piece of driftwood.

Skye handed Summer a clipboard with a blank seal sighting form. She peered through the binoculars and dictated information to Summer. "It's a young harbor seal, highly alert with his head raised. He is resting."

Summer filled in the blanks on the form.

"This has been very interesting." The woman extended her cell phone toward Skye. "Could I trouble you to take a photo for us?"

Skye accepted the phone. "Stand right here and I'll take a few shots of you both with the seal in the background."

She handed back the phone. Summer and Skye watched the pair holding hands strolling away from them up the beach.

"How cute were they?" Summer continued gazing at the couple. She yearned for their kind of love—still holding hands after forty years.

"Hey stranger." Summer switched her focus toward the female voice sounding from behind her.

"Bonney. It's so good to see you." Summer opened her arms and hugged her friend warmly.

"You too, honey. I was hoping you were home for the wedding," Bonney said.

Bonney was officially clad like Summer and Skye, with a tote bag slung over her shoulder and a camera held in hand. "How does our little buddy look?" She focused through the viewfinder and zoomed in before snapping photos in succession.

"He looks healthy and very alert. His eyes followed you walking toward him. Can you please take a picture of his left eye? I think I see some blood," Skye said.

Summer smiled. Skye didn't need photographic evidence; her sister already knew everything about this seal without using the binoculars or zoom lens.

Bonney complied with Skye's request using her telephoto lens. The trio hunched over Bonney's camera inspecting the stills and agreeing that the injury was a small cut and nothing to worry about.

While they followed protocol, the beach remained deserted. Skye sent a summary text to K.C. "Bonney, let's set up perimeter barriers and post the signs. Summer, will you please text Charlotte and ask her to coordinate the volunteers' checking on him periodically?"

"Sure." Summer slipped her phone out of her pocket and composed the message. When she was done, she grabbed a sign that included the warning that seals were protected by the Marine Animal Protection Act and touching, feeding or harassing seals in any way was illegal. *"Shh, I am trying to sleep. Keep 100 feet away."* She drove the post into the sand and then posted another sign until the perimeter was secure.

In the parking lot, Bonney, Skye and Summer chatted for a few minutes catching up with news about the wedding and the antics of Bonney's grandchildren.

"It was great seeing you, Bonney. I don't know when I'll be back. Hopefully for turtle nesting season. I'll only sit a nest if you and Tim are the parents." Summer hugged her.

"I'll look forward to that." Bonney opened her car door and turned toward Skye. "There's a meeting Tuesday night. Will you be able to make it?"

"Absolutely." Skye tossed her tote bag into the back seat of the jeep and then slipped into the driver seat next to Summer.

"What meeting?"

"The Administration has approved seismic testing along the entire Eastern seaboard preceding exploratory drilling for oil. We're mobilizing to fight this decision. It makes me sick thinking about what will happen to our marine animals if we allow this to happen."

"Let me know if there is anything that I can do to help you." There was no mistaking the sorrow in Skye's voice. Her sister was a sensitive, gentle soul and her relationship with the marine life surrounding the island was intimate and deeply personal. "I'll check and see what you can do legally to try to stop it when I get back to the office."

"Thanks, that would be a huge help. Now we better hustle so that you can change for your flight."

****

Her suitcase was in the backseat, tears were shed, hugs were given, promises to return were made to her parents and Summer had taken her seat in Skye's jeep bound for Norfolk International Airport.

"Thanks again for driving me. Um. Since…"

Thankfully, Skye interjected before she had to explain Vinnie's taking the rental car without Summer. "No problem. I had to make a run to Norfolk this week anyway to drop off those paintings in the back. Today worked out perfectly for me. I make this drive at least once a month."

"I'm so proud of you." Summer gently touched her sister's arm.

"Thanks. It's been quite a ride. You know me, the solo art shows are the hardest. I'm happiest alone in my studio. But my agent, Ronnie won't tolerate my reclusiveness and pushes me to show my work. I've taken a few months off from traveling just to paint. But Ronnie has things lined up for Spring."

"Any chance you're coming to New York?"

"Not this season. I'm heading to the West coast. I have Lynn's wedding in Palm Springs coming up, so Ronnie decided to take advantage of the trip and has scheduled showings in a few galleries in California."

"That is so exciting." Summer agreed with Ronnie. Skye needed to get out from behind her easel and meet people.

"I guess."

"When is Lynn's wedding?"

"May. I'm her Maid of Honor. I can't wait to see her. It's been too long since we've gotten together. I'll leave the week before the wedding for my dress fitting. And her friends are organizing a bachelorette party."

"You'll have a great time."

Skye nodded.

The jeep ate up a few miles while Summer and Skye sat, seemingly out of conversation.

"Okay. Let's talk about the pachyderm in the car."

Summer burst out laughing. "You sound just like Dad."

"I do, don't I? But what happened with Vinnie? Why did he leave?"

Summer gazed at her lap twisting the emerald bracelet on her wrist. "My technical expert traced the endpoint of the money transfers. To Vinnie's sister's savings account."

Skye whistled. "And you did what about that info?"

"I confronted him."

"What did he say?"

"He didn't say anything during my rant and demands for explanation. When I pressed him, he said we were done and walked away. I was too pissed to go after him. I thought I'd let him cool off some and try again. But he had already packed, taken my rental car and left by the time I got back to the inn." Anger mushroomed inside Summer again.

"Did you try to call him?"

"Why? He left me with no explanation. I wanted him to tell me how that money wound up in his sister's account," she snapped.

Skye remained silent.

Remorse replaced her anger. "I'm sorry I barked at you, Skye. What do you think about all this?"

"I think he didn't explain the money in his sister's account because he has no clue how it got there."

"What about the expensive gifts he gave everyone for Christmas? What about this bracelet?" She waved her arm in Skye's direction.

Skye braked at a stoplight along Route 158, touched her fingertips to Summer's bracelet and closed her eyes.

"This is not a new bracelet." Her voice rang with authority.

The light turned green and she let go of Summer's wrist accelerating the car. "There's a lot of love attached to your bracelet. I think it's been in his family for a long time and it was very special that he gave this heirloom to you."

Summer's stomach sank. "Damn. Really? Why didn't he tell me that?"

"I can't speak for him but maybe he was hurt that

you questioned his innocence. He left because you didn't trust him."

Tears stung the corners of Summer's eyes. "I guess I'll have to apologize. But I'm still nowhere with his case. I know you don't like Vinnie. But do you have any feelings about the money?"

"I haven't been too nice to him myself. But I have nothing against Vinnie now. I held him responsible for putting Bree in danger when she was shot. I've come to realize that Bree's a big girl and she was just as responsible as Vinnie. I was touched by his thoughtful Christmas gifts. Most of all, I like the way he looks at you when you're unaware."

"I love him, Skye."

"I know."

"What am I going to do?"

"Well first of all you're going to trace that money. You have the best people working for you. Push them hard to get it done."

"You don't think Vinnie had anything to do with it?"

"No. I'm positive he's innocent. I know we said it before, but you need to find that ring."

"It's an FBI Academy ring. Vinnie has one."

"The ring Mom saw isn't his. She described the fingers. They're thin. Definitely a man's hands, but nothing like Vinnie's. Mom saw more this morning. I forgot to tell you with the excitement about the seal. She said the man was typing on a gold keyboard. She's never seen one like it before."

The serious lead thrilled Summer. "That's huge, Skye. Thanks. I'll inform my team." Her optimism faded thinking about where she and Vinnie had left things. "I still don't know how to deal with him."

"Find the answers. Then apologize. You and Vinnie belong together."

****

Skye pulled up to the curb fronting the departures area for American Airlines. Summer opened the door and sprung out of the jeep. She hoisted her carry-on and briefcase out of the back seat and deposited them on the sidewalk.

She turned toward Skye and threw her arms around her as the tears started to flow. "Thank you for everything. I miss you already," she blubbered. "I'll talk to you soon."

"You bet. I'll let you know how the meeting goes."

"Drive safe. Love you." With a quick wave Summer trudged through the automatic doors.

She stopped inside and watched Skye steer away from the curb letting unchecked tears run down her cheeks.

Chapter 26

Summer wasn't surprised at the caller ID readout she noticed as she had taken her seat on the plane. The phone had trilled, and she had debated sending Tricia to voicemail. But she had enough time before mandatory setting the phone in airplane mode, and she was interested in what Vinnie's sister had to say. Pressing the green dot on the screen to accept the call, she answered with a brisk, "Hi Tricia."

"Oh, Summer. Thank God I reached you. I'm losing my mind here and I have never seen Vinnie more upset. When he told me why; I almost had a stroke. You *have* to believe I…we didn't steal anything."

"I actually do believe that. But I'm still at a loss explaining your account balance."

Soft weeping sounded in Summer's ear. Tricia's voice quavered responding, "I'm sure you are. I don't know how the money wound up there, either. I'm an idiot. I thought Chuck Roberts had forced a settlement from Barry. Remember when I mentioned that when we met at the mall Christmas shopping?"

Summer searched her memory and recalled how excited Tricia had seemed at lunch relating her ability to pay off the house and have money left over to give the boys a nice Christmas. The pieces didn't exactly fall into place, but at least Summer had an innocent explanation that she could accept. "I do remember now your mentioning that Chuck must have worked a miracle forcing Barry to do the right thing. But what led to you to believe the funds were a settlement? Chuck didn't ask you to sign anything. Or did he?"

"No. Not anything other than the initial paperwork. That's why I'm an idiot just assuming that he had somehow coerced Barry into depositing money in our account. But you *have* to believe me. I didn't take money from the FBI. And neither did Vinnie," Tricia sobbed.

Tricia's distress pierced Summer with regret. Her heart yearned to return to "the before". Before Mike Haws blew her romance apart. Before she had reason to distrust the man she loved. Why didn't Vinnie stay to thrash out Mike's findings with her? How could he sneak away?

"You saw Vinnie in person, I take it?" She couldn't resist asking, to anchor him in her mind and pretend he hadn't left her.

"Yes. I called you the minute he left."

Summer wouldn't hunt him down even though guilt at accusing him invaded her, partially supplanting earlier anger. "Where did he go...just in case I need to get in touch with him after my flight lands?"

"I think the restaurant. I've got to warn you..."

Summer's concentration on the call was broken when the booming PA announcement prevented her from hearing the end of Tricia's sentence. "...door is closed. At this time, all portable electronic devices must be..."

"Tricia, I have to go," Summer said. "The flight is departing. Do you want me to call you when I land?"

"No, no. Unless you have more questions for me,

that is."

"Not right now. I'm sorry this new information is so upsetting. But I'll untangle this as soon as I can. Bye."

"What do I do with the money?" Tricia's muted voice sounded from the phone just as Summer powered it down.

Good question. Better to do nothing until she could solve the mystery of the money's origin. She'd send Tricia a text responding to her question when she landed. Summer tossed the phone into her briefcase, toed the case under the seat in front of her, leaned back in the seat and gazed vacantly through the porthole. The jet surged forward propelling her deeper against the backrest in opposing momentum. And then the plane soared up off the runway reducing the ships in the sprawl of the Norfolk Naval Station to gray dots.

She closed her eyes tightly in a vain effort to blank her mind, rest—float above the clouds unencumbered by the weight of her problems. But Vinnie was there with her; the playful, sexy light in his blue eyes dimmed by shock at her accusations. Giving up on even the slightest escape, Summer leaned down and dragged her briefcase out from under the seat, propped it in her lap and slipped out her laptop.

Setting the briefcase aside, she wrestled her tray table into position, switched on her computer and connected to Wi-Fi. First she composed an email to Mike Haws: "Mike, I'll have my office supply you with a formal letter of request to the SAC if necessary—let me know if you have pushback—but I need you to evaluate the computers of the following personnel to establish a link with the proxy server you have identified: Paul Muñoz, Bob Finelli, King Pouw and John Morphy. I hope you can work with the same contact at the Bureau who allowed you to inspect my client's laptop. I'm especially interested in locating a computer with an unusual gold keyboard—a lead I've just received. Thank you, SL"

She had just opened a new email window to compose directions to Barbara when the incoming mail bell tone sounded. Summer minimized her work in progress and double clicked on Haws's response. "Already checked Muñoz out. Clean. No gold keyboard. Will work on the others. I have rapport with IT at the FBI. I don't anticipate problems. Mike"

She typed a quick, "Thanks," in response and then discarded the unfinished email to her assistant. Satisfied that at least she had taken *some* action, she stowed the laptop and sagged in the seat. *I should finish reading my book. Or maybe do the Times crossword puzzle.*

Normally the prospect of pleasant entertainment at 35,000 feet where contact with the outside world was optional delighted her. But the stranger in the seat next to her was a poor substitute for Vinnie Carlucci. She wondered if he had asked Jack to help him with alternate flight arrangements that morning. *Whatever. Merry Christmas. Yeah right…Stop, Summer.*

The duration of the flight passed in a daze. On the ground she navigated deplaning, car hailing, and journeying home by reflex. Arriving home, just blocks from Vinnie's condo, held no welcome or anticipation. Her little Christmas tree with fairy lights set on automatic timer twinkled in the corner of her living room. She mentally vowed to take it down as soon as she could muster the energy. Not up to any task, she drifted to a perch on the sofa.

Summer gazed dully at the light spectacle of the city that no matter how dispirited she felt; she could only describe as magical. But the magic that night didn't uplift or inspire.

She had demolished magic with Vinnie that weekend. Spending her holiday saturated in love and good fortune in his acceptance of all that her heritage as a sister of the legend entailed had conjured magic. He had delighted in her truth! A miracle.

Summer snapped her fingers: poof. She had shattered him with her doubts. What choice had she? She lifted her eyes heavenward wagging her head.

The phone in her hand teased her with the temptation to call him and… And what? She lacked a solution and until she unearthed all the facts that *had* to point away from Vinnie and Tricia, she had nothing worth saying to him. He wouldn't listen anyway.

She checked her watch. Ten o'clock. Too early to go to bed. But she longed for the oblivion of slumber like she had on the plane. Not only to gain respite from circular thinking, but maybe she also might experience a mind-clearing view of the path through the maze of incriminating evidence.

Frustration pecked at her. Deciding to use the phone to connect with her only available touchstone, she dialed Skye.

"Mind spinning?" Skye answered.

"Yep."

"I know."

"Any suggestions?"

"Of course. You know what to do."

Summer closed her eyes angling her head into the

crook of her left arm. "Dream."

"Dream," Skye said simultaneously.

"I'll let you know what I see. *If* I see."

"Sounds good. Night, Summer."

"Goodnight."

Summer moved off the couch in slow motion toward the kitchen. She plugged her phone into the charger, turned off lights around the condo and shuffled down the hall into the bathroom. It seemed a gargantuan effort to wash her face, brush her teeth and change into pajamas. Her emotional exhaustion might fuel sleep after all. Snuggled under her comforter, she prayed to the Sacred Source for the power to see Vinnie's truth.

Hours before dawn, Summer's prayer was answered. In the dream a man's tapered fingers with light brown hair on his knuckles, hovering over a gleaming, golden keyboard, swam into her consciousness. The vision cleared, crystalline, in perfect focus, and the fingers began typing rapidly. The chunky Academy ring bobbed up and down with the movements.

As if a lens widened the angle, male forearms came into view. A red pin striped shirt, cuffs rolled up to his elbows. *Come on, come on.* Her inner voice willed the vision to expand and reveal all. But the scene remained the same: typing fingers on the end of slim forearms.

Summer studied the surroundings for clues finding nothing concrete nor familiar. The desk or table beneath the keyboard wasn't visible at all. The details of the room beyond the man's arms were blurred, an indistinct watery gray. But then…

In inches, her field of vision widened: a bicep,

shoulder, neck… *Then.* A full profile. Sandy blond hair. Curly. Maybe permed. A pert nose. No beard stubble. Fair skin. Distinctly *not* Vinnie.

Recognition exploded in her mind. Electrified, Summer launched out of sleep and leaped out of bed. "Thank you, thank you, thank you Sacred Source!"

She strode toward her bedroom door, spun on a heel and sped back to the bedside table to check the time. "Damn," she said at the 4:00AM digital readout.

Summer put on a robe and left her bedroom anyway, too itchy to set the necessary steps in motion for further sleep. "Coffee would be good."

On a beeline for her coffee maker, she didn't care that she talked to an empty apartment. All she cared about was proving what she now knew. A litigator didn't prevail in court by pointing a finger and proclaiming, "I dreamed that *this* man is guilty." Nope.

She had to assemble the right plan. And her Rain Man was key.

Summer filled the coffee carafe with water and dumped the contents into the coffee machine. She started the brewing process and paced in circles in the kitchen, her cellphone in hand.

It's too early and rude to text.

Deciding to fire off an email to ask him to call immediately when he woke, her heart somersaulted with glee when Mike Haws called seconds later.

"Thank you for calling so quickly," Summer sang out.

"Yes, Ms. Layton. What can I do for you?" He sounded as sharp and clear-headed as usual.

"Scrap the list I provided you yesterday. I still want you to find the gold keyboard, either at a workstation or personal computer. And you need to tie the computer to the proxy server and the trail of the missing money from the Informants Fund. But there's only one name now on the list. I'm sure you'll find what we need to establish the chain of evidence against him."

"All right…"

She wondered what kind of expression Mike wore: the logical man faced with his crazy illogical employer. "Still there, Mike?"

"I am. But ma'am?"

"Yes, Mike?"

"When we're done with this investigation, will you please…?"

"Explain?" she guessed.

"Yes."

She burst out laughing. "I'll try."

Chapter 27

Vinnie weaved through the bustling restaurant, amazed that not a single table remained empty at lunchtime. Later that New Year's Eve from the dinner hour on, his father had already turned away reservations, but the crowd now had to have taken his dad by surprise.

He halted at a table of eight elderly women. "Mrs. Marconi, you look gorgeous today. How can Mr. Marconi let you out of his sight?" Vinnie smiled as the octogenarians seemed to perk up, preening at his attention.

"Dominic." Vinnie beckoned a waiter over to the table. "Can you please bring a bottle of champagne over to my favorite ladies here?"

The waiter nodded, smiled and then headed to the bar.

"Now you ladies behave yourselves tonight."

Their bawdy laughter sounded as he turned away with a smile. He worked the room of guests, a mind clearing distraction, stopping at tables along the way to the kitchen, exchanging pleasantries and checking that no request went unfulfilled.

Vinnie pushed through the swinging door into the kitchen.

His dad looked up from the stainless steel worktable. "What are you doing here?"

"Well, that's a nice greeting, Pops." He chuckled. "Good to see you too."

He gave his father a hug and then grabbed an apron off a wall hook.

"I'm happy to see you, too. But didn't you get the message that we had everything covered today? I sent texts."

"Sorry, no. I had a problem with my phone. I have to get it fixed on my way home."

He'd never tell his father that he had to buy a new phone; the old one beyond salvage. Currently all three pieces of the smartphone resided in his trash; the direct result of heaving it against the wall in frustration after nearly calling Summer's number repeatedly and then changing his mind at the last second. She should call him. She owed *him* an apology—whether he accepted it or not, he had to have one from the lady.

"Your mother has been calling you and she's worried. Your sister thinks you blame her for this mess with the money; so, she's upset, too. Call them."

"I will as soon as I get a new phone. I promise."

"Good boy. Then you should call Summer." He cocked his head and gestured, stop with the upturned palm of his hand. "Misunderstandings happen."

Vinnie frowned. "Really? A misunderstanding? She made it crystal clear that she questioned my honesty. Has mom ever distrusted you?"

"No. I can't say that she has. But did Summer say she doesn't trust you?"

"Not in so many words. But she insinuated plenty pushing me to explain how the money wound up in Tricia's account."

"Did you tell her you didn't know how it

happened?"

Vinnie thought back to the day on the beach. He had a clear memory of how shocked he was when Summer told him about the money in the account. And how paralyzed with fury he became at her leading questions. "I didn't say anything. She seemed sure that I had something to do with it. I could hear the distrust in her voice—read it in her eyes."

"Bullshit."

Vinnie arched his eyebrows. His dad cursed rarely. But when he did, his family paid attention.

A slow smile bloomed on his father's face. "You and I both know that Carlucci men have…healthy egos. I think Summer kicked you in your ego that day. How dare she think you stole money? How dare she not trust you explicitly? Does this ring a bell?"

Vinnie had to grin back at his dad.

"Have you tried to see Summer's side? She's a ballbuster lawyer. I liked that about her right from the start. I wouldn't have given her the nod to defend you if she weren't. She was blindsided by potentially incriminating information about her client. She had to deal with it immediately. And what did that client do?"

"Okay, Dad. I get the point. Maybe I could have handled it better. I'll think about it. Thanks for the advice." He wrapped the apron belt around his waist once and started to tie it.

Dad shook his head and held out a hand. "I'll take the apron. You go. Get a new phone. Then call your mother and put her mind at ease. Call Tricia, too, while you're at it. Wish them Happy New Year."

"You sure you don't need me to help out here?"

"Of course, I'm sure. Happy New Year, son. I

know that this is gonna be a very good year for you."

Vinnie patted Dad's back. "From your mouth to God's ears. Happy New Year, Dad. I love you."

****

A biting cold wind whipped the ends of the scarf around Summer's face and neck running from the cab to her office door. She kicked the snow off her boots and trudged inside missing the warm weather of home. Jake had called her early that morning and asked her to spring one of their client's spoiled kids from jail. Summer rarely handled their elite clients' family woes and wouldn't enjoy the task today, but Jake would host a huge New Year's Eve party and was tied up organizing. So, she'd arrange the little brat's release.

Technically, Summer didn't need to come to the office to tackle the job, but the walls of her condo closed in on her since her return from North Carolina and she seized that opportunity to escape.

She strode down the carpeted hallway and caught sight of her assistant seated at her desk outside Summer's office. "Barbara? I told you to take the day off."

Barbara looked up from her desk. "I know, Ms. Layton. But I had a few things I wanted to finish and it's so much easier to get work done when the phones aren't ringing."

"I guess I don't have any messages."

"There were only a few questions on voice mail from the prosecutor's office about the Tyson case, but I handled it."

"Mike Haws didn't call?"

"No, he didn't."

Summer wanted to hear that Vinnie called, and

almost asked Barbara. But she knew the answer. No, he didn't call. No, he wasn't going to call. If Summer wanted to connect with him, she would have to make the first move.

Summer unwound her scarf and unbuttoned her coat. "Do you and Cindy have any plans for the night?"

"We sure do." Barbara's face lit with her smile at the mention of her wife's name. "Cindy's picking up Ray's pizza on her way home from work. We'll change into flannel pajamas, open a couple bottles of wine and watch the ball drop on TV. A perfect evening."

Summer smiled back at her. "It does sound perfect."

"Are you going to Mr. Levant's party?"

"I might. I haven't decided. But honestly, pizza and wine sound pretty darn good."

Summer stepped into her office, stopped under the doorframe, and faced Barbara. "Now I want you to get out of here immediately. That's an order," she said smiling. "And Barbara, Happy Healthy New Year."

"Thank you, Ms. Layton. Happy New Year to you, too. I'll just straighten my desk."

She drifted to her desk and made the necessary calls to complete Jake's request, finishing with a call to the parents with instructions to bring their son home later that day. Summer disconnected the call and then checked her cell phone. No messages. Damn.

This is ridiculous, waiting for the phone to ring like a heartsick teenager. Before she could change her mind, she selected Vinnie's contact and connected the call. The phone rang three times and she was about to hang up.

But his voicemail recording played, and her heart

somersaulted at the sound of his resonant, masculine voice. *"I can't pick up the phone, leave a message."*

The brief greeting struck her as typical of Vinnie: to the point and direct. She could be direct, too.

"Call me." She disconnected.

Summer sagged in her chair. *Well that wasn't satisfying.*

She booted up her computer and checked emails, hoping to gain some satisfaction from clearing her workload before the New Year holiday. Her text indicator dinged startling her.

Eagerly, she seized the phone and read the text. *You were right, Ms. Layton. Can we meet?*

I'm on my way to your hotel. Meet in the lobby? She fired back. And then she laid the phone down on her desk, shrugged into her coat, and wound the scarf around her neck keeping her eyes glued on the screen.

Please come to room 2011. I have my equipment set up to show you what I've found.

Will do.

****

Summer flew out of the cab in front of the Marriott Residence Inn, her heart racing nonstop. Too fired up to wait for an elevator she pounded up two flights of stairs and hammered on the door to room 2011.

Mike Haws swung open the door grinning at her.

He directed Summer over to his desk where three juxtaposed monitors glowed fluorescent like an improvised command center. Taking a seat, he tapped the keyboard and pointed to the first screen. "Here is the proxy server I identified initially. I traced the EFT from Carlucci's bank account to this server and the EFT to the Warner's joint account."

Summer peered at the screen unable to decipher the symbols and letters combinations. "I'll take your word for it."

Mike tapped on the keyboard and strings of data appeared on the central monitor. "I'm sorry it took me so long to connect the dots after you gave me Wellington's name. He's been off the grid since we spoke. No recent credit card usage or banking transactions. I found that odd. It bothered me."

She smiled at his admission believing that nothing could bother the unflappable Michael Haws.

"It's best I don't go into detail about access to flight logs...or whatever. But I located him at his family's home on Martha's Vineyard where the Wellington's spend holidays. Tyler Wellington used his mother's computer to special order a gold wireless keyboard, delivered to Buttercup Wellington the day after Labor Day."

"*Buttercup?*"

"His mother's legal name."

Summer burst out laughing, delighted when the usually taciturn Mike joined in.

He cleared his throat. "Wellington used his mother's computer to route the EFT's from the Informants' Fund to your client's account and then to the proxy server, etc. I've confirmed a deposit of $10,000 to Wellington's money market account, also, confirming the trail of the entire missing funds. Nice, hiding behind your mommy, right?"

Summer threw back her head and cackled in glee. "I can't thank you enough, Mike."

"A pleasure." He pointed to third monitor. "I immediately provided this dossier to my contact at the

FBI."

Summer leaned over Mike's shoulder and peered at the screen. Mostly English was involved in the text.

"He reviewed it at my request and informed Agents Ashley and McMillan," Mike continued. "My understanding is that FBI personnel are en route to Martha's Vineyard to seize the hardware and arrest Wellington. Special Agent Ashley thought you'd like to inform Mr. Carlucci that he is fully reinstated with retroactive pay. Also, I believe his team will be honored with awards for the last assignment completed under Carlucci's leadership."

"My God, Mike. This is amazing. I'll arrange a bonus for your work during the holidays. I hope we have a chance to work together again. If you ever need a reference, please don't hesitate to contact me."

"Thanks, ma'am. Happy New Year."

"To you, too."

Downstairs in the lobby, Summer pirouetted, her spirits soaring. She *had* to let Vinnie know. Without hesitation she dialed his number. Again, his voicemail recording played in her ear. At the prompt she sang out, "Vinnie call me. I have fantastic news."

She absolutely had to share this news, or she'd explode. *Tricia, of course.*

Vinnie's sister answered the call on the first ring. "Summer, thank God. I'm going out of my mind. I haven't heard from Vinnie...sorry." Tricia took a deep breath. "Do you have news?"

"I do. It's over, Tricia. Vinnie has been cleared. I haven't been able to reach him."

"Thank you, thank you, thank you," Tricia said, her voice thick with emotion. "I haven't heard from him either. But you have made my day! What do I do about my bank account?"

"Sit tight on that. An arrest is in progress. I'll get instructions from the FBI shortly, I'm sure."

"Now I can start the new year off right." She chuckled. "I still don't have money from my soon to be ex, but that's another story."

"That will turn out just fine. You'll see."

"I believe you. Happy New Year, Summer. Thank you *so* much."

"Happy New Year, Tricia. Give my love to the boys."

Grinning nonstop on the cab ride home, she directed the driver to stop at Ray's for takeout Sicilian pizza. Barbara and Cindy's New Year's Eve plans sounded just right. She fantasized that Vinnie would retrieve her message, rush over to her place and shower her with gratitude. They'd spend the night naked in each other's arms—eating pizza in between sessions of glorious, passionate love making.

A few hours closer to midnight, cold pizza congealed in the box on her kitchen counter and Summer anticipated spending New Year's Eve alone.

She tried Vinnie's number. Again, she reached his voicemail recording.

"You're acting like a baby," she groused. Having no other choice, she left the message about his reinstatement and hung up.

Stomping into her bathroom, she filled the tub with the hottest water she could stand and added a fragrant bath bomb. The aroma of lily of the valley filled the steamy room as she stripped off her clothes. Lowering herself into the tub gingerly, she relaxed as stress seeped out of her. She laid her head on the edge of the tub, letting her mind drift.

Maybe I'll go to Jake's party. Or maybe I'll curl up on the couch in my pajamas.

She closed her eyes and floated in a pleasant daze.

In the dream, Summer shaded her eyes with her hand enjoying the rear view of Vinnie wading into the surf, diving beneath a wave and swimming out beyond the breakers with sure strokes. Appreciation turned to alarm at the sight of ominous dorsal fins a few feet ahead of him. Help me help him, she begged her sisters who lazed on a beach blanket and pointedly ignored her. She called upon the Sacred Source to grant her power like Skye's and was electrified with the transformative surge. Now within the sleek dolphin body, she could speed to him. Tow him to safety. He accepted the ride and she whisked him back to shore, emerging from the shallows on shaky legs. Relief flooded through her and she reached for his hand, grateful beyond words to the Sacred Source for supplying the ability to save him. Brusquely he swatted her hand away rejecting her touch. She stood at the water's edge watching him stalk away from her, helpless to reach him.

A drumming sounded jolting her awake. The pounding on her front door continued becoming more insistent.

Disoriented and disturbed from the dream, she sloshed out of the tub, dried her body quickly, wrapped the oversized towel around her and tucked the edges over her breasts. Summer padded to the front door and peeked through the peephole. Elation burst inside and she swung wide the door for Vinnie.

The grimace he wore hardly matched her mood. *Didn't he get my message? Why does he look so angry?*

He waved a checkbook in front of her face. "I've come to pay you for your services."

Chapter 28

Summer had a white-knuckle grip on the doorknob. His stormy gaze lasered into her eyes, and for the first time, she fully appreciated Vinnie's physical ability to take down criminals. With a check book as his weapon he loomed, threatening and coiled to pounce. The dream. Was he about to swat her away just when she had saved him from the sharks?

Not if she swatted him away first.

"*Services?*" she spat out glaring back at him. "Exactly *which* services have I provided that you're willing to pay for?"

She presented her back to him and marched away. Summer sensed his entering her condo, confirmed as he slammed shut the door.

"Stop," he boomed.

"I don't take orders from you."

Summer strode into her living room. His looming body heat close behind her further stoked her anger. She spun on her heel and squared off, nose to nose, for her frontal assault. "You can't afford *any* of my services."

Vinnie narrowed his eyes. A muscle in his jaw twitched.

Summer held his gaze poised to do battle. She caught a glimmer in his eyes—challenge, maybe humor—a subtle shift in the charged atmosphere.

His chest heaved and he expelled a breath. Breaking eye contact he dropped his gaze to the floor and pursed his lips, wagging his head. "You Layton sisters…"

Fury erupted inside her. "What the hell does *that* mean?" She dipped her head to force his eyes to meet hers. "Are we interchangeable? I look just like Bree, so when she wouldn't have you, I was…next?"

His brows knit and his muscles bunched visibly. "You can't be serious."

She glared back at him. Her heart pounded so wildly that surely, he heard every drumbeat.

"Right, Summer." His baritone voice dripped with sarcasm. "You're done with me, so now I move on to Skye."

Logic alluded Summer. The confrontation had swerved toward the absurd, but in that moment her wounded heart prevented her steering the conversation back on track. She wasn't done with Vinnie. She wanted *everything* with him. Did this mean he wasn't done with her? And her dream wouldn't prevail?

She exhaled a breath. "Let's take a step back."

"Okay." He relaxed his stance and his frown faded. But the alert, guarded expression in his eyes remained.

"You haven't explained why you came here today. To pay legal fees, I assume. Are you firing me?"

"No…well, yes. I guess I am."

"I see. Why is that?"

"You don't believe I'm innocent." His voice remained level delivering his statement. But the hurt in his eyes nearly swamped her.

"I never said that."

"In so many words…"

She splayed her fingers and held up her hand, stop. "I never expressed a single word questioning your innocence. By the way, it's not necessary that my clients *are* innocent. Everyone is entitled to the best defense possible."

"You see? That's why I'm here. I don't want you defending me even though you think I might be guilty. I need a new lawyer." He knit his brows again and storm clouds swirled in his sea blue eyes.

Despite his threatening posture, Summer began to enjoy toying with him. Obviously, he had no idea that she had already proven him innocent. "Why didn't you answer me when I asked for an explanation of the deposit in Tricia's account?"

"I didn't have an answer."

"Right. When confronted with the seeming accusation, your answer *should* have been, 'This is freaking unbelievable, Summer. I have no idea how the money landed in my sister's bank account.' Or something to that effect."

"Yeah. So? I didn't like your implying that Tricia stole the money, either. I *freaking* didn't like your accusations at all."

"I didn't accuse, I questioned. And yet, you chose not to answer any of my valid questions. Instead, you turned tail and left me. Without a rental car, to boot."

The pang of conscience mirrored in his eyes. "I'm sorry. You didn't deserve that treatment. I realize you were just doing your job. Let me write your check, Summer. I won't bother you again."

Her stomach sank anticipating the anguish losing him would bring. Now she needed to steer this onto the right track. "Why haven't you answered my calls?"

His face lit with his smile. "You called me?"

Satisfaction that the prospect of her calling him obviously brought him pleasure replaced any trace of anger. "I did. *Several* times, in fact."

His eyes danced. "My phone is broken. I haven't had a chance to replace it yet. I might have demo'd it over you."

"Over intending to fire me?"

"No." His gaze bored into her eyes again. This time his hooded eyes held a different physical threat: ravishing her right there on the living room floor. "I…think I should fire you, Summer. I realize I don't want you to be my lawyer."

"I…"

He kissed her, smothering further discussion, encircling his arms around her shoulders and pressing her to his solid chest. She melted at his touch and welcomed the delicious surrender in the harbor of his embrace. When he slowly ended the kiss, she smiled up at him.

"What I'm trying to tell you, Counselor, is I don't want you to be my lawyer. I want you to be my wife. *If* you can trust me. I have never lied to you, Summer. I am innocent. And I do love you."

Summer's head spun, unsure that she had heard him correctly. "Did you just *propose*?"

He gave her a crooked grin. "Probably not the romantic gesture of your dreams. But, yeah. Will you marry me?"

My dreams. Jubilation burst inside her. Vinnie had rejected her professionally when he swatted her hand away in the dream. He was still hers. *Thank you, Sacred Source.* "I love you, too, and I'm *very* sorry if it seemed that I didn't trust you when I questioned you on the beach. We were both blindsided by Mike Haws's preliminary findings. I always believed you were innocent. And if you had a phone, you'd know that I've proven it. It's over, Vin. You're fully reinstated with back pay and there's talk of commendations for your team for your last assignment."

Vinnie let out a whoop. He clamped his arms around her waist and squeezed the breath out of her hauling her straight off her feet and launching her into a couple of spinning gyrations. Setting her back down on the floor, he held her at arms' length beaming her a dazzling smile.

He had never looked more handsome. Summer rocked on her feet beaming back at him, dizzy from the circular motions and the heady elation of finally delivering the news he had longed to hear.

"I can't believe it. How?"

The dizziness subsided and Summer held out her hand. "Sit with me. I'll explain everything."

She gently towed him to the leather sectional and sat down, just then registering the lovely gleaming city, dressed in holiday illumination, beyond her windowpanes. Her *Charlie Brown* Christmas tree glowed pretty with white fairy lights in the corner of the room. He plopped down next to her and clasped both of her hands in his. Reflections of Christmas lights glimmered in his soft eyes. His touch set off delicious shivers through her. Gazing into his eyes, she related the facts about his exoneration.

He covered his chin with his hand and shook his head. "Tyler Wellington? I thought the kid hero worshipped me. Why the hell would he do this to me?

Hell—to anybody at the Bureau? And involve my sister? He must hate me. Although I don't know why."

"I'm not sure, either, Vin. He struck me as a narcissistic tool. Maybe he had something to prove? One thing for sure, if he evaded detection by someone like Mike Haws this long, he's a damn good hacker. Maybe that was the point? At the very least he must be pathologically jealous of your position."

"Yeah, wow." He shook his head as if to clear it. "Shit. I have to call Tricia. Can I borrow your phone?"

"I already spoke with her. I called her right after I left you the message."

Vinnie leaned back against the sofa cushion wrapping an arm around Summer's shoulder and drawing her close to his side. She nestled against him enjoying the view of the city lights, content and brimming with happiness.

He jerked upright and turned to face her. "Hey. My proposal. You never answered me. Was that on purpose?"

"No." She grinned at him.

"No, what?"

"No, it wasn't on purpose. I got carried away telling you the charges were dropped."

He ran a hand through his close cropped, raven hair. And then dropped to one knee on the floor, cramped in between her coffee table and sofa, holding out upturned palms toward her.

She giggled, placing her hands in his, gazing at him expectantly.

"Summer Layton," he said. "Even though you are a carbon copy of two other women, there is only you for me. Only one Summer. You are the love of my life.

Will you marry me?"

"Yes, Vincente Carlucci. I'll marry you. *If* you're sure you can handle…my legendary inheritance."

He gave her a wicked grin and yanked on her arms. She pitched forward tumbling off the sofa. Vinnie caught her easily and balanced her sitting on his bent thigh. "I figure I'll lose every arm-wrestling contest. Can you handle marriage to an FBI agent? I'm gone a lot. And it's possible we'll be on opposite sides in the court room someday."

"I can handle all that. I'm proud of what you do."

"Ditto."

In one swift move he laid her prone on the sofa, straddled her and arched over her trembling body to kiss her senseless. Easing back on his haunches, he smiled down at her. "It's almost midnight. Do you have wine or something we can toast with? We have a lot to celebrate."

She nodded. "Uh huh. I have a couple bottles of red and white wine."

"Good." He unfurled from the couch and reached a handhold to Summer.

She clasped his hand letting him tow her to her feet.

In the kitchen he tipped a finger on the edge of the cardboard box and peered at the hardened pizza. He arched an eyebrow and glanced at Summer.

"On the way home from the meeting with Mike Haws after leaving you a voicemail message, I stopped and bought the pizza. I had a fantasy that you'd rush over here after hearing the message and we'd eat pizza, naked in bed, watching the ball drop in Times Square."

"Ah," he said taking the wine bottle out of her hand

and removing the cork. "I think I'll skip the pizza, but the naked part? I think that fantasy is about to come true."

She carried the wine glasses. He brought the bottle, strolling down the hallway with his free arm wrapped around her, his hand branding her hip with his emanating heat. Laughing she set the glasses down on her nightstand and switched on the TV. Thirty seconds remained in the countdown.

He filled their glasses and offered one to Summer. She sat down on the foot of her bed and he took a seat next to her. At the top of the ten second countdown, he clinked his glass against hers. "Thank you, Summer. Happy New Year, my love."

"Happy New Year, Vinnie. I love you." She took a sip of wine and then followed Vinnie's lead setting her glass aside.

At the ringing in of the new year, Summer and Vinnie locked in an embrace tilting backward to stretch out on the mattress. He propped up over her smiling. "Now for the naked part."

Vinnie stripped his sweater off, up over his head.

Her phone rang with the triplets' distinctive ring tone—*Sisters* sung by Rosemary Clooney. She smiled and held up a finger. "Just a sec."

Connecting the call on speakerphone, she sang out, "Happy New Year. You're on speaker. Vinnie's here with me."

"We know," Skye said.

"Happy New Year, darling," Mom said. "And to you, too, Vinnie."

"Happy New Year, Kay."

"Thank you so much, Mom, for the lead. My vision

centered on the gold keyboard and I saw Tyler Wellington."

"Vision? Gold keyboard?" Vinnie said.

Summer patted his arm. "I'll explain later."

"Hold on, I'm conferencing in Bree," Skye said.

A few seconds later, newlywed Bree joined the conversation wishing everyone happy new year, her voice ringing with happiness.

And then her sisters and mother chorused, "Welcome to the family, Vinnie. When's the wedding?"

A word about the author...

K.M. Daughters is the pen name for team writers and sisters Pat Casiello and Kathie Clare. The pen name is dedicated to the memory of their parents, "K"ay and "M"ickey Lynch.

K.M. Daughters is a multi-award-winning author of 16 romance genre and mainstream fiction novels.

The "Daughters" are wives, mothers and grandmothers residing in the Chicago suburbs and on the Outer Banks, North Carolina.

Visitors are most welcome at:

http://www.kmdaughters.com
www.kmdaughters.com

www.ingramcontent.com/pod-product-compliance
Lightning Source LLC
Chambersburg PA
CBHW070055030726
47506CB00002B/482